GLOBAL Reading SAFARI

GLOBAL Reading SAFARI

REFLECTIONS IN FICTION

EDITED BY JAMES BARRY

BREBEUF COLLEGE SCHOOL

Nelson Canada

I(T)P ™

International Thomson Publishing
The trademark ITP is used under licence

© Nelson Canada,
A Division of Thomson Canada Limited, 1994

All rights in this book are reserved.

Published in Canada by
Nelson Canada,
A Division of Thomson Canada Limited
1120 Birchmount Road
Scarborough, Ontario
M1K 5G4

ISBN 0-17-603980-5
Teacher's Guide 0-17-603988-0

Managing Editor: Jean Stinson
Developmental Editor: David Friend
Project Editor: Tara Shields
Senior Production Editor: Sandra Manley
Art Director: Bruce Bond
Series Design: Tracy Walker
Cover Design: Liz Nyman
Cover Illustration: Pol Turgeon
Typesetting: Zenaida Merjudio

Printed and bound in Canada by
Best Gagné Book Manufacturers

1234567890 / BGBM / 2109876543

Canadian Cataloguing in Publication Data

Main entry under title:

Global reading safari

ISBN 0-17-603980-5

1. Short stories.   I. Barry, James, date.

PN6120.2.G56 1993 808.83'1 C93-094478-X

Reviewers

The publishers thank the following people
who contributed their valuable expertise
during the development of this book:

Patti Buchanan, Vancouver, B.C.
Anne Carrier, Toronto, Ont.
Shirley-Dale Easley, Fredericton, N.B.
Graham Foster, Calgary, Alta.
Dan Kral, Regina, Sask.

The editor thanks Caroline Cobham,
David Friend, Carolyn Madonia,
Tara Shields, Joseph Griffin, and
Anna Barry for their time, insights,
and hard work in helping to prepare
this global read.

**As requested by individual copyright
holders, some selections may retain
original spellings, punctuation, usage,
and style of measurement.**

CONTENTS

III IDENTITY AND SOCIETY

IV THE CLEVER PERSON

V RELATIONSHIPS

VI POLITICS AND POWER

VII DECISIONS

INTRODUCTION

These stories offer a global perspective on fiction — from oral folk tradition to the contemporary literary scene. They were selected because readers enjoyed them. They were the stories that wouldn't go away.

Transcending the boundaries of language and nationality can have electrifying and illuminating results. Readers take pride in stories that spring from their own, perhaps overlooked, traditions. Comparative literature is one of the best mirrors reflecting the common human spirit around the globe. It is also one of the cheapest forms of travel.

Storytelling has always been a vehicle for teaching us who we are and who we could be. These stories were selected not only for their literary merit but also for the values they explore. Like a good friend, a good story tells the truth, but, as Emily Dickinson would say, tells it slant.

These stories mesh the old with the new. Homer's story of the Cyclops is from the ninth century B.C. The Canadian story "Young Man's Folly" won *The Toronto Star* Short Story Contest in 1992.

The best anthology, of course, is the one you compile from your own reading. We hope some of these stories will become part of your personal collection.

Dedicated to the many students across the country who read the book and candidly offered their opinions.

James Barry
Editor

CANADA

UNITED STATES
OF AMERICA

MEXICO

TRINIDAD

THE
NETHERLANDS
SCOTLAND
IRELAND
GERMANY
ENGLAND
FRANCE
HUNGARY
ITALY
SPAIN
GREECE

NIGERIA

ARGENTINA

RUSSIA

ARMENIA

TURKEY

ISRAEL

EGYPT

PEOPLE'S REPUBLIC OF
CHINA

JAPAN

INDIA

PAKISTAN

VIETNAM

KENYA

SOUTH
AFRICA

NEW
ZEALAND

How Mosquitoes Came to Be

RETOLD BY RICHARD ERDOES
AND ALFONSO ORTIZ

Long ago there was a giant who loved to kill humans . . .

Long ago there was a giant who loved to kill humans, eat their flesh, and drink their blood. He was especially fond of human hearts. "Unless we can get rid of this giant," people said, "none of us will be left," and they called a council to discuss ways and means.

One man said, "I think I know how to kill the monster," and he went to the place where the giant had last been seen. There he lay down and pretended to be dead.

Soon the giant came along. Seeing the man lying there, he said, "These humans are making it easy for me. Now I don't even have to catch and kill them; they might die right on my trail, probably from fear of me!"

The giant touched the body. "Ah, good," he said, "this one is still warm and fresh. What a tasty meal he'll make; I can't wait to roast his heart."

The giant flung the man over his shoulder, and the man let his head hang down as if he were dead. Carrying the man home, the giant dropped him in the middle of the floor right near the fireplace. Then he saw that there was no firewood and went to get some.

As soon as the monster had left, the man got up and grabbed the giant's huge skinning knife. Just then the giant's son came in, bending low to enter. He was still small as giants go, and the man held the big knife to his throat. "Quick, tell me, where's your father's heart? Tell me or I'll slit your throat!"

The giant's son was scared. He said, "My father's heart is in his left heel."

Just then the giant's left foot appeared in the entrance, and the man swiftly plunged the knife into the heel. The monster screamed and fell down dead.

Yet the giant still spoke: "Though I'm dead, though you killed me, I'm going to keep on eating you and all the other humans in the world forever!"

"That's what you think!" said the man. "I'm about to make sure that you never eat anyone again." He cut the giant's body into pieces and burned each one in the fire. Then he took the ashes and threw them into the air for the winds to scatter.

Instantly, each of the particles turned into a mosquito. The cloud of ashes became a cloud of mosquitoes, and from the midst the man heard the giant's voice laughing, saying, "Yes, I'll eat you people until the end of time."

And as the monster spoke, the man felt a sting, and a mosquito started sucking his blood, and then many mosquitoes stung him, and he began to scratch himself.

A Letter to God

BY GREGORIO LÓPEZ Y FUENTES

TRANSLATED FROM THE SPANISH BY DONALD A. YATES

Not a leaf remained on the trees. The corn was totally destroyed. The flowers were gone from the kidney-bean plants. Lencho's soul was filled with sadness.

The house—the only one in the entire valley—sat on the crest of a low hill. From this height one could see the river and, next to the corral, the field of ripe corn dotted with the kidney-bean flowers that always promised a good harvest.

The only thing the earth needed was a rainfall, or at least a shower. Throughout the morning Lencho—who knew his fields intimately—had done nothing else but scan the sky toward the northeast.

"Now we're really going to get some water, woman."

The woman, who was preparing supper, replied:

"Yes, God willing."

The oldest boys were working in the field, while the smaller ones were playing near the house, until the woman called to them all:

"Come for dinner...."

It was during the meal that, just as Lencho had predicted, big drops of rain began to fall. In the northeast huge mountains of clouds could be seen approaching. The air was fresh and sweet.

The man went out to look for something in the corral for no other reason than to allow himself the pleasure of feeling the rain on his body, and when he returned he exclaimed:

"Those aren't raindrops falling from the sky, they're new coins. The big drops are ten-centavo pieces and the little ones are fives...."

With a satisfied expression he regarded the field of ripe corn with its kidney-bean flowers, draped in a curtain of rain. But suddenly a strong wind began to blow and together with the rain very large hailstones began to fall. These truly did resemble new silver coins. The boys, exposing themselves to the rain, ran out to collect the frozen pearls.

"It's really getting bad now," exclaimed the man, mortified. "I hope it passes quickly."

It did not pass quickly. For an hour the hail rained on the house, the garden, the hillside, the cornfield, on the whole valley. The field was white, as if covered with salt. Not a leaf remained on the trees. The corn was totally destroyed. The flowers were gone from the kidney-bean plants. Lencho's soul was filled with sadness. When the storm had passed, he stood in the middle of the field and said to his sons:

"A plague of locusts would have left more than this.... The hail has left nothing: this year we will have no corn or beans...."

That night was a sorrowful one:

"All our work, for nothing!"

"There's no one who can help us!"

"We'll all go hungry this year...."

But in the hearts of all who lived in that solitary house in the middle of the valley, there was a single hope: help from God.

"Don't be so upset, even though this seems like a total loss. Remember, no one dies of hunger!"

"That's what they say: no one dies of hunger...."

All through the night, Lencho thought only of his one hope: the help of God, whose eyes, as he had been instructed, see everything, even what is deep in one's conscience.

Lencho was an ox of a man, working like an animal in the fields, but still he knew how to write. The following Sunday, at daybreak, after having convinced himself that there is a protecting spirit, he began to write a letter which he himself would carry to town and place in the mail.

It was nothing less than a letter to God.

"God," he wrote, "if you don't help me, my family and I will go hungry this year. I need a hundred pesos in order to resow the field and to live until the crop comes, because the hailstorm...."

He wrote "To God" on the envelope, put the letter inside and, still troubled, went to town. At the post office he placed a stamp on the letter and dropped it into the mailbox.

One of the employees, who was a postman and also helped at the post office, went to his boss laughing heartily and showed him the letter to God. Never in his career as a postman had he known that address. The postmaster—a fat, amiable fellow—also broke out laughing, but almost immediately he turned serious and, tapping the letter on his desk, commented:

"What faith! I wish I had the faith of the man who wrote this letter. To believe the way he believes. To hope with the confidence that he knows how to hope with. Starting up a correspondence with God!"

So, in order not to disillusion that prodigy of faith, revealed by a letter that could not be delivered, the postmaster came up with an idea: answer the letter. But when he opened it, it was evident that to answer it he needed something more than good will, ink, and paper. But he stuck to his resolution: he asked for money from his employee, he himself gave part of his salary, and several friends of his were obliged to give something "for an act of charity."

It was impossible for him to gather together the hundred pesos, so he was able to send the farmer only a little more than half. He put the bills in an envelope addressed to Lencho and with them a letter containing only a single word as a signature: GOD.

The following Sunday Lencho came a bit earlier than usual to ask if there was a letter for him. It was the postman himself who handed the letter to him, while the postmaster, experiencing the contentment of a man who has performed a good deed, looked on from the doorway of his office.

Lencho showed not the slightest surprise on seeing the bills—such was his confidence—but he became angry when he counted the money.... God could not have made a mistake, nor could he have denied Lencho what he had requested!

Immediately, Lencho went up to the window to ask for paper and ink. On the public writing table, he started in to write, with much wrinkling of his brow, caused by the effort he had to make to express his ideas. When he finished, he went to the window to buy a stamp which he licked and then affixed to the envelope with a blow of his fist.

The moment that the letter fell into the mailbox the postmaster went to open it. It said:

"God: of the money that I asked for, only seventy pesos reached me. Send me the rest, since I need it very much. But don't send it to me through the mail, because the post-office employees are a bunch of crooks. Lencho."

"Tell all the Truth but tell it slant"
Emily Dickinson

A Fable

BY ROBERT FOX

The young man rose from his seat and stood before the girl's mother. He cleared his throat very carefully for a long time.

The young man was clean shaven and neatly dressed. It was early Monday morning and he got on the subway. It was the first day of his first job and he was slightly nervous; he didn't know exactly what his job would be. Otherwise he felt fine. He loved everybody he saw. He loved everybody on the street and everybody disappearing into the subway and he loved the world because it was a fine clear day and he was starting his first job.

Without kicking anybody, the young man was able to find a seat on the Manhattan bound train. The car filled quickly and he looked up at the people standing over him envying his seat. Among them were a mother and daughter who were going shopping. The daughter was a beautiful girl with blonde hair and soft looking skin, and he was immediately attracted to her.

"He's staring at you," the mother whispered to the daughter.

"Yes, mother, I feel so uncomfortable. What shall I do?"

"He's in love with you."

"In love with me? How can you tell?"

"Because I'm your mother."

"But what shall I do?"

"Nothing. He'll try to talk to you. If he does, answer him. Be nice to him. He's only a boy."

The train reached the business district and many people got off. The girl and her mother found seats opposite the young man. He continued to look at the girl who occasionally looked to see if he was looking at her.

The young man found a good pretext for standing in giving his seat to an elderly man. He stood over the girl and her mother. They whispered back and forth and looked up at him. At another stop, the seat next to the girl was vacated and the young man blushed, but quickly took it.

"I knew it," the mother said between her teeth. "I knew it, I *knew* it."

The young man cleared his throat and tapped the girl. She jumped.

"Pardon me," he said. "You're a very pretty girl."

"Thank you," she said.

"Don't talk to him," her mother said. "Don't answer him; I'm warning you. Believe me."

"I'm in love with you," he said to the girl.

"I don't believe you," the girl said.

"Don't answer him," the mother said.

"I really do," he said. "In fact, I'm so much in love with you that I want to marry you."

"Do you have a job?" she said.

"Yes, today is my first day. I'm going to Manhattan to start my first day of work."

"What kind of work will you do?" she asked.

"I don't know exactly," he said. "You see, I didn't start yet."

"It sounds exciting," she said.

"It's my first job but I'll have my own desk and handle a lot of papers and carry them around in a briefcase, and it will pay well, and I'll work my way up."

"I love you," she said.

"Will you marry me?"

"I don't know. You'll have to ask my mother."

The young man rose from his seat and stood before the girl's mother. He cleared his throat very carefully for a long time. "May I have the honor of having your daughter's hand in marriage?" he said, but he was drowned out by the subway noise.

The mother looked up at him and said, "What?" He couldn't hear her either, but he could tell by the movement of her lips, and by the way her face wrinkled up that she said, what.

The train pulled to a stop.

"May I have the honor of having your daughter's hand in marriage!" he shouted, not realizing there was no subway noise. Everybody on the train looked at him, smiled, and then they all applauded.

"Are you crazy?" the mother asked.

The train started again.

"What?" he said.

"Why do you want to marry her?" she asked.

"Well, she's pretty—I mean, I'm in love with her."

"Is that all?"

"I guess so," he said. "Is there supposed to be more?"

"No. Not usually," the mother said. "Are you working?"

"Yes. As a matter of fact, that's why I'm going into Manhattan so early. Today is the first day of my first job."

"Congratulations," the mother said.

"Thanks," he said. "Can I marry your daughter?"

"Do you have a car?" she asked.

"Not yet," he said. "But I should be able to get one pretty soon. And a house, too."

"A house?"

"With lots of rooms."

"Yes, that's what I expected you to say," she said. She turned to her daughter. "Do you love him?"

"Yes, mother, I do."

"Why?"

"Because he's good, and gentle, and kind."

"Are you sure?"

"Yes."

"Then you really love him."

"Yes."

"Are you sure there isn't anyone else that you might love and might want to marry?"

"No, mother," the girl said.

"Well, then," the mother said to the young man. "Looks like there's nothing I can do about it. Ask her again."

The train stopped.

"My dearest one," he said. "Will you marry me?"

"Yes," she said.

Everybody in the car smiled and applauded.

"Isn't life wonderful?" the boy asked the mother.

"Beautiful," the mother said.

The conductor climbed down from between the cars as the train started up, and straightening his dark tie, approached them with a solemn black book in his hand.

The Two Pickpockets

. . . he suddenly found that his own pocketbook had been taken.

There was a provincial pickpocket who was very successful at his work, and he thought he'd go up to London and see what he could do there. So he went up to London, and he was even more successful.

One day he was busy in Oxford Street when he suddenly found that his own pocketbook had been taken. He looked round and saw a very attractive blond girl walking away. He was sure that she was the one who had picked his pocket so he followed her and got his pocketbook back from her. He was so much taken by her cleverness in robbing him that he suggested that they should go into partnership together. And so they did, and succeeded brilliantly.

At length the provincial pickpocket thought, "We're the best pickpockets in London. If we married we could breed up a race of the best pickpockets in the world." So he asked the girl, and she was quite agreeable, and they were married, and in due time a beautiful little baby boy was born to them. But the poor little fellow was deformed. His right arm was bent to his chest, and the little fist tightly clenched. And nothing they could do would straighten it.

The poor parents were much distressed. "He'll never make a pickpocket," they said, "with a paralyzed right arm." They took him at once to the doctor, but the doctor said he was too young, they must wait. But they didn't want to wait; they took him to one doctor after another, and at last—because they were very rich by this time—to the best child specialist they could hear of.

The specialist took out his gold watch, and felt the pulse on the little paralyzed arm. "The flow of blood seems normal," he said. "What a bright little fellow he is for his age! He's focusing his eyes on my watch." He took the chain out of his waistcoat, and swung the watch to and fro, and the baby's eyes followed it. Then the little bent arm straightened out towards the watch, the little clenched fingers opened to take it, and down dropped the midwife's gold wedding ring.

A Catch Tale

BY CHARLIE SLANE

Suddenly, I came nose to nose with this great, black bear.

You don't see bears around as often as you used to. But I remember seeing one once when I was out picking raspberries. It was the end of August and it was hot. It was a real scorcher! And there I was, down on my knees making my way around the raspberry canes. Suddenly, I came nose to nose with this great, black bear.

He was doing the same thing, of course. He was eating the raspberries, stripping them off with his big paw and stuffing them in his mouth. He was surprised and annoyed that I was picking his berries, because he growled and got up on his hind legs. Well, I didn't hang around.

I took off down the old woods road, and when I looked back he was coming along after me on all fours. Bears can run pretty fast. I can run pretty fast, too. I was running the mile in about two minutes, at least. But so was the bear and he was right behind me.

I ran and ran and ran. It was awful hot. The sweat was just pouring off me. I'd look back every once in a while, and the bear seemed to be getting a little closer. So I put on a little more effort and I ran for an awful long time. I was getting tired, too. But the bear was still coming on. He wasn't getting any farther away. In fact, he was just as close as he could be.

So I ran and ran and ran. I ran for an awful long time. And just when I thought I couldn't run another step, I came to this lake. It was frozen over a little bit. There was just an inch of ice over it, and I knew that it would hold me if I ran over it real fast, and I knew if the bear followed me, it wouldn't hold him.

So I ran out onto the ice, and I stopped in the middle. And there came the bear, charging after me. He paused for a minute when he saw me out there, then he ran right out on the ice. He got just about halfways when the ice cracked and gave way and down he went and drowned. That was the end of him.

"Hey! That can't be true. You said it was summertime and awful hot. There couldn't be any ice on the lake then!"

Yup, it's true all right. It was summertime when I started running. But like I said, I ran for an awful long time.

The Princess and the Tin Box

BY JAMES THURBER

. . . all her life she had been glutted with precious stones and priceless metals . . .

Once upon a time, in a far country, there lived a king whose daughter was the prettiest princess in the world. Her eyes were like the cornflower, her hair was sweeter than the hyacinth, and her throat made the swan look dusty.

From the time she was a year old, the princess had been showered with presents. Her nursery looked like Cartier's window. Her toys were all made of gold or platinum or diamonds or emeralds. She was not permitted to have wooden blocks or china dolls or rubber dogs or linen books, because such materials were considered cheap for the daughter of a king.

When she was seven, she was allowed to attend the wedding of her brother and throw real pearls at the bride instead of rice. Only the nightingale, with his lyre of gold, was permitted to sing for the princess. The common blackbird, with his boxwood flute, was kept out of the palace grounds. She walked in silver-and-samite slippers to a sapphire-and-topaz bathroom and slept in an ivory bed inlaid with rubies.

On the day the princess was eighteen, the king sent a royal ambassador to the courts of five neighboring kingdoms to announce that he would give his daughter's hand in marriage to the prince who brought her the gift she liked the most.

The first prince to arrive at the palace rode a swift white stallion and laid at the feet of the princess an enormous apple made of solid gold which he had taken from a dragon who had guarded it for a thousand years. It was placed on a long ebony table set up to hold the gifts of the princess's suitors. The second prince, who came on a gray charger, brought her a nightingale made of a thousand diamonds, and it was placed beside the golden apple. The third prince, riding on a black horse, carried a great jewel box made of platinum and sapphires, and it was placed next to the diamond nightingale. The fourth prince, astride a fiery yellow horse, gave the princess a gigantic heart made of rubies and pierced by an emerald arrow. It was placed next to the platinum-and-sapphire jewel box.

Now the fifth prince was the strongest and handsomest of all the five suitors, but he was the son of a poor king whose realm had been overrun by mice and locusts and wizards and mining engineers so that there was nothing much of value left in it. He came plodding up to the palace of the princess on a plow horse and he brought her a small tin box filled with mica and feldspar and hornblende which he had picked up on the way.

The other princes roared with disdainful laughter when they saw the tawdry gift the fifth prince had brought to the princess. But she examined it with great interest and squealed with delight, for all her life she had been glutted with precious stones and priceless metals, but she had never seen tin before or mica or feldspar or hornblende. The tin box was placed next to the ruby heart pierced with an emerald arrow.

"Now," the king said to his daughter, "you must select the gift you like best and marry the prince that brought it."

The princess smiled and walked up to the table and picked up the present she liked the most. It was the platinum-and-sapphire jewel box, the gift of the third prince.

"The way I figure it," she said, "is this. It is a very large and expensive box, and when I am married, I will meet many admirers who will give me precious gems with which to fill it to the top. Therefore, it is the most valuable of all the gifts my suitors have brought me and I like it the best."

The princess married the third prince that very day in the midst of great merriment and high revelry. More than a hundred thousand pearls were thrown at her and she loved it.

Moral: All those who thought the princess was going to select the tin box filled with worthless stones instead of one of the other gifts will kindly stay after class and write one hundred times on the blackboard "I would rather have a hunk of aluminum silicate than a diamond necklace."

"Storytelling is vital to human health. It gives us workable metaphors for our lives."

Clarence Major

Action Will Be Taken

An Action-Packed Story

BY HEINRICH BÖLL

TRANSLATED FROM THE GERMAN BY LEILA VENNEWITZ

I must have paused too long, for Wunsiedel, who seldom raised his voice, shouted at me: "Answer! Answer, you know the rules!"

Probably one of the strangest interludes in my life was the time I spent as an employee in Alfred Wunsiedel's factory. By nature I am inclined more to pensiveness and inactivity than to work, but now and again prolonged financial difficulties compel me—for pensiveness is no more profitable than inactivity—to take on a so-called job. Finding myself once again at a low ebb of this kind, I put myself in the hands of the employment office and was sent with seven other fellow-sufferers to Wunsiedel's factory, where we were to undergo an aptitude test.

The exterior of the factory was enough to arouse my suspicions: the factory was built entirely of glass brick, and my aversion to well-lit buildings and well-lit rooms is as strong as my aversion to work. I became even more suspicious when we were immediately served breakfast in the well-lit, cheerful coffee shop: pretty waitresses brought us eggs, coffee and toast, orange juice was served in tastefully designed jugs, goldfish pressed their bored faces against the sides of pale-green aquariums. The waitresses were so cheerful that they appeared to be bursting with good cheer. Only a strong effort of will—so it seemed to me—restrained them from singing away all day long.

They were as crammed with unsung songs as chickens with unlaid eggs.

Right away I realized something that my fellow-sufferers evidently failed to realize: that this breakfast was already part of the test; so I chewed away reverently, with the full appreciation of a person who knows he is supplying his body with valuable elements. I did something which normally no power on earth can make me do: I drank orange juice on an empty stomach, left the coffee and egg untouched, as well as most of the toast, got up, and paced up and down in the coffee shop, pregnant with action.

As a result I was the first to be ushered into the room where the questionnaires were spread out on attractive tables. The walls were done in a shade of green that would have summoned the word "delightful" to the lips of interior decoration enthusiasts. The room appeared to be empty, and yet I was so sure of being observed that I behaved as someone pregnant with action behaves when he believes himself unobserved: I ripped my pen impatiently from my pocket, unscrewed the top, sat down at the nearest table and pulled the questionnaire toward me, the way irritable customers snatch at the bill in a restaurant.

Question No. 1: Do you consider it right for a human being to possess only two arms, two legs, eyes, and ears?

Here for the first time I reaped the harvest of my pensive nature and wrote without hesitation: "Even four arms, legs and ears would not be adequate for my driving energy. Human beings are very poorly equipped."

Question No. 2: How many telephones can you handle at one time?

Here again the answer was as easy as simple arithmetic: "When there are only seven telephones," I wrote, "I get impatient; there have to be nine before I feel I am working to capacity."

Question No. 3: How do you spend your free time?

My answer: "I no longer acknowledge the term free time—on my fifteenth birthday I eliminated it from my vocabulary, for in the beginning was the act."

I got the job. Even with nine telephones I really didn't feel I was working to capacity. I shouted into the mouthpieces: "Take immediate action!" or: "Do something!—We must have some action—Action will be taken—Action has been taken—Action should be taken." But as a rule—for I felt this was in keeping with the tone of the place—I used the imperative.

Of considerable interest were the noon-hour breaks, when we consumed nutritious foods in an atmosphere of silent good cheer. Wunsiedel's factory was swarming with people who were obsessed with telling you the story of their lives, as indeed vigorous personalities are fond of doing. The story of their lives is more important to them than their lives, you have only to press a button, and immediately it is covered with spewed-out exploits.

Wunsiedel had a right-hand man called Broschek, who had in turn made a name for himself by supporting seven children and a paralyzed wife by working night-shifts in his student days, and successfully carrying on four business agencies, besides which he had passed two examinations with honors in two years. When asked by reporters: "When do you sleep, Mr. Broschek?" he had replied: "It's a crime to sleep!"

Wunsiedel's secretary had supported a paralyzed husband and four children by knitting, at the same time graduating in psychology and German history as well as breeding shepherd dogs, and she had become famous as a night-club singer where she was known as *Vamp Number Seven.*

Wunsiedel himself was one of those people who every morning, as they open their eyes, make up their minds to act. "I must act," they think as they briskly tie their bathrobe belts around them. "I must act," they think as they shave, triumphantly watching their beard hairs being washed away with the lather: these hirsute vestiges are the first daily sacrifices to their driving energy. The more intimate functions also give these people a sense of satisfaction: water swishes, paper is used. Action has been taken. Bread gets eaten, eggs are decapitated.

With Wunsiedel, the most trivial activity looked like action: the way he put on his hat, the way—quivering with energy—he buttoned up his overcoat, the kiss he gave his wife, everything was action.

When he arrived at his office he greeted his secretary with a cry of "Let's have some action!" And in ringing tones she would call back: "Action will be taken!" Wunsiedel then went from department to

department, calling out his cheerful: "Let's have some action!" Everyone would answer: "Action will be taken!" And I would call back to him too, with a radiant smile, when he looked into my office: "Action will be taken!"

Within a week I had increased the number of telephones on my desk to eleven, within two weeks to thirteen, and every morning on the streetcar I enjoyed thinking up new imperatives, or chasing the words *take action* through various tenses and modulations: for two whole days I kept saying the same sentence over and over again because I thought it sounded so marvelous: "Action ought to have been taken;" for another two days it was: "Such action ought not to have been taken."

So I was really beginning to feel I was working to capacity when there actually was some action. One Tuesday morning—I had hardly settled down at my desk—Wunsiedel rushed into my office crying his "Let's have some action!" But an inexplicable something in his face made me hesitate to reply, in a cheerful gay voice as the rules dictated: "Action will be taken!" I must have paused too long, for Wunsiedel, who seldom raised his voice, shouted at me: "Answer! Answer, you know the rules!" And I answered, under my breath, reluctantly, like a child who is forced to say: I am a naughty child. It was only by a great effort that I managed to bring out the sentence: "Action will be taken," and hardly had I uttered it when there really was some action: Wunsiedel dropped to the floor. As he fell he rolled over onto his side and lay right across the open doorway. I knew at once, and I confirmed it when I went slowly around my desk and approached the body on the floor: he was dead.

Shaking my head I stepped over Wunsiedel, walked slowly along the corridor to Broschek's office, and entered without knocking. Broschek was sitting at his desk, a telephone receiver in each hand, between his teeth a ballpoint pen with which he was making notes on a writing pad, while with his bare feet he was operating a knitting machine under the desk. In this way he helps to clothe his family. "We've had some action," I said in a low voice.

Broschek spat out the ballpoint pen, put down the two receivers, reluctantly detached his toes from the knitting machine.

"What action?" he asked.

"Wunsiedel is dead," I said.

"No," said Broschek.

"Yes," I said, "come and have a look!"

"No," said Broschek, "that's impossible," but he put on his slippers and followed me along the corridor.

"No," he said, when we stood beside Wunsiedel's corpse, "no, no!" I did not contradict him. I carefully turned Wunsiedel over onto his back, closed his eyes, and looked at him pensively.

I felt something like tenderness for him, and realized for the first time that I had never hated him. On his face was that expression which one sees on children who obstinately refuse to give up their faith in Santa Claus, even though the arguments of their playmates sound so convincing.

"No," said Broschek, "no."

"We must take action," I said quietly to Broschek.

"Yes," said Broschek, "we must take action."

Action was taken: Wunsiedel was buried, and I was delegated to carry a wreath of artificial roses behind his coffin, for I am equipped with not only a penchant for pensiveness and inactivity but also a face and figure that go extremely well with dark suits. Apparently as I walked along behind Wunsiedel's coffin carrying the wreath of artificial roses I looked superb. I received an offer from a fashionable firm of funeral directors to join their staff as a professional mourner. "You are a born mourner," said the manager, "your outfit would be provided by the firm. Your face—simply superb!"

I handed in my notice to Broschek, explaining that I had never really felt I was working to capacity there; that, in spite of the thirteen telephones, some of my talents were going to waste. As soon as my first professional appearance as a mourner was over I knew: This is where I belong, this is what I am cut out for.

Pensively I stand behind the coffin in the funeral chapel, holding a simple bouquet, while the organ plays Handel's *Largo*, a piece that does not receive nearly the respect it deserves. The cemetery café is my regular haunt; there I spend the intervals between my professional engagements, although sometimes I walk behind coffins which I have not been engaged to follow, I pay for flowers out of my own pocket and join the welfare worker who walks behind the coffin of some homeless person. From time to time I also visit Wunsiedel's grave, for after all I owe it to him that I discovered my true vocation, a vocation in which pensiveness is essential and inactivity my duty.

It was not till much later that I realized I had never bothered to find out what was being produced in Wunsiedel's factory. I expect it was soap.

INNOCENCE AND EXPERIENCE II

The Sniper

BY LIAM O'FLAHERTY

Here and there through the city, machine guns and rifles broke the silence of the night . . .

The long June twilight faded into night. Dublin lay enveloped in darkness but for the dim light of the moon that shone through fleecy clouds, casting a pale light as of approaching dawn over the streets and the dark waters of the Liffey. Around the beleaguered Four Courts the heavy guns roared. Here and there through the city, machine guns and rifles broke the silence of the night, spasmodically, like dogs barking on lone farms. Republicans and Free Staters were waging civil war.

On a rooftop near O'Connell Bridge, a Republican sniper lay watching. Beside him lay his rifle and over his shoulders were slung a pair of field glasses. His face was the face of a student, thin and ascetic, but his eyes had the cold gleam of the fanatic. They were deep and thoughtful, the eyes of a man who is used to looking at death.

He was eating a sandwich hungrily. He had eaten nothing since morning. He had been too excited to eat. He finished the sandwich, and taking a flask of whisky from his pocket, he took a short draught. Then he returned the flask to his pocket. He paused for a moment, considering whether he should risk a smoke. It was dangerous. The flash might be seen in the darkness, and there were enemies watching. He decided to take the risk.

Placing a cigarette between his lips, he struck a match, inhaled the smoke hurriedly and put out the light. Almost immediately, a bullet flattened itself against the parapet of the roof. The sniper took another whiff and put out the cigarette. Then he swore softly and crawled away to the left.

Cautiously he raised himself and peered over the parapet. There was a flash and a bullet whizzed over his head. He dropped immediately. He had seen the flash. It came from the opposite side of the street.

He rolled over the roof to a chimney stack in the rear, and slowly drew himself up behind it, until his eyes were level with the top of the parapet. There was nothing to be seen—just the dim outline of the opposite housetop against the blue sky. His enemy was under cover.

Just then an armored car came across the bridge and advanced slowly up the street. It stopped on the opposite side of the street, fifty yards ahead. The sniper could hear the dull panting of the motor. His heart beat faster. It was an enemy car. He wanted to fire, but he knew it was useless. His bullets would never pierce the steel that covered the gray monster.

Then round the corner of a side street came an old woman, her head covered by a tattered shawl. She began to talk to the man in the turret of the car. She was pointing to the roof where the sniper lay. An informer.

The turret opened. A man's head and shoulders appeared, looking toward the sniper. The sniper raised his rifle and fired. The head fell heavily on the turret wall. The woman darted toward the side street. The sniper fired again. The woman whirled round and fell with a shriek into the gutter.

Suddenly from the opposite roof a shot rang out and the sniper dropped his rifle with a curse. The rifle clattered to the roof. The sniper thought the noise would wake the dead. He stopped to pick the rifle up. He couldn't lift it. His forearm was dead. "I'm hit," he muttered.

Dropping flat onto the roof, he crawled back to the parapet. With his left hand he felt the injured right forearm. The blood was oozing through the sleeve of his coat. There was no pain—just a deadened sensation, as if the arm had been cut off.

Quickly he drew his knife from his pocket, opened it on the breastwork of the parapet, and ripped open the sleeve. There was a small hole where the bullet had entered. On the other side there was no hole. The bullet had lodged in the bone. It must have fractured it. He bent the arm below the wound. The arm bent back easily. He ground his teeth to overcome the pain.

Then taking out his field dressing, he ripped open the packet with his knife. He broke the neck of the iodine bottle and let the bitter fluid drip into the wound. A paroxysm of pain swept through him. He placed the cotton wadding over the wound and wrapped the dressing over it. He tied the ends with his teeth.

Then he lay still against the parapet, and, closing his eyes, he made an effort of will to overcome the pain.

In the street beneath, all was still. The armored car had retired speedily over the bridge, with the machine gunner's head hanging lifeless over the turret. The woman's corpse lay still in the gutter.

The sniper lay still for a long time nursing his wounded arm and planning escape. Morning must not find him wounded on the roof. The enemy on the opposite roof covered his escape. He must kill that enemy and he could not use his rifle. He had only a revolver to do it. Then he thought of a plan.

Taking off his cap, he placed it over the muzzle of his rifle. Then he pushed the rifle slowly upward over the parapet, until the cap was visible from the opposite side of the street. Almost immediately, there was a report, and a bullet pierced the center of the cap. The sniper slanted the rifle forward. The cap slipped down into the street. Then catching the rifle in the middle, the sniper dropped his left hand over the roof and let it hang, lifelessly. After a few moments he let the rifle drop to the street. Then he sank to the roof, dragging his hand with him.

Crawling quickly to the left, he peered up at the corner of the roof. His ruse had succeeded. The other sniper, seeing the cap and rifle fall, thought that he had killed his man. He was now standing before a row of chimney pots, looking across, with his head clearly silhouetted against the western sky.

The Republican sniper smiled and lifted his revolver above the edge of the parapet. The distance was about fifty yards—a hard shot in the dim light, and his right arm was paining him like a thousand devils. He took a steady aim. His hand trembled with eagerness. Pressing his lips together, he took a deep breath through his nostrils and fired.

He was almost deafened with the report and his arm shook with the recoil.

Then when the smoke cleared he peered across and uttered a cry of joy. His enemy had been hit. He was reeling over the parapet in his death agony. He struggled to keep his feet, but he was slowly falling forward, as if in a dream. The rifle fell from his grasp, hit the parapet, fell over, bounded off the pole of a barber's shop beneath and then clattered on the pavement.

Then the dying man on the roof crumpled up and fell forward. The body turned over and over in space and hit the ground with a dull thud. Then it lay still.

The sniper looked at his enemy falling and he shuddered. The lust of battle died in him. He became bitten by remorse. The sweat stood out in beads on his forehead. Weakened by his wound and the long summer day of fasting and watching on the roof, he revolted from the sight of the shattered mass of his dead enemy. His teeth chattered, he began to gibber to himself, cursing the war, cursing himself, cursing everybody.

He looked at the smoking revolver in his hand, and with an oath he hurled it to the roof at his feet. The revolver went off with the concussion and the bullet whizzed past the sniper's head. He was frightened back to his senses by the shock. His nerves steadied. The cloud of fear scattered from his mind and he laughed.

Taking the whisky flask from his pocket, he emptied it at a draught. He felt reckless under the influence of the spirit. He decided to leave the roof now and look for his company commander, to report. Everywhere around was quiet. There was not much danger in going through the streets. He picked up his revolver and put it in his pocket. Then he crawled down through the skylight to the house underneath.

When the sniper reached the laneway on the street level, he felt a sudden curiosity as to the identity of the enemy sniper whom he had killed. He decided that he was a good shot, whoever he was. He wondered did he know him. Perhaps he had been in his own company before the split in the army. He decided to risk going over to have a look at him. He peered around the corner into O'Connell Street. In the upper part of the street there was a heavy firing, but around here all was quiet.

The sniper darted across the street. A machine gun tore up the ground around him with a hail of bullets, but he escaped. He threw himself face downward beside the corpse. The machine gun stopped.

Then the sniper turned over the dead boy and looked into his brother's face.

Pita of the Deep Sea

BY MICHAEL ANTHONY

He could hear the terrible roar which from the deep had sounded like a whisper of music. He looked back a little. There was only a tiny streak of blood behind him.

Pita panicked. There was nothing he could do. He was trapped. Trapped with hundreds of others. The Monster had come and was slowly, surely, dragging them from the deep. He swam through the excited crowd to try the bottom. Then he tried the top again. The great Monster had encircled them completely. There were millions of holes in its great hands, but none large enough. If only they were a little larger. Pita tried to push himself through one of the holes again. He squeezed and squeezed. Great tails lashed around him. Not only he but the whole crowd were in desperation. He tried to ease himself through. The thread-limbs pressed against his eyes. If only his head could get through. He pushed again, hard, and the pain quivered through his body. Down to his tail. He turned around. But it was no use trying it from that end. His tail was much wider than his head. There was nothing he could do. He heard the breakers roaring above now. That meant they were nearing the shore. Pita whipped his tail in fury. The Monster was gradually closing its hands. The crowd was being heaped against each other. He was knocked about by the giant tails. Good thing he was so small and could avoid being crushed. Around him were his friends and his dreaded enemies. The bonito was there, the killer shark was there. None of them thought of him now. They were all trying to escape. The killer shark, too. Shark, bonito, herring, cavali—they were all the same to him. A giant swordfish charged the threads desperately. The shark turned on its belly in vain to swallow the Monster. It swallowed a jellyfish. There were cries now above the surface. Below, the Monster grated on sand. The shore! They had reached the shore! Frantically Pita flung himself against one of the tiny holes. He gave a cry as the scales tore from his back—then a cry of joy. He was free! Free!

He lunged forward below the surface. He could feel the density of the breakers pushing down on him. He could hear the terrible roar which from the deep had sounded like a whisper of music. He looked back a little. There was only a tiny streak of blood behind him. He would be all right. He would be all right. Down, he went. Further away and down. Faster, faster he swam. His tail whipped the white foam, pushing him forward like a spear. Down he sped, rejoicing in his tiny-ness. If he was only a little bigger he would have been dying on the shore now. The fateful shore! There had been those who had actually come back from that world. This was one of the greatest mysteries. It was hard to believe that any fish had come back from the shore. But some said they had been there, and had talked of that awesome place. A place of no water and no fish. It was hard to believe this. But so had it been to believe about the Monster. But the Monster was real enough now. His mother had always warned him. He looked back a little. There was no more blood now. Down, he swam. Deeper, further. Deep, deep, until the sound of the breakers was only a bitter memory, and the sea was not sandy but blue and clear, and until, far, far away in the distance, green with the fern and the tender moss, he saw the rocks of home.

A thrill ran through him. He squirted through the water as if a new verve had possessed his body. His tail whipped the foam white and frothy.

"Mother!" he thought, "Mother!" And he dived headlong towards the green rock.

"Mother, I am home," he gurgled.

The mother stared at him between the rocks. She noticed the bruised back. She was cross, yet the very fact that he had returned made her feel happy inside.

"Pita!" she exclaimed.

"I am home," he said.

"Wherever have you been to? Whatever happened?"

She was sure he had gone among the rocks playing and had lost his way. And that he had bruised his back swimming carelessly, or romping with the shingles. Pita was like that. He had always gone away far and played. He had always run away to meet the corals and the anemones and his other friends of the deep sea.

"Where have you been?" she said.

"Mother—" Pita hesitated, "Mother—the Monster."

The mother went cold with shock. Her eyes gleamed white and there was fear and horror in them.

"Pita, I warned you! I warned you! You wouldn't hear! Why did you go near the surface!"

"Mother—"

"Keep away from the surface, I always tell you! Keep away from the shore!"

"Mother, the Monster is everywhere."

"He can't come between the rocks. He never comes here."

"Mother, I can't stay all day between the rocks. I have friends everywhere. This morning I promised the corals—"

"This morning you promised nothing!" gulped the mother. "You nearly promised your life. Keep here between the rocks. Play with the moss and the fern. Here you are safe."

"The Monster isn't always here," said Pita. "Sometimes I swim out to my friends. We see the wonderful things. Sometimes we go up to the surface to see the sun. It is dark here below. Up there it is bright and very strange. When I grow up I will go often to see the sun, and to hear the music of the waves, and to watch the winds play on the roof of the sea."

"Hush up," the mother gulped. "It is more beautiful here between the rocks. It is more beautiful here because it is safe. Tell me, how did you escape? It is very odd. No one escapes the Monster."

"Oh," said Pita, and he told her. He told her how he was just playing and how very suddenly he found himself against the Great Hands of the Monster. He told her how terrified he was and how he swam down to the bottom to escape, but he could not. And even at the top he could not. For the hands were everywhere. The hands with the million tiny holes. He told her how there were hundreds of others caught like him, even the killer shark. She gulped and shrunk back, and he said yes, the killer shark. And he told her how the Great Hands had gradually closed around them and pushed them all together and how they were all frightened and desperate, even the killer shark. He told her how the breakers had pounded over them and how they were dragged on the sands of the shore, and how he had actually heard the voices of the shore. Then he told her how he had flung himself desperately against one of the holes, while the thread-limbs cut at him and the pain shot through him, but how he had discovered himself free at last in the wide ocean. And he laughed as he said this part for he remembered himself speeding through the water, faster than barracuda, faster than anything.

But the mother did not laugh. In fact she was gloomier than before. For Pita was a wayward fish. She knew she couldn't change him. She knew that with all her advice she couldn't prevail upon him to keep away from the open deep, and from the surface, and from the sound of the breakers near the shore. She knew, too, as well as he, that it was his tinyness that saved him. But he was growing fast. In the next few months he would be no baby any more. She shuddered to think what would happen then if he made such a mistake again. Certainly that would be the end. Yet, as he grew he would become quicker. The fully-grown carite was perhaps the fastest fish in the sea. But as far as she had heard, the hands of the Monster were deep and wide and stretched far beyond the bounds of speed. Therefore she turned away sadly and swam to a dark corner of the rock to meditate.

The fully-grown carite was, indeed, the fastest fish in the sea. Pita no longer feared the barracuda, the shark, the swordfish. In the earlier months these had seemed to him so very fast. Now, with his long streamlined body, he could outstrip them with the greatest ease.

The mother was so proud. Pita was as handsome as he was enormous. But he was not so enormous as to be ungainly. Sometimes at play, or just to be showing off, he would go past the rocks like a silver flash. And she would smile. Yes, he had grown up but he was still fond of play.

And now he was so popular that his friends would not leave him alone. Every day he sported with the dolphins and corals and the anemones. And at night he came back to dream among the ferns.

Secretly his mother would be amused with his tales. Sometimes she stayed up just to hear.

"Quiet," she would say, "be quiet and go to sleep!" And he would gurgle teasingly among the rocks, and she would listen to his tales of the deep, about his pranks with the pretty corals and anemones. But about his new friend, the moonfish, Pita said nothing. He had met her at the distant rocks.

As the days passed he thought of the moonfish more and more. She was whom he dreamed of when he lay among the ferns. There he saw her eyes again, sparkling like the crystal depths. There again he saw her tinted scales, gleaming like mirrors of silver. She was Iona, the Pride of the Sea. Thinking of her, Pita became more and more wistful till even his mother noticed and was puzzled. But Pita kept silent. All his friends of the deep knew, though, and together they talked about it. They talked of how Pita stared blindly into water, and how once he nearly swam in the way of a killer shark. They talked of Iona the Beautiful, and they envied her. For they knew what would be. And now the dolphins waited on the reefs in vain, and the corals, broken-hearted, murmured their low, sad song.

Eventually Pita spoke to his mother, for he would go away. She wept because she, too, knew what would be. She asked who was this Iona and Pita was surprised. All the sea knew, he said. In the heights and in the depths. From the waters near the shore, to the waters of the limitless bounds. Even the wonderful moon in the wind-water above the sea knew of her, for they had played together and he had given his magic to her.

He said he would go away to the distant rocks and before many tides he would return. Then would he bring back, he said, the greatest treasure of his days. He would bring back his bride and her daughter— the Pride of the Sea.

The mother listened with great pain. She realized that in this way Pita was lost to her. And she knew that she could not forbid this marriage even if she would have wanted to. Therefore she warned him again of the open sea, for it was still the terrible season of the Great Hands. And she told him of the ways to go. The ways which were difficult but safest. Then her heart lifted a little, for the marriage was good. As for the Monster of the Great Hands, the Providence which guided Pita so long would guide him again. She swam through the rocks looking about her busily. For now she had to prepare a home for her son, and for the beautiful Iona—the Pride of the Sea.

The bay was deep and wide and the winds played on the floor of the ocean. It was a beautiful month for the fishing, although it was the mating season. In the mating season you did not catch the fish plentifully, but if you were young and you went out with the sea calm and the breeze fresh, and with the sun lighting up the palm-fringed shore, sometimes you laughed aloud for the sheer joy of living and you hardly thought of the fish at all.

Thus had it been with these fishermen crossing the breakers. But now they cast their nets out with some enthusiasm because of the unexpected sight below. Halfway down, the water was foamy and rippling. The sign of fish.

Quickly they encircled the fish. They watched the leaden weights of the nets sink to the bottom. This would make their day. It came almost too easily. They watched each other, for it was very unusual to come upon a school of fish in the mating season.

Soon they were back on shore hauling the catch in. They hauled as the fish struggled in the nets and the breakers chattered along the bay. They pulled and pulled still amazed at their fortune, and when the nets dragged on sand and they could see the host of fins and tails flapping and lashing up the water, they were even more astonished.

They dragged the catch right out on dry beach. There were hundreds of fish and crabs and corals. Even anemones.

"Look," said one of the fishermen, pulling out a shiny flat fish from the living heap. Nearby a carite beat violently, gulping and leaping about the sand. The fishermen were looking at the shiny fish.

"It's ages," said the one with the fish, "years—since we brought in one of these." He held the fish high. Its eyes gleamed as sparkling as the crystal depths and its scales were like mirrors of silver.

"Moonfish," he said, more to himself. He was experienced and he knew it. "Look at her! Pretty eh?" he smiled. "She's like some—like some Pride of the Sea!"

The carite nearby beat furiously.

"The oldest story is the story of flight, the search for greener pastures."
Guy Vanderhaeghe

You Are Now Entering the Human Heart

BY JANET FRAME

I wanted to see more of the Franklin Institute and the Natural Science Museum across the street, but a journey through the human heart would be fascinating.

I looked at the notice. I wondered if I had time before my train left Philadelphia for Baltimore in one hour. The heart, ceiling-high, occupied one corner of the large exhibition hall, and from wherever you stood in the hall you could hear its beating, *thum-thump-thum-thump*. It was a popular exhibit, and sometimes, when there were too many children about, the entrance had to be roped off, as the children loved to race up and down the blood vessels and match their cries to the heart's beating. I could see that the heart had already been punished for the day—the floor of the blood vessel was worn and dusty, the chamber walls were covered with marks, and the notice "You Are Now Taking the Path of a Blood Cell Through the Human Heart" hung askew. I wanted to see more of the Franklin Institute and the Natural Science Museum across the street, but a journey through the human heart would be fascinating. Did I have time?

Later. First, I would go across the street to the Hall of North America, among the bear and the bison, and catch up on American flora and fauna.

I made my way to the Hall. More children, sitting in rows on canvas chairs. An elementary class from a city school, under the control of an elderly teacher. A museum attendant holding a basket, and all eyes gazing at the basket.

"Oh," I said. "Is this a private lesson? Is it all right for me to be here?"

The attendant was brisk. "Surely. We're having a lesson in snake-handling," he said. "It's something new. Get the children young and teach them that every snake they meet is not to be killed. People seem to think that every snake has to be knocked on the head. So we're getting them young and teaching them."

"May I watch?" I said.

"Surely. This is a common grass snake. No harm, no harm at all. Teach the children to learn the feel of them, to lose their fear."

He turned to the teacher. "Now, Miss—Mrs.—" he said.

"Miss Aitcheson."

He lowered his voice. "The best way to get through to the children is to start with teacher," he said to Miss Aitcheson. "If they see you're not afraid, then they won't be."

She must be near retiring age, I thought. A city woman. Never handled a snake in her life. Her face was pale. She just managed to drag the fear from her eyes to someplace in their depths, where it lurked like a dark stain. Surely the attendant and the children noticed?

"It's harmless," the attendant said. He'd been working with snakes for years.

Miss Aitcheson, I thought again. A city woman born and bred. All snakes were creatures to kill, to be protected from, alike the rattler, the copperhead, king snake, grass snake—venom and victims. Were there not places in the South where you couldn't go into the streets for fear of the rattlesnakes?

Her eyes faced the lighted exit. I saw her fear. The exit light blinked, hooded. The children, none of whom had ever touched a live snake, were sitting hushed, waiting for the drama to begin; one or two looked afraid as the attendant withdrew a green snake about three feet long from the basket and with a swift movement, before the teacher could protest, draped it around her neck and stepped back, admiring and satisfied.

"There," he said to the class. "Your teacher has a snake around her neck and she's not afraid."

Miss Aitcheson stood rigid; she seemed to be holding her breath.

"Teacher's not afraid, are you?" the attendant persisted. He leaned forward, pronouncing judgement on her, while she suddenly jerked her head and lifted her hands in panic to get rid of the snake. Then, seeing the children watching, she whispered, "No, I'm not afraid. Of course not." She looked around her.

"Of course not," she repeated sharply.

I could see her defeat and helplessness. The attendant seemed unaware, as if his perception had grown a reptilian covering. What did she care for the campaign for the preservation and welfare of copperheads and rattlers and common grass snakes? What did she care about someday walking through the woods or the desert and deciding between killing a snake and setting it free, as if there would be time to decide, when her journey to and from school in downtown Philadelphia held enough danger to occupy her? In two years or so, she'd retire and be in that apartment by herself and no doorman, and everyone knew what happened then, and how she'd be afraid to answer the door and to walk after dark and carry her pocketbook in the street. There was enough to think about without learning to handle and love the snakes, harmless and otherwise, by having them draped around her neck for everyone, including the children—most of all the children—to witness the outbreak of her fear.

"See, Miss Aitcheson's touching the snake. She's not afraid of it at all."

As everyone watched, she touched the snake. Her fingers recoiled. She touched it again.

"See, she's not afraid. Miss Aitcheson can stand there with a beautiful snake around her neck and touch it and stroke it and not be afraid."

The faces of the children were full of admiration for the teacher's bravery, and yet there was a cruelly persistent tension; they were waiting, waiting.

"We have to learn to love snakes," the attendant said. "Would someone like to come out and stroke teacher's snake?"

Silence.

One shamefaced boy came forward. He stood petrified in front of the teacher.

"Touch it," the attendant urged. "It's a friendly snake. Teacher's wearing it around her neck and she's not afraid."

The boy darted his hand forward, rested it lightly on the snake, immediately withdrew his hand. Then he ran back to his seat. The children shrieked with glee.

"He's afraid," someone said. "He's afraid of the snake." The attendant soothed. "We have to get used to them, you know. Grownups are not afraid of them, but we can understand that when you're small you might be afraid, and that's why we want you to learn to love them. Isn't that right, Miss Aitcheson? Isn't that right? Now who else is going to be brave enough to touch teacher's snake?"

Two girls came out. They stood hand in hand, side by side, and stared at the snake and then at Miss Aitcheson.

I wondered when the torture would end. The two little girls did not touch the snake, but they smiled at it and spoke to it and Miss Aitcheson smiled at them and whispered how brave they were.

"Just a minute," the attendant said. "There's really no need to be brave. It's not a question of bravery. The snake is *harmless*, absolutely *harmless*. Where's the bravery when the snake is harmless?"

Suddenly the snake moved around to face Miss Aitcheson and thrust its flat head toward her cheek. She gave a scream, flung up her hands, and tore the snake from her throat and threw it on the floor, and rushing across the room, she collapsed into a small canvas chair beside the Bear Cabinet and started to cry.

I didn't feel I should watch any longer. Some of the children began to laugh, some to cry. The attendant picked up the snake and nursed it. Miss Aitcheson, recovering, sat helplessly exposed by the small piece of useless torture. It was not her fault she was city-bred, her eyes tried to tell us. She looked at the children, trying in some way to force their admiration and respect; they were shut against her. She was evicted from them and from herself and even from her own fear-infested tomorrow, because she could not promise to love and preserve what she feared. She had nowhere, at that moment, but the small canvas chair by the Bear Cabinet of the Natural Science Museum.

I looked at my watch. If I hurried, I would catch the train from Thirtieth Street. There would be no time to make the journey through the human heart. I hurried out of the museum. It was freezing cold. The icebreakers would be at work on the Delaware and the Susquehanna; the mist would have risen by the time I arrived home. Yes, I would just catch the train from Thirtieth Street. The journey through the human heart would have to wait until some other time.

"Storytelling is a personal art that makes public what is private and makes private what is public. By choosing this or that story to tell, I reveal much about myself."

Jane Yolen

Winter Oak

BY YURI NAGIBIN

Translated from the Russian by Helena Goscilo

As soon as they entered the forest and the heavily snow-laden fir branches closed behind them, they were transported into another, enchanted world of peace and quiet.

The snow that had fallen during the night covered the narrow path leading from Uvarovka to the school, and its course could be surmised only by the faint broken shadow on the glistening carpet of snow. The teacher trod cautiously in her small fur-trimmed boots, ready to withdraw her foot if the snow proved treacherous.

It was only a half-kilometre to the school, and the teacher had merely thrown a short fur jacket over her shoulders, and tied a light woollen kerchief on her head. It was bitter cold, and there was a fierce wind besides, which swept the freshly-fallen snow off the frozen snow crust and showered her with it from head to foot. But the twenty-four-year-old teacher liked all that. She liked it when the frost bit her nose and cheeks, when the wind blew under her fur jacket and stung her body with the cold. Turning her back to the wind, she saw behind the thick footprints of her pointed shoes, like the tracks of some wild animal, and that, too, appealed to her.

The fresh January morning, saturated with light, awakened in her joyful thoughts about life and about herself. It was only two years since she'd come from college, and already she'd acquired the reputation of a competent, experienced teacher of Russian. They knew and appreciated her everywhere—in Uvarovka, Kuzminky, Black Gully, the peat settlement, and the stud farm—and they respectfully called her Anna Vasilyevna.

A man was coming across the field in her direction. "What if he won't step aside to let me by?" thought Anna Vasilyevna with lively apprehension. "Two people can't fit onto the path, and if you step aside you sink into the snow in a second." But she knew inwardly that there wasn't a person in the district who wouldn't step aside for the teacher from Uvarovka.

They drew level. It was Frolov, a warden at the stud farm.

"Good morning, Anna Vasilyevna!" Frolov raised his fur hat above his solid, close-cropped head.

"What are you doing! Put it back on, it's freezing!"

Frolov probably wanted to pull his fur over his eyes himself, but now he delayed on purpose, wanting to show that the cold didn't affect him at all. A sheepskin coat fitted his trim light body snugly, and in his hand he held a slender snake-like whip with which he kept hitting his white felt boots, which were turned down below the knee.

"How's my Lyosha? He's not acting up?" Frolov asked deferentially.
"Of course he is. All normal children act up. Just so it doesn't go too far," replied Anna Vasilyevna, conscious of her pedagogical experience.

Frolov grinned:

"My Lyoshka's quiet, he takes after his father!"

He stepped aside and, sinking up to his knees in the snow, he looked no taller than a fifth-grader. Anna Vasilyevna nodded condescendingly to him and went on her way....

The two-story building, with its wide windows painted with frost, stood behind a low fence right beside the highway; its red walls cast a reddish light on the snow all the way up to the highway. The school had been built on the road on the side away from Uvarovka because it was attended by children from all around: from the nearby villages, from the stud farm, from the oilworkers' sanatorium, and from the distant peat settlement. And now along the highway from both directions hoods, kerchiefs, caps, hats, earmuffs, and bashlyks[1] streamed toward the school gates.

"Good morning, Anna Vasilyevna!" sounded every second, some of the greetings ringing and clear, others muffled and barely audible beneath the scarves and kerchiefs bundled up to the eyes.

Anna Vasilyevna's first lesson was with the fifth-grade "A" group. The shrill bell signalling the beginning of classes hadn't ceased ringing when Anna Vasilyevna entered the classroom. The children rose together, greeted her, and sat down in their seats. It took a while for it to get quiet. Desk tops banged, benches creaked, someone sighed loudly, evidently bidding farewell to the carefree morning mood.

"Today we'll finish analyzing parts of speech...."

The class grew quiet, and one could hear a heavy truck crawling and skidding along the highway.

Anna Vasilyevna remembered how nervous she used to get the previous year before classes began, and she used to repeat to herself like a schoolgirl during an exam. "A noun is a part of speech.... a noun is a part of speech..." And she also remembered how a strange fear had tormented her: what if they won't understand?

Anna Vasilyevna smiled at the recollection, adjusted the pin in her heavy knot of hair, and in a calm, even voice, feeling her calmness like a warmth through her body, began:

"A noun is a part of speech that denotes an object. In grammar an object is the name for anything about which one can ask who or what it is. For example: 'Who is he?' 'A student.' Or 'What is it?' 'A book'...."

"Can I come in?"

In the half-open doorway stood a small figure in worn felt boots on which sparkles of melting frost were dissolving. His round face, stung by the bitter cold, glowed as though rubbed with beets, and his eyebrows were silvered with frost.

"Late again, Savushkin?" Like the majority of young teachers, Anna Vasilyevna liked to be strict, but right now her question sounded almost plaintive.

Interpreting the teacher's words as permission to enter the classroom, Savushkin quickly stole to his seat. Anna Vasilyevna saw the boy put his oilskin bag in the desk and ask his neighbour something without turning his head—probably what she was explaining.

Savuskhin's lateness grieved Anna Vasilyevna as an annoying little incident that ruined a day which had begun well. The geography teacher, a small, dried-up old lady who resembled a night moth, had complained to her that Savushkin kept coming in late. She complained a lot in general—about the noise in the classroom, the students' inattentiveness. "The first morning lessons are so difficult!" the old woman had sighed. "Yes, for those who can't hold their students' attention and make their lessons interesting," Anna Vasilyevna had thought then with self-assurance, and had offered to change hours with her. Now she felt guilty before the old woman, who was perceptive enough to have sensed a challenge and a reproach in Anna Vasilyevna's obliging offer.

"Is everything clear?" Anna Vasilyevna addressed the class.

"Yes!... Yes!..." the children chorused in response.

"Fine. Then give me examples."

It was very quiet for a few seconds, then someone said hesitantly: "Cat."

"Right," said Anna Vasilyevna, instantly recalling that the year before the first example had also been "cat." And then all bonds seemed to break loose:

"Window!" "Table!" "House!" "Road!"

"Right," said Anna Vasilyevna.

The class seethed with happy excitement. Anna Vasilyevna was surprised at the joy with which the children named objects that were familiar to them as though they perceived a new, unusual significance in them. The range of examples kept expanding, but during the first moments the children stuck to the most familiar tangible things: wheel... tractor... well... starling's nest....

But from a desk in the back where fat Vasyatka was sitting there came the thin but insistent sound of:

"Tack... tack... tack..."

And someone said tentatively:

"Town..."

"Town—good!" Anna Vasilyevna approved.

And then they were off:

"Street..." "Subway..." "Tram..." "Film"

"That'll do," said Anna Vasilyevna. "I can see you understand it."

The voices died down somehow reluctantly; only fat Vasyatka still kept on droning his unacknowledged "tack." And suddenly, as if roused from sleep, Savushkin rose from his desk and cried out clearly:

"Winter oak!"

The children burst out laughing.

"Quiet!" Anna Vasilyevna slapped her palm on the desk.

"Winter oak!" Savushkin repeated, without noticing either his classmates' laughter or the teacher's peremptory shout. He said it differently from the other students. The words burst from his heart like a confession, like a joyful mystery which his brimming heart hadn't the strength to hold back.

Anna Vasilyevna couldn't understand his strange excitement, and hiding her irritation with difficulty, she said:

"Why 'winter'? Simply 'oak'!"

"What's an oak! A winter oak, now that's a real noun!"

"Sit down, Savushkin. That's what lateness does. 'Oak' is a noun, but we haven't yet studied what 'winter' is. Be so good as to come to the teacher's room during the main break."

"So much for your winter oak!" tittered someone at the back desk.

Savushkin sat down, smiling at his own thoughts, totally unaffected by the teacher's threat.

"A difficult boy," thought Anna Vasilyevna.

The lesson continued.

"Sit down," said Anna Vasilyevna when Savushkin entered the teacher's room.

The boy sank into the soft armchair with pleasure and rocked several times on its springs.

"Be so good as to explain why you invariably come late to school."

"I really don't know, Anna Vasilyevna." He spread his hands in an adult gesture. "I leave a whole hour before school starts."

How difficult it was to arrive at the truth in the simplest matter. Many of the children lived much farther away than Savushkin, and yet none of them spent more than an hour getting there.

"You live in Kuzminky?"

"No, at the sanatorium."

"And you're not ashamed to say that you leave an hour before class? It's a fifteen-minute walk from the sanatorium to the highway, and it doesn't take more than half an hour to get here from the highway."

"But I don't use the highway. I take a short cut, throughn the forest," said Savushkin as though he himself was quite surprised at the fact.

"'Through,' not 'throughn,'" Anna Vasilyevna corrected him mechanically.

She suddenly felt upset and sad, as she always did when she came up against a child's lies. She remained silent, hoping that Savuskhin would say: "I'm sorry, Anna Vasilyevna, I got carried away playing snowballs with the other kids,"—or something just as simple and ingenuous, but he only regarded her with his big grey eyes as if to say, "So we've cleared it all up. What else do you want from me?"

"It's sad, Savushkin, very sad! I'll have to talk with your parents."

"There's only my mother, Anna Vasilyevna," Savushkin smiled.

Anna Vasilyevna blushed slightly. She remembered Savushkin's mother—a shower nurse," as her son called her. She worked at the sanatorium hydrotherapy section—a thin timid-looking woman with hands that were white and flaccid, as though made of cloth, because of the hot water. She was alone (her husband had been killed during World War II), and she fed and brought up three other children besides Kolya.

Savushkina undoubtedly had enough worries without this business.

"Do come, Anna Vasilyevna, she'll be glad to see you!"

"Unfortunately, nothing of what I have to say will make her glad. Does she have the morning shift?"

"No, the second, starting at three."

"Very well, then. I finish at two. You'll take me there after class...."

The path along which Savushkin led Anna Vasilyevna started right at the back of the school grounds. As soon as they entered the forest and the heavily snow-laden fir branches closed behind them, they were transported into another, enchanted world of peace and quiet. The magpies and crows flying from tree to tree shook the branches, knocked off the cones, and from time to time broke off the brittle dry twigs that they caught with their wings. But nothing made any sound.

It was totally white all around. Only high up the crowns of the tall weeping birches tossed by the wind stood out, and the slender branches seemed drawn in Indian ink on the blue mirror-like surface of the sky.

The path ran alongside a stream—now on a level with it, obediently following all the windings of its course, now climbing up high to wind along the sheer steep slope.

Occasionally the trees would part to expose sunlit cheery clearings, crisscrossed with hares' tracks that resembled a watch chain. There were larger tracks too, in the form of a shamrock, which belonged to some large animal. The tracks led into the innermost depths of the forest, to the wind-fallen wood.

"An elk's been through here!" said Savushkin, as though he were speaking of a good acquaintance, when he saw Anna Vasilyevna's interest in the tracks. "Don't be frightened," he added in response to the glance the teacher cast at the dense forest. "Elks are peaceful."

"You've seen one?" Anna Vasilyevna asked excitedly.

"An elk? A real live one?" Savushkin sighed. "No, I never had the chance to. I've seen his little pellets."

"What?"

"Droppings," Savushkin explained shyly.

Gliding under the arch of a bowed willow, the path ran down to the stream again. In places the stream was covered by a thick blanket of snow, in others, it was trapped in a sheer armor of ice, and occasionally amid the ice and snow free-flowing water peeped out with dark eyes.

"Why isn't it completely frozen?" asked Anna Vasilyevna.

"There are warm springs gushing in it. Look, can you see them spurting?"

Bending over the unfrozen patch of water, Anna Vasilyevna made out a thin thread extending from the bottom; it burst into tiny bubbles without reaching the water's surface. The very slender stem with its small bubbles resembled a lily of the valley.

"There are simply tons of these springs here!" said Savushkin enthusiastically. "That's why the stream runs even under the snow."

He brushed the snow aside, and some pitch-black but transparent water became visible.

Anna Vasilyevna noticed that the snow that fell in the water didn't melt, but thickened instantly and sagged in the water like gelatinous greenish algae. She liked that so much that she started knocking snow into the water with the toe of her boot, feeling happy when especially intricate shapes formed from a large lump of snow. She'd begun enjoying herself, and didn't immediately notice that Savushkin had gone on and was waiting for her. He'd sat down high in the fork of a branch that hung over the stream. Anna Vasilyevna caught up with Savushkin. At that point the activity of the warm springs ended; the stream was covered with a thin film of ice. Swift light shadows rushed about along its marbled surface.

"Look how thin the ice is, you can even see the current!"

"What do you mean, Anna Vasilyevna! I rocked the branch, and that's the shadow moving."

Anna Vasilyevna held her tongue. Perhaps here in the forest she'd do well to keep quiet.

Savushkin set off again, walking in front of the teacher, bending slightly and gazing about him concentratedly.

And the forest led them on and on with its complicated tangled paths. There seemed no end to the trees, snowdrifts, silence, and twilight shot through with sunshine.

In the distance a smoky blue chink appeared unexpectedly. The trees thinned out and it became open and fresh. And then the chink turned into a wide clear space which appeared in front of them flooded with sunlight; something glittered, sparkled, and warmed with icy stars.

The path skirted a nut bush and the forest immediately opened up in all directions. In the midst of the clearing, in white glistening garments, stood an oak as enormous and magnificent as a cathedral. The trees seemed to part respectfully to allow their older companion to spread out in full force. Its lower branches stretched out in a tent over the clearing. The snow had filled the deep crevices of the bark, and the trunk, which was so wide that it would have taken three men to get their arms around it, looked as if it were shot through with silver thread. It had hardly shed any of the foliage which had dried up during the fall; the oak was covered with snow-capped leaves to the very top.

"There it is, the winter oak!"

Anna Vasilyevna stepped timidly toward the oak and the mighty magnanimous forest sentinel quietly shook a branch to her in greeting.

Totally unaware of what was passing in his teacher's heart, Savushkin was messing about at the foot of the oak, treating the oak simply as his old acquaintance.

"Look, Anna Vasilyevna!"

With an effort he pushed aside a lump of snow whose underside was plastered with earth and the remains of rotting grass. There in the hole lay a little ball wrapped in rotting leaves as thin as a cobweb. Sharp points of needles protruded through the leaves, and Anna Vasilyevna guessed that it was a hedgehog.

"He's wrapped himself up well!"

Savushkin carefully covered the hedgehog with its modest blanket. Then he dug up the snow at another root. A tiny grotto with a fringe of icicles on its opening was revealed. A brown frog was sitting in it as if it were made of cardboard; its skin, tightly stretched along its bones, looked as though it were lacquered. Savushkin touched the frog, but it didn't stir.

"It's pretending it's dead," Savushkin laughed, "But just let the sun warm it up a bit, and boy, will it jump!"

He continued guiding Anna Vasilyevna through his world. There were many other guests who'd taken shelter at the foot of the oak: bugs, lizards, insects. Some were hiding under the roots, others had burrowed in the cracks of the bark; grown thin, as though they were hollow, they were hibernating through the winter. The powerful tree, brimming with life, had gathered around itself so much vital warmth that the poor creatures couldn't have found themselves a better dwelling. Anna Vasilyevna was staring with joyous interest at the secret life of the forest, so unfamiliar to her, when she heard Savushkin's anxious exclamation:

"Oh, we'll be too late to catch mother!"

Anna Vasilyevna quickly lifted her hand to look at her watch—it was a quarter past three. She felt as though she were caught in a trap. And mentally begging the oak forgiveness for her petty human deceit, she said:

"Well, Savushkin, that only shows that a short cut isn't necessarily the best way. You'll have to start taking the highway."

Savushkin didn't answer, merely lowering his head.

"My God!" Anna Vasilyevna thought painfully. "What clearer way of admitting my impotence?" She remembered that day's class and all her other classes: how poor, dry, and cold were her comments on the word, on language, on those things without which man, helpless in his feelings, is mute before the world—on their beautiful language, which was as fresh, beautiful, and rich as life was bounteous and beautiful.

And she considered herself a competent teacher! She'd taken no more than one stride, perhaps, along the path for which a whole lifetime isn't sufficient. And where was it, this path? To find it wasn't simple or easy, like finding the key to a miser's casket. But in the joy with which the children had yelled out "tractor," "well," and "starling's nest," a joy she now understood, the first landmark was dimly visible to her.

"Thank you for the walk, Savushkin. Of course, you can take this route too."

"Thank you, Anna Vasilyevna!"

Savushkin blushed: he badly wanted to tell the teacher that he'd never be late again, but he was afraid of lying. He raised the collar of his jacket and pulled the cap with earflaps lower over his eyes.

"I'll walk you..."

"There's no need, Savushkin. I'll make it by myself."

He glanced doubtfully at the teacher, then picked up a stick from the ground and breaking off its bent end, held it out to Anna Vasilyevna.

"If an elk jumps out, let him have it across the back and he'll run for all he's worth. Better still, simply wave the stick, and that'll be enough for him. Or else he'll get offended and leave the forest for good."

"All right, Savushkin. I won't hit him."

After she'd gone a short distance Anna Vasilyevna for the last time glanced around at the oak, lightly pink in the rays of the sunset, and saw a small dark figure at the foot of it: Savushkin hadn't left, he was watching over his teacher from a distance. And suddenly Anna Vasilyevna realized that the most wonderful thing in the forest wasn't the winter oak, but the small person in the worn felt boots and the patched cheap clothes, the son of a shower nurse and a soldier who'd perished for his country—a marvellous and mysterious citizen of the future.

She waved her hand to him and quietly made her way along the winding path.

NOTE

[1]bashlyk: a protective hood with long ends to wrap around the neck

The Black Dog

BY J. BERNLEF

TRANSLATED FROM THE DUTCH BY FRANK SCIMONE

He looked around him. A bed spring, a smashed orange crate. Not a person in sight. Nobody who could see them here. Nobody to help his father.

"There's a fire at Voorthuyzen's bakery on Main Street," his father had said during breakfast. "A large blazing fire," he had added.

Half an hour later he shuffled back, his head lowered. His father had laughed at him. His mother had found it childish that he responded so angrily to his father's joke.

It was Saturday, the first of April. Secretly he had wished his father dead.

Now it was the second of April. You can forget a lot in twenty-four hours. He took the usual Sunday stroll with his father.

Behind the still-closed outdoor wooden swimming pool the sandy land stretched ruggedly toward the pale green backdike. While he dodged through the holes and half-caved-in huts of unknown boys in search of possible treasures, his father whistled softly through his teeth and smoked a Player's from a pale blue pack, his shiny black raincoat folded in four over his left arm, for he never trusted the weather report, especially not in April.

At the edge of the dike his father sat staring for a long time in the direction of the three chimney stacks of the electric plant while he, the son, watched the schools of nearly transparent sticklebacks and the scurrying of pitch-black water beetles at the foot of a ditch.

These were always the best hours of the week, all alone with his father, who now took off his glasses and wiped them with a chamois cloth which he removed from a front compartment in his purse. As if he wanted to get a better look at the three upright brick-red chimneys of the power plant.

Sitting on top of the dike in clear weather you could even see the ships slowly sailing through the Connecting Canal on their way to the sea.

These were the best hours of the week because his father didn't do a thing, but just sat there silently and every now and then gave him a short wave whenever he, sitting in a hunched position, would look up from the side of the ditch. He listened to the shrill cries of the peewits and the seagulls in the pasture in front of him. A lightly spotted rabbit jumped clumsily through the short grass.

When his father had finished smoking another Player's he made the usual gesture. Time to return. Actually it was only a short walk to the backdike, but the town's last row of houses still seemed to be far away.

A large black dog ran toward them over the dunes of sand in enormous lopsided leaps. A Bouvier de Flandres. You could tell by the trimmed ears lying flat against his head.

The dog began to jump around them, barking wildly.

"Just keep on walking." His father had barely finished the sentence before he had to use both hands to keep the raving dog at bay. Savagely, with his head shaking, the animal settled his jaws into the black raincoat.

Only now did he notice the flecks of foam flying out of his mouth, the yellowish glare in his eyes and the unusual rigid manner in which the dog fixed his paws, jerking at a flap of the coat with all his might while his father frantically held on to it with both hands. Every now and then the dog's black body trembled as if it were undergoing an electric shock.

He looked around him. A bed spring, a smashed orange crate. Not a person in sight. Nobody who could see them here. Nobody to help his father.

Suddenly the dog let go of the coat. His father lost his balance, stumbled over backwards, and the dog immediately plunged toward him with a wide-open mouth full of foam and threads of bloody slime. Lying on the ground his father gave the dog such a kick with one of his black shoes that the dog tottered a few steps sideways and stood in a daze for a few moments, as if the blow had brought him to his senses.

Then the dog shook his pelt and bent down, the front paws spread out before him, snarling at the ground. His father had jumped up, the shredded raincoat still in his hands. His left hand was bleeding.

A Dodge hobbled over the sandy land loudly blowing its horn. For the first time he dared to do something. He ran toward the stub-nosed car, his thin boy's arms swaying above his head. Come here. Come here. The driver, a man with a thick bald head and red cheeks, leaned out of the lowered side window.

"That dog," he shouted gasping and pointing. "That dog is biting my father to death!"

The man appeared startled by his announcement and accelerated. The car lunged ahead. He ran after the car, which rode in a circle around his father and the dog twice. His father made a motion to the driver. The car then made an abrupt turn and joltingly disappeared in the direction of the main road. And the dog sprung up again with his mouth wide open.

"Go away," his father screamed. "Run. Go home. Hurry up."

He had to. Without even looking he ran from his father who would now surely be bitten to death by the dog.

He began to cross the sandy land, through the Sunday streets, along parks and lampposts, along the closed front doors of friends' homes, the fence of the nursery school, the pharmacy with its brown bottles in the window.

His father, bitten to death by a black wolf-dog. Covered with foam and slime. Bleeding all over.

He ran crying with quivering lips. Everywhere sat silent people across from each other in bay windows.

Panting, he let himself fall against the door of his house. He pressed the bell without letting go. He leaned against the door with such force that when it was opened he slowly glided together with the door's panel into the hallway.

From the open space of the landing above he heard his mother's voice. Who was there? He stumbled up the stairs.

He couldn't utter a word, only shake his wailing head. His mother gathered him up. What is wrong? What had happened?

Finally he sat plopped down in one of the armchairs in the living room. She went to the kitchen and came back with a wet washcloth which she brusquely rubbed over his face.

"What happened exactly? Quiet down and tell me."

He could only wail, his drawn-up knees pressed against his chest. She could not understand it. Only he knew what he had wished upon his father while walking back from the nonexistent fire that Saturday morning.

"Daddy is dead."

He hardly felt the hard lashing blow on his cheek. His head jerked to the side and bumped against the headrest. It was as if his insides were filling up with ice water. He vaguely heard doors slamming. Then it became silent. In front of him a striped blue washcloth lay on the carpet.

He let his legs sink to the floor, stood up and walked to the window. The field in front of the door was deserted. Because it was Sunday there were no playing children to be seen. He stood high above the ground and looked out over the lot, the pastures, the canal and the rows of dully shining greenhouses in the distance.

"I'm never going onto the street again," he said loudly.

He turned around. The chairs, the table, the piano, the light rug with the cheerful orange rectangles; he stood in a room that suddenly had nothing to do with home anymore.

Filled with panic he leaped into the side room and grabbed the portrait on his father's desk. His father and mother, arm in arm and laughing, somewhere in a garden.

"That was made when you were not here yet."

Then this could also be possible. That everything would continue as before, the room, the dike, his mother, the school, only his father was not there anymore. A dog which grew ever bigger and blacker while his father got weaker and smaller until he completely disappeared.

He had thought of it first, then he had said it and now it had happened.

From a thin silver frame his father and mother smiled at him. From a time in which he had not existed.

Perhaps that was why he sat behind the desk as if turned to stone, the photo pressed between both hands, when the door opened and he heard his father's voice. As if he still lived. He put the portrait down. With his eyes closed he turned around. He heard his father laughing. Only then did he dare to look.

One of his father's arms was in a white sling. He laughed and leaned with his good arm on the marble mantel shelf. He was really alive. Both of them lived, he and his father, at the same time.

The door opened yet again and his mother entered, a tray in her hands. A teapot, three white cups and three saucers. Three spoons, a sugar pot. He could not keep his eyes from these things.

They went to sit at the table, each at his own place. His father on the left, his mother to his right. Walls and furniture surrounded them. His mother poured the tea. A thin golden-yellow stream that softly splashed into the cups. All three of them stirred their teaspoons at the same time.

He sat at the head of the table peering at a stain on the wallpaper and suddenly everything came to him from the dark spot on the wall as if from out of a hole. The fire in the not burning bakery, the picture from the time he had not yet existed, and his bitten-to-death living father, who patted his head with his free hand and said there was no reason to cry.

"They did away with him right away," he heard his father say. "One shot through the head and that was it."

A Company of Laughing Faces

BY NADINE GORDIMER

Somewhere there was a moment's stay of uneasiness; but a great unfolding impulse, the blind turn of a daisy toward the sun, made her go calmly with him along the corridor, under his influence . . .

When Kathy Hack was seventeen her mother took her to Ingaza Beach for the Christmas holidays. The Hacks lived in the citrus-farming district of the Eastern Transvaal, and Kathy was an only child; "Mr. Hack wouldn't let me risk my life again," her mother confided at once, when ladies remarked, as they always did, that it was a lonely life when there was only one. Mrs. Hack usually added that she and her daughter were like sisters anyway; and it was true that since Kathy had left school a year ago she had led her mother's life, going about with her to the meetings and afternoon teas that occupied the ladies of the community. The community was one of retired businessmen and mining officials from Johannesburg who had acquired fruit farms to give some semblance of productivity to their leisure. They wore a lot of white linen and created a country-club atmosphere in the village where they came to shop. Mr. Hack had the chemist's shop there, but he too was in semi-retirement and he spent most of his afternoons on the golf course or in the club.

The village itself was like a holiday place, with its dazzling white buildings and one wide street smelling of flowers; tropical trees threw shade and petals, and bougainvillaea climbed over the hotel. It was not a rest that Mrs. Hack sought at the coast, but a measure of gaiety and young company for Kathy. Naturally, there were few people under forty-five in the village and most of them had grown-up children who were married or away working or studying in the cities. Mrs. Hack couldn't be expected to part with Kathy—after all, she *is* the only one, she would explain—but, of course, she felt, the child must get out among youngsters once in a while. So she packed up and went on the two-day journey to the coast for Kathy's sake.

They travelled first class, and Mrs. Hack had jokingly threatened Mr. Van Meulen, the station master, with dire consequences if he didn't see to it that they had a carriage to themselves. Yet though she had insisted that she wanted to read her book in peace and not be bothered with talking to some woman, the main-line train had hardly pulled out of Johannesburg station before she and Kathy edged their way along the train corridors to the dining car, and, over tea, Mrs. Hack at once got into conversation with the woman at the next table. There they sat for most of the afternoon; Kathy looking out of the window through the mist of human warmth and teapot steam in which she had drawn her name with her forefinger and wiped a porthole with her fist, her mother talking gaily and comfortingly behind her. "... yes, a wonderful place for youngsters, they tell me. The kids really enjoy themselves there.... Well, of course, everything they want, dancing every night. Plenty of youngsters their own age, that's the thing.... *I* don't mind, I mean, I'm quite content to chat for half an hour and go off to my bed...."

Kathy herself could not imagine what it would be like, this launching into the life of people her own age that her mother had in store for her; but her mother knew all about it and the idea was lit up inside the girl like a room made ready, with everything pulled straight and waiting.... Soon—very soon now, when they got there, when it all began to happen—life would set up in the room. She would know she was young. (When she was a little girl, she had often asked, but what is it like to *be* grown-up? She was too grown-up now to be able to ask, but what do you mean by "being young," "oh, to be young"—what is it I ought to feel?) Into the lit-up room would come the young people of her own age who would convey the secret quality of being that age; the dancing; the fun. She had the vaguest idea of what this fun would be; she had danced, of course, at the monthly dances at the club, her ear on a level with the strange breathing noises of middle-aged partners who were winded by whisky. And the fun, the fun? When she tried to think of it she saw a blur, a company of laughing faces, the faces among balloons in a Mardi Gras film, the crowd of bright-skinned, bright-eyed faces like glazed fruits, reaching for a bottle of Coca-Cola on a roadside hoarding.

The journey passed to the sound of her mother's voice. When she was not talking, she looked up from time to time from her knitting, and smiled at Kathy as if to remind her. But Kathy needed no reminder; she thought of the seven new dresses and the three new pairs of shorts in the trunk in the van.

When she rattled up the dusty carriage shutters in the morning and saw the sea, all the old wild joy of childhood gushed in on her for a moment—the sight came to her as the curl of the water along her ankles and the particular sensation, through her hands, of a wooden spade lifting a wedge of wet sand. But it was gone at once. It was the past. For the rest of the day, she watched the sea approach and depart, approach and depart as the train swung towards and away from the shore through green bush and sugar cane, and she was no more aware of it than her mother, who, without stirring, had given the token recognition that Kathy had heard from her year after year as a child: "Ah, I can smell the sea."

The hotel was full of mothers with their daughters. The young men, mostly students, had come in groups of two or three on their own. The mothers kept "well out of the way," as Mrs. Hack enthusiastically put it; kept, in fact, to their own comfortable adult preserve—the veranda and the card room—and their own adult timetable—an early, quiet breakfast before the young people, who had been out till all hours, came in to make the dining room restless; a walk or a chat, followed by a quick bathe and a quick retreat from the hot beach back to the cool of the hotel; a long sleep in the afternoon; bridge in the evening. Any young person who appeared among them longer than to snatch a kiss and fling a casual good-bye between one activity and the next was treated with tolerant smiles and jolly remarks that did not conceal a feeling that she really ought to run off—she was there to enjoy herself wasn't she? For the first few days Kathy withstood this attitude stolidly; she knew no one and it seemed natural that she would accompany her mother. But her mother made friends at once, and Kathy became a hanger-on, something her schoolgirl ethics had taught her to despise. She no longer followed her mother onto the veranda. "Well, where are you off to, darling?" "Up to change." She and her mother paused in the foyer; her mother was smiling, as if she caught a glimpse of the vista of the morning's youthful pleasures. "Well, don't be too late for lunch. All the best salads go first." "No, I won't." Kathy went evenly up the stairs, under her mother's eyes.

In her room, that she shared with her mother, she undressed slowly and put on the new bathing suit. And the new Italian straw hat. And the new sandals. And the new bright wrap, printed with sea horses. The disguise worked perfectly; she felt the blessed thrill of belonging. This was the world for which she had been brought up, and now, sure enough, when the time had come, she looked the part. Yet it was a marvel to her, just as it must be to the novice when she puts her medieval hood over her shaved head and suddenly is a nun.

She went down to the beach and lay all morning close by, but not part of, the groups of boys and girls who crowded it for two hundred yards, lying in great ragged circles that were constantly broken up and re-formed by chasing and yelling, and the restless to-and-fro of those who were always getting themselves covered with sand in order to make going into the water worthwhile, or coming back out of the sea to fling a wet hand down in someone's warm lap. Nobody spoke to her except two huge louts who tripped over her ankles and exclaimed a hoarse, "Gee, I'm sorry"; but she was not exactly lonely—she had the satisfaction of knowing that at least she was where she ought to be, down there on the beach with the young people.

Every day she wore another of the new dresses or the small tight shorts—properly, equipment rather than clothes—with which she had been provided. The weather was sufficiently steamy hot to be described by her mother, sitting deep in the shade of the veranda, as glorious. When, at certain moments, there was that pause that comes in the breathing of the sea, music from the beach tearoom wreathed up to the hotel, and at night, when the dance was in full swing down there, the volume of music and voices joined the volume of the sea's sound itself, so that, lying in bed in the dark, you could imagine yourself under the sea, with the waters sending swaying sound waves of sunken bells and the cries of drowned men ringing out from depth to depth long after they themselves have touched bottom in silence.

She exchanged smiles with other girls, on the stairs; she made a fourth, at tennis; but these encounters left her again, just exactly where they had taken her up—she scarcely remembered the mumbled exchange of names, and their owners disappeared back into the anonymous crowd of sprawled bare legs and sandals that filled the hotel. After three days, a young man asked her to go dancing with him at the Coconut Grove, a rickety bungalow on piles above the lagoon. There was to be a party of eight or more—she didn't know. The idea pleased her mother; it was just the sort of evening she liked to contemplate for Kathy. A jolly group of youngsters and no nonsense about going off in "couples."

The young man was in his father's wholesale tea business; "Are you at varsity?" he asked her, but seemed to have no interest in her life once that query was settled. The manner of dancing at the Coconut Grove was energetic and the thump of feet beat a continuous talc-like dust out of the wooden boards. It made the lights twinkle, as they do at twilight. Dutifully, every now and then the face of Kathy's escort, who was called Manny and was fair, with a spongy nose and small far-apart teeth in a wide grin, would appear close to her through the bright dust and he would dance with her. He danced with every girl in turn, picking them out and returning them to the pool again with obvious enjoyment and a happy absence of discrimination. In the intervals, Kathy was asked to dance by other boys in the party; sometimes a bold one from some other party would come up, run his eye over the girls, and choose one at random, just to demonstrate an easy confidence. Kathy felt helpless. Here and there were girls who did not belong to the pool, boys who did not rove in predatory search simply because it was necessary to have a girl to dance with. A boy and a girl sat with hands loosely linked, and got up to dance time and again without losing this tenuous hold of each other. They talked, too. There was a lot of guffawing and some verbal sparring at the table where Kathy sat, but she found that she had scarcely spoken at all, the whole evening. When she got home and crept into bed in the dark, in order not to waken her mother, she was breathless from dancing all night, but she felt that she had been running, a long way, alone, with only the snatches of voices from memory in her ears.

She did everything everyone else did, now, waking up each day as if to a task. She had forgotten the anticipation of this holiday that she had had; that belonged to another life. It was gone, just as surely as what the sea used to be was gone. The sea was a shock of immersion in cold water, nothing more, in the hot sandy morning of sticky bodies, cigarette smoke, giggling, and ragging. Yet inside her was something distressing, akin to the thickness of not being able to taste when you have a cold. She longed to break through the muffle of automatism with which she carried through the motions of pleasure. There remained in her a desperate anxiety to succeed in being young, to grasp, not merely fraudulently to do, what was expected of her.

People came and went, in the life of the hotel, and their going was not noticed much. They were replaced by others much like them or who became like them, as those who enter into the performance of a rite inhabit a personality and a set of actions preserved in changeless continuity by the rite itself. She was lying on the beach one morning in a crowd when a young man dropped down beside her, turning his head quickly to see if he had puffed sand into her face, but not speaking to her. She had seen him once or twice before; he had been living at the hotel for two or three days. He was one of those young men of the type who are noticed; he no sooner settled down, lazily smoking, addressing some girl with exaggerated endearments and supreme indifference, than he would suddenly get up again and drop in on some other group. There he would be seen in the same sort of ease and intimacy; the first group would feel both slighted and yet admiring. He was not dependent upon anyone; he gave or withheld his presence as he pleased, and the mood of any gathering lifted a little when he was there, simply because his being there was always unexpected. He had brought to perfection the art, fashionable among the boys that year, of leading a girl to believe that he had singled her out for his attention, "fallen for her," and then, the second she acknowledged this, destroying her self-confidence by one look or sentence that made it seem that she had stupidly imagined the whole thing.

Kathy was not surprised that he did not speak to her; she knew only too well that she did not belong to that special order of girls and boys among whom life was really shared out, although outwardly the whole crowd might appear to participate. It was going to be a very hot day; already the sea was a deep, hard blue and the sky was taking on the gauzy look of a mirage. The young man—his back was half turned to her—had on a damp pair of bathing trunks and on a level with her eyes, as she lay, she could see a map-line of salt emerging white against the blue material as the moisture dried out of it. He got into some kind of argument, and his gestures released from his body the smell of oil. The argument died down and then, in relief at a new distraction, there was a general move up to the beach tearoom where the crowd went every day to drink variously coloured bubbly drinks and to dance, in their bathing suits, to the music of a gramophone. It was the usual straggling procession; "Aren't you fellows coming?"—the nasal, complaining voice of a girl. "Just a sec, what's happened to my glasses?..." "All right, don't *drag* me, man—" "Look what you've done!" "I don't want any more blisters, thank you very much, not after last night...." Kathy lay watching them troop off, taking her time about following. Suddenly there was a space of sand in front of her, kicked up and tousled, but empty. She felt the sun, that had been kept off her right shoulder by the presence of the young man, strike her; he had got up to follow the others. She lay as if she had not heard when suddenly he was standing above her and had said, shortly, "Come for a walk." Her eyes moved anxiously. "Come for a walk," he said, taking out of his mouth the empty pipe that he was sucking. She sat up; going for a walk might have been something she had never done before, was not sure if she could do.

"I know you like walking."

She remembered that when she and some others had limped into the hotel from a hike the previous afternoon, he had been standing at the reception desk, looking up something in a directory. "All right," she said, subdued and got up.

They walked quite briskly along the beach together. It was much cooler down at the water's edge. It was cooler away from the crowded part of the beach, too; soon they had left it behind. Each time she opened her mouth to speak, a mouthful of refreshing air came in. He did not bother with small talk—not even to the extent of an exchange of names. (Perhaps, despite his air of sophistication, he was not really old enough to have acquired any small talk. Kathy had a little stock, like premature grey hairs, that she had found quite useless at Ingaza Beach.) He was one of those people whose conversation is an interior monologue that now and then is made audible to others. There was a ship stuck like a tag out at sea, cut in half by the horizon, and he speculated about it, its size in relation to the distance, interrupting himself with thrown-away remarks, sceptical of his own speculation, that sometimes were left unfinished. He mentioned something an anonymous "they" had done "in the lab"; she said, taking the opportunity to take part in the conversation, "What do you do?"

"Going to be a chemist," he said.

She laughed with pleasure. "So's my father!"

He passed over the revelation and went on comparing the performance of an MG sports on standard commercial petrol with the performance of the same model on a special experimental mixture. "It's a lot of tripe, anyway," he said suddenly, abandoning the plaything of the subject. "Crazy fellows tearing up the place. What for?" As he walked he made a rhythmical clicking sound with his tongue on the roof of his mouth, in time to some tune that must have been going round in his head. She chattered intermittently and politely, but the only part of her consciousness that was acute was some small marginal awareness that along this stretch of gleaming, sloppy sand he was walking without making any attempt to avoid treading on the dozens of small spiral-shell creatures who sucked themselves down into the ooze at the shadow of an approach.

They came to the headland of rock that ended the beach. The rocks were red and smooth, the backs of centuries-warm, benign beasts;

then a gaping black seam, all crenellated with turban-shells as small and rough as crumbs, ran through a rocky platform that tilted into the gnashing, hissing sea. A small boy was fishing down there, and he turned and looked after them for a few moments, perhaps expecting them to come to see what he had caught. But when they got to the seam, Kathy's companion stopped, noticed her; something seemed to occur to him; there was the merest suggestion of a pause, a reflex of a smile softened the corner of his mouth. He picked her up in his arms, not without effort, and carried her across. As he set her on her feet she saw his unconcerned eyes, and they changed, in her gaze, to the patronizing, preoccupied expression of a grown-up who has swung a child in the air. The next time they came to a small obstacle, he stopped again, jerked his head in dry command, and picked her up again, though she could quite easily have stepped across the gap herself. This time they laughed, and she examined her arm when he had put her down. "It's awful, to be grabbed like that, without warning." She felt suddenly at ease, and wanted to linger at the rock pools, poking about in the tepid water for seaweed and the starfish that felt, as she ventured to tell him, exactly like a cat's tongue. "I wouldn't know," he said, not unkindly. "I haven't got a cat. Let's go." And they turned back towards the beach. But at anything that could possibly be interpreted as an obstacle, he swung her carelessly into his arms and carried her to safety. He did not laugh again, and so she did not either; it seemed to be some very serious game of chivalry. When they were down off the rocks, she ran into the water and butted into a wave and then came flying up to him with the usual shudders and squeals of complaint at the cold. He ran his palm down her bare back and said with distaste, "Ugh. What did you do that for."

And so they went back to the inhabited part of the beach and continued along the path up to the hotel, slowly returning to that state of anonymity, that proximity without contact, that belonged to the crowd. It was true, in fact, that she still did not know his name, and did not like to ask. Yet as they passed the beach tearoom, and heard the shuffle of bare sandy feet accompanying the wail and fall of a howling song, she had a sudden friendly vision of the dancers.

After lunch was the only time when the young people were in possession of the veranda. The grown-ups had gone up to sleep. There was an unwritten law against afternoon sleep for the young people; to admit a desire for sleep would have been to lose at once your fitness to be one of the young crowd: "Are you crazy?" The enervation of exposure to the long hot day went on without remission.

It was so hot, even in the shade of the veranda, that the heat seemed to increase gravity; legs spread, with more than their usual weight, on the grass chairs, feet rested heavily as the monolithic feet of certain sculptures. The young man sat beside Kathy, constantly relighting his pipe; she did not know whether he was bored with her or seeking out her company, but presently he spoke to her monosyllabically, and his laconicism was that of long familiarity. They dawdled down into the garden, where the heat was hardly any worse. There was bougainvillaea, as there was at home in the Eastern Transvaal—a huge, harsh shock of purple, papery flowers that had neither scent nor texture, only the stained-glass colour through which the light shone violently. Three boys passed with swinging rackets and screwed-up eyes, on their way to the tennis courts. Someone called, "Have you seen Micky and them?"

Then the veranda and garden were deserted. He lay with closed eyes on the prickly grass and stroked her hand—without being aware of it, she felt. She had never been caressed before, but she was not alarmed because it seemed to her such a simple gesture, like stroking a cat or a dog. She and her mother were great readers of novels and she knew, of course, that there were a large number of caresses—hair and eyes and arms and even breasts—and an immense variety of feelings that would be attached to them. But this simple caress sympathized with her in the heat; she was so hot that she could not breathe with her lips closed and there was on her face a smile of actual suffering. The buzz of a fly round her head, the movement of a leggy red ant on the red earth beneath the grass made her aware that there were no voices, no people about; only the double presence of herself and the unknown person breathing beside her. He propped himself on his elbow and quickly put his half-open lips on her mouth. He gave her no time for surprise or shyness, but held her there, with his wet warm mouth; her instinct to resist the kiss with some part of herself—inhibition, inexperience—died away with the first ripple of its impulse, was smoothed and lost in the melting, boundaryless quality of physical being in the hot afternoon. The salt taste that was in the kiss—it was the sweat on his lip or on hers; his cheek, with its stipple of roughness beneath the surface, stuck to her cheek as the two surfaces of her own skin stuck together wherever they met. When he stood up, she rose obediently. The air seemed to swing together, between them. He put his arm across her shoulder—it was heavy and uncomfortable, and bent her head—and began to walk her along the path toward the side of the hotel.

"Come on," he said, barely aloud, as he took his arm away at the dark archway of an entrance. The sudden shade made her draw a deep breath. She stopped. "Where are you going?" He gave her a little urging push. "Inside," he said, looking at her. The abrupt change from light to dark affected her vision; she was seeing whorls and spots, her heart was plodding. Somewhere there was a moment's stay of uneasiness; but a great unfolding impulse, the blind turn of a daisy toward the sun, made her go calmly with him along the corridor, under his influence: her first whiff of the heady drug of another's will.

In a corridor of dark doors he looked quickly to left and right and then opened a door softly and motioned her in. He slipped in behind her and pushed home the old-fashioned bolt. Once it was done, she gave him a quick smile of adventure and complicity. The room was a bare little room, not like the one she shared with her mother. This was the old wing of the hotel, and it was certain that the push-up-and-down window did not have a view of the sea, although dingy striped curtains were drawn across it, anyway. The room smelled faintly of worn shoes, and the rather cold, stale, male smells of dead cigarette ends and ironed shirts; it was amazing that it could exist, so dim and forgotten, in the core of the hotel that took the brunt of a blazing sun. Yet she scarcely saw it; there was no chance to look round in the mood of curiosity that came upon her; like a movement down to earth. He stood in front of her, their bare thighs touching beneath their shorts, and kissed her and kissed her. His mouth was different then, it was cool, and she could feel it, delightfully, separate from her own. She became aware of the most extraordinary sensation; her little breasts, that she had never thought of as having any sort of assertion of life of their own, were suddenly inhabited by two struggling trees of feeling, one thrusting up, uncurling, spreading toward each nipple. And from his lips, it came, this sensation! From his lips! This person she had spoken to for the first time that morning. How pale and slow were the emotions engendered, over years of childhood, by other people, compared to this! You lost the sea, yes, but you found this. When he stopped kissing her she followed his mouth like a calf nuzzling for milk.

Suddenly he thrust his heavy knee between hers. It was a movement so aggressive that he might have hit her. She gave an exclamation of surprise and backed away, in his arms. It was the sort of exclamation that, in the context of situations she was familiar with, automatically brought a solicitous apology—an equally startled "I'm sorry! Did I hurt you!" But this time there was no apology. The man was fighting with her; *he did not care* that the big bone of his knee had bruised hers. They struggled clumsily, and she was pushed backwards and landed up sitting on the bed. He stood in front of her, flushed and burning-eyed, contained in an orbit of attraction strong as the colour of a flower, and he said in a matter-of-fact, reserved voice, "It's all right. I know what I'm doing. There'll be nothing for you to worry about." He went over to the chest of drawers, while she sat on the bed. Like a patient in a doctor's waiting room; the idea swept into her head. She got up and unbolted the door. "Oh no," she said, a whole horror of prosaicness enveloping her, "I'm going now." The back of the stranger's neck turned abruptly away from her. He faced her, smiling exasperatedly, with a sneer at himself. "I thought so. I thought that would happen." He came over and the kisses that she tried to avoid smeared her face. "What the hell did you come in here for then, hey? Why did you come?" In disgust, he let her go.

She ran out of the hotel and through the garden down to the beach. The glare from the sea hit her, left and right, on both sides of her face; her face that felt battered out of shape by the experience of her own passion. She could not go back to her room because of her mother; the idea of her mother made her furious. She was not thinking at all of what had happened, but was filled with the idea of *her mother*, lying there asleep in the room with a novel dropped open on the bed. She stumbled off over the heavy sand toward the rocks. Down there, there

was nobody but the figure of a small boy, digging things out of the wet sand and putting them in a tin. She would have run from anyone, but he did not count; as she drew level with him, ten yards off, he screwed up one eye against the sun and gave her a crooked smile. He waved the tin. "I am going to try them for bait," he said. "See these little things?" She nodded and walked on. Presently the child caught up with her, slackening his pace conversationally. But they walked on over the sand that the ebbing tide had laid smooth as a tennis court, and he did not speak. He thudded his heels into the firmness.

At last he said, "That was me, fishing on the rocks over there this morning."

She said with an effort, "Oh, was it? I didn't recognize you." Then, after a moment: "Did you catch anything?"

"Nothing much. It wasn't a good day." He picked a spiral shell out of his tin and the creature within put out a little undulating body like a flag. "I'm going to try these. No harm in trying."

He was about nine years old, thin and hard, his hair and face covered with a fine powder of salt—even his eyelashes held it. He was at exactly the stage of equidistant remoteness: he had forgotten his mother's lap, and had no inkling of the breaking voice and growing beard to come. She picked one of the spirals out of the tin, and the creature came out and furled and unfurled itself about her fingers. He picked one of the biggest. "I'll bet this one'd win if we raced them," he said. They went nearer the water and set the creatures down when the boy gave the word "Go!" When the creatures disappeared under the sand, they dug them out with their toes. Progressing in this fashion, they came to the rocks, and began wading about in the pools. He showed her a tiny hermit crab that had blue eyes; she thought it the most charming thing she had ever seen and poked about until she found one like it for herself. They laid out on the rock five different colours of starfish, and discussed possible methods of drying them; he wanted to take back some sort of collection for the natural-history class at his school. After a time, he picked up his tin and said, with a responsible sigh, "Well, I better get on with my fishing." From the point of a particularly high rock, he turned to wave at her.

She walked along the water's edge back to the hotel. In the room, her mother was spraying cologne down the front of her dress. "Darling, you'll get boiled alive, going to the beach at this hour." "No," said Kathy, "I'm used to it now." When her mother had left the room, Kathy went to the dressing table to brush her hair, and running her tongue over her dry lips, tasted not the salt of the sea, but of sweat; it came to her as a dull reminder. She went into the bathroom and washed her face and cleaned her teeth, and then quickly powdered her face again.

Christmas was distorted, as by a thick lens, by swollen, rippling heat. The colours of paper caps ran on sweating foreheads. The men ate flaming puddings in their shirt-sleeves. Flies settled on the tinsel snow of the Christmas tree.

Dancing in the same room on Christmas Eve, Kathy and the young man ignored each other with newly acquired adult complicity. Night after night Kathy danced, and did not lack partners. Though it was not for Mrs. Hack to say it, the new dresses *were* a great success. There was no girl who looked nicer. "K. is having the time of her life," wrote Mrs. Hack to her husband. "Very much in the swing. She's come out of herself completely."

Certainly Kathy was no longer waiting for a sign; she had discovered that this was what it was to be young, of course, just exactly this life in the crowd that she had been living all along, silly little ass that she was, without knowing it. There it was. And once you'd got into it, well, you just went on. You clapped and booed with the others at the Sunday night talent contests, you pretended to kick sand in the boys' faces when they whistled at your legs; squashed into an overloaded car, you yelled songs as you drove, and knew that you couldn't have any trouble with a chap (on whose knees you found yourself) getting too fresh, although he could hold your hand adoringly. The thickness of skin required for all this came just as the required suntan did; and everyone was teak-brown, sallow-brown, homogenized into a new leathery race by the rigorous daily exposure to the fierce sun. The only need she had, these days, it seemed, was to be where the gang was; then the question of what to do and how to feel solved itself. The crowd was flat or the crowd was gay; they wanted to organize a beauty contest or trail to the beach at midnight for a watermelon feast.

One afternoon someone got up a hike to a small resort a few miles up the coast. This was the sort of jaunt in which brothers and sisters who really were still too young to qualify for the crowd were allowed to join; there were even a few children who tagged along. The place itself was strange, with a half-hidden waterfall, like a rope, and great tiers of overhanging rock stretching out farther and farther, higher and higher, over a black lagoon; the sun never reached the water. On the other side, where the sea ran into the lagoon at high tide, there was open beach, and there the restless migration from Ingaza Beach settled. Even there, the sand was cool; Kathy felt it soothing to her feet as she struggled out of the shorts and shirt she had worn over her bathing suit while she walked. She swam steadily about, dipping to swim underwater when the surface began to explode all over the place with the impact of the bodies of the boys who soon clambered up the easier reaches of rock and dived from them. People swam close under the wide roof of rock and looked up; hanging plants grew there, and the whole undersurface was chalky, against its rust-streaked blackness, with the droppings of swallows that threaded in and out of the ledges like bats. Kathy called out to someone from there and her voice came ringing down at her: "...al-l-low!" Soon the swimmers were back on the sand, wet and restless, to eat chocolate and smoke. Cold drinks were brought down by an Indian waiter from the little hotel overlooking the beach; two girls buried a boy up to the neck in sand; somebody came out of the water with a bleeding toe, cut on a rock. People went off exploring, there was always a noisy crowd clowning in the water, and there were always a few others lying about talking on the sand. Kathy was in such a group when one of the young men came up with his hands on his hips, lips drawn back from his teeth thoughtfully, and asked, "Have you seen the Bute kid around here?" "What kid?" someone said. "Kid about ten, in green trunks. Libby Bute's kid brother." "Oh, I know the one you mean. I don't know—all the little boys were playing around on the rocks over there, just now." The young man scanned the beach, nodding. "Nobody knows where he's got to."

"The kids were all together over there, only a minute ago."

"I know. But he can't be found. Kids say they don't know where he is. He might have gone fishing. But Libby says he would have told her. He was supposed to tell her if he went off on his own."

Kathy was making holes in the sand with her forefinger. "Is that the little boy who goes fishing up on the rocks at the end of our beach?"

"Mm. Libby's kid brother."

Kathy got up and looked round at the people, the lagoon, as if she was trying to reinterpret what she had seen before. "I didn't know he was here. I don't remember seeing him. With those kids who were fooling around with the birds' nests?"

"That's right. He was there." The young man made a little movement with his shoulders and wandered off to approach some people farther along. Kathy and her companions went on to talk of something else. But suddenly there was a stir on the beach; a growing stir. People were getting up; others were coming out of the water. The young man hurried past again; "He's not found," they caught from him in passing. People began moving about from one knot to another, gathering suppositions, hoping for news they'd missed. Centre of an awkward, solicitous, bossy circle was Libby Bute herself, a dark girl with long hands and a bad skin, wavering uncertainly between annoyance and fear. "I suppose the little tyke's gone off to fish somewhere, without a word. I don't know. Doesn't mean a thing that he didn't have his fishing stuff with him, he's always got a bit of string and a couple of pins." Nobody said anything. "He'll turn up," she said; and then looked round at them all.

An hour later, when the sun was already beginning to drop from its afternoon zenith, he was not found. Everyone was searching for him with a strange concentration, as if, in the mind of each one, an answer, the remembrance of where he was, lay undisturbed, if only one could get at it. Before there was time for dread, like doubt, like dew, to form coldly, Kathy Hack came face to face with him. She was crawling along the first ledge of rock because she had an idea he might have got it into his head to climb into what appeared to be a sort of cave behind the waterfall and be stuck there, unable to get out and unable to make himself heard. She glanced down into the water, and saw a glimmer of light below the surface. She leant over between her haunches and he was looking at her, not more than a foot below the water, where, shallow over his face, it showed golden above its peat-coloured depths. The water was very deep there, but he had not gone far. He lay held up by the just-submerged rock that had struck the back of his head as he had fallen backwards into the lagoon. What she felt was not shock, but recognition. It was as if he had had a finger to his lips, holding the two of them there, so that she might not give him away. The water moved but did not move him; only his little bit of short hair was faintly obedient, leaning the way of the current, as the green beard of the rock did. He was as absorbed as he must have been in whatever it was he was doing when he fell. She looked at him, looked at him, for a minute, and then she clambered back to the shore and went on with the search. In a little while, someone else found him, and Libby Bute lay screaming on the beach, saliva and sand clinging round her mouth.

Two days later, when it was all over, and more than nine pounds had been collected among the hotel guests for a wreath, and the body was on the train to Johannesburg, Kathy said to her mother, "I'd like to go home." Their holiday had another week to run. "Oh I know," said Mrs. Hack with quick sympathy. "I feel the same myself. I can't get that poor little soul out of my mind. But life has to go on darling, one can't take the whole world's troubles on one's shoulders. Life brings you enough troubles of your own, believe me." "It's not that at all," said Kathy. "I don't like this place."

Mrs. Hack was just feeling herself nicely settled, and would have liked another week. But she felt that there was the proof of some sort of undeniable superiority in her daughter's great sensitivity; a superiority they ought not to forgo. She told the hotel proprietor and the other mothers that she had to leave; that was all there was to it: Kathy was far too much upset by the death of the little stranger to be able simply to go ahead with the same zest for holiday pleasures that she had enjoyed up till now. Many young people could do it, of course; but not Kathy. She wasn't made that way, and what was she, her mother, to do about it?

In the train going home they did not have a carriage to themselves, and very soon Mrs. Hack was explaining to their lady travelling companion—in a low voice, between almost closed teeth, in order not to upset Kathy—how the marvellous holiday had been ruined by this awful thing that had happened.

The girl heard, but felt no impulse to tell her mother—knew, in fact, that she would never have the need to tell anyone the knowledge that had held her secure since the moment she looked down into the lagoon: the sight, there, was the one real happening of the holiday, the one truth and the one beauty.

"Fiction writers are thoughtful interpreters of the world."
Annie Dillard

IDENTITY AND SOCIETY   III

Heartache

BY ANTON CHEKHOV

TRANSLATED FROM THE RUSSIAN BY AVRAHM YARMOLINSKY

Iona feels the hunchback's wriggling body and quivering voice behind his back. He hears abuse addressed to him, sees people, and the feeling of loneliness begins little by little to lift from his heart.

"TO WHOM SHALL I TELL MY SORROW?"

Evening twilight. Large flakes of wet snow are circling lazily about the street lamps which have just been lighted, settling in a thin soft layer on roofs, horses' backs, people's shoulders, caps. Iona Potapov, the cabby, is all white like a ghost. As hunched as a living body can be, he sits on the box without stirring. If a whole snowdrift were to fall on him, even then, perhaps, he would not find it necessary to shake it off. His nag, too, is white and motionless. Her immobility, the angularity of her shape, and the stick-like straightness of her legs make her look like a penny gingerbread horse. She is probably lost in thought. Anyone who has been torn away from the plow, from the familiar gray scenes, and cast into this whirlpool full of monstrous lights, of ceaseless uproar and hurrying people, cannot help thinking.

Iona and his nag have not budged for a long while. They had driven out of the yard before dinnertime and haven't had a single fare yet. But now evening dusk is descending upon the city. The pale light of the street lamps changes to a vivid color and the bustle of the street grows louder.

"Sleigh to the Vyborg District!" Iona hears. "Sleigh!"

Iona starts, and through his snow-plastered eyelashes sees an officer in a military overcoat with a hood.

"To the Vyborg District!" repeats the officer. "Are you asleep, eh? To the Vyborg District!"

As a sign of assent Iona gives a tug at the reins, which sends layers of snow flying from the horse's back and from his own shoulders. The officer gets into the sleigh. The driver clucks to the horse, cranes his neck like a swan, rises in his seat and, more from habit than necessity, flourishes his whip. The nag, too, stretches her neck, crooks her stick-like legs and irresolutely sets off.

"Where are you barging in, damn you?" Iona is promptly assailed by shouts from the massive dark wavering to and fro before him. "Where the devil are you going? Keep to the right!"

"Don't you know how to drive? Keep to the right," says the officer with vexation.

A coachman driving a private carriage swears at him; a pedestrian who was crossing the street and brushed against the nag's nose with his shoulder, looks at him angrily and shakes the snow off his sleeve. Iona fidgets on the box as if sitting on needles and pins, thrusts out his elbows and rolls his eyes like a madman, as though he did not know where he was or why he was there.

"What rascals they all are," the officer jokes. "They are doing their best to knock into you or be trampled by the horse. It's a conspiracy."

Iona looks at his fare and moves his lips. He wants to say something, but the only sound that comes out is a wheeze.

"What is it?" asks the officer.

Iona twists his mouth into a smile, strains his throat and croaks hoarsely: "My son, sir... er, my son died this week."

"H'm, what did he die of?"

Iona turns his whole body around to his fare and says, "Who can tell? It must have been a fever. He lay in the hospital only three days and then he died.... It is God's will."

"Get over, you devil!" comes out of the dark. "Have you gone blind, you old dog? Keep your eyes peeled!"

"Go on, go on," says the officer. "We shan't get there until tomorrow at this rate. Give her the whip!"

The driver cranes his neck again, rises in his seat, and with heavy grace swings his whip. Then he looks around at the officer several times, but the latter keeps his eyes closed and is apparently indisposed to listen. Letting his fare off in the Vyborg District, Iona stops by a teahouse and again sits motionless and hunched on the box. Again the wet snow paints him and his nag white. One hour passes, another....

Three young men, two tall and lanky, one short and hunch-backed, come along swearing at each other and loudly pound the pavement with their galoshes.

"Cabby, to the Police Bridge!" the hunchback shouts in a cracked voice. "The three of us... twenty kopecks!"

Iona tugs at the reins and clucks to his horse. Twenty kopecks is not fair, but his mind is not on that. Whether it is a ruble or five kopecks, it is all one to him now, so long as he has a fare.... The three young men, jostling each other and using foul language, go up to the sleigh and all three try to sit down at once. They start arguing about which two are to sit and who shall be the one to stand. After a long ill-tempered and abusive altercation, they decide that the hunchback must stand up because he is the shortest.

"Well, get going," says the hunchback in his cracked voice, taking up his station and breathing down Iona's neck. "On your way! What a cap you've got, brother! You won't find a worse one in all Petersburg—"

"Hee hee... hee, hee... " Iona giggles, "as you say—"

"Well, then, 'as you say,' drive on. Are you going to crawl like this all the way, eh? D'you want to get it in the neck?"

"My head is splitting," says one of the tall ones. "At the Dukmasovs' yesterday, Vaska and I killed four bottles of cognac between us."

"I don't get it, why lie?" says the other tall one angrily. "He is lying like a trouper."

"Strike me dead, it's the truth!"

"It is about as true as that a louse sneezes."

"Hee, hee," giggles Iona. "The gentlemen are feeling good!"

"Faugh, the devil take you!" cries the hunchback indignantly.

"Will you get a move on, you old pest, or won't you? Is that the way you drive? Give her a crack of the whip! Giddap, devil! Giddap! Let her feel it!"

Iona feels the hunchback's wriggling body and quivering voice behind his back. He hears abuse addressed to him, sees people, and the feeling of loneliness begins little by little to lift from his heart. The hunchback swears till he chokes on an elaborate three-decker oath and is overcome by cough. The tall youths begin discussing a certain Nadezhda Petrovna. Iona looks round at them. When at last there is a lull in the conversation for which he has been waiting, he turns around and says: "This week... er... my son died."

"We shall all die," says the hunchback, with a sigh wiping his lips after his coughing fit. "Come, drive on, drive on. Gentlemen, I simply cannot stand this pace! When will he get us there?"

"Well, you give him a little encouragement. Biff him in the neck!"

"Do you hear, you old pest? I'll give it to you in the neck. If one stands on ceremony with fellows like you, one may as well walk. Do you hear, you old serpent? Or don't you give a damn what we say?"

And Iona hears rather than feels the thud of a blow on his neck.

"Hee, hee," he laughs. "The gentlemen are feeling good. God give you health!"

"Cabby, are you married?" asks one of the tall ones.

"Me? Hee, hee! The gentlemen are feeling good. The only wife for me now is the damp earth.... Hee, haw, haw! The grave, that is!... Here my son is dead and me alive.... It is a queer thing, death comes in at the wrong door.... It don't come for me, it comes for my son...."

And Iona turns round to tell them how his son died, but at that point the hunchback gives a sigh of relief and announces that, thank God, they have arrived at last. Having received his twenty kopecks, for a long while Iona stares after the revelers, who disappear into a dark entrance. Again he is alone and once more silence envelops him. The grief which has been allayed for a brief space comes back again and wrenches his heart more cruelly than ever. There is a look of anxiety and torment in Iona's eyes as they wander restlessly over the crowds moving to and fro on both sides of the street. Isn't there someone among those thousands who will listen to him? But the crowds hurry past, heedless of him and his grief. His grief is immense, boundless. If his heart were to burst and his grief to pour out, it seems that it would flood the whole world, and yet no one sees it. It has found a place for itself in such an insignificant shell that no one can see it in broad daylight.

Iona notices a doorkeeper with a bag and makes up his mind to speak to him.

"What time will it be, friend?" he asks.

"Past nine. What have you stopped here for? On your way!"

Iona drives a few steps away, hunches up and surrenders himself to his grief. He feels it is useless to turn to people. But before five minutes are over, he draws himself up, shakes his head as though stabbed by a sharp pain and tugs at the reins.... He can bear it no longer.

"Back to the yard!" he thinks. "To the yard!"

And his nag, as though she knew his thoughts, starts out at a trot. An hour and a half later, Iona is sitting beside a large dirty stove. On the stove, on the floor, on benches are men snoring. The air is stuffy and foul. Iona looks at the sleeping figures, scratches himself, and regrets that he has come home so early.

"I haven't earned enough to pay for the oats," he reflects. "That's what's wrong with me. A man that knows his job... who has enough to eat and has enough for his horse don't need to fret."

In one of the corners a young driver gets up, hawks sleepily and reaches for the water bucket.

"Thirsty?" Iona asks him.

"Guess so."

"H'm, may it do you good, but my son is dead, brother... did you hear? This week in the hospital.... What a business!"

Iona looks to see the effect of his words, but he notices none. The young man has drawn his cover over his head and is already asleep. The old man sighs and scratches himself. Just as the young man was thirsty for water so he thirsts for talk. It will soon be a week since his son died and he hasn't talked to anybody about him properly. He ought to be able to talk about it, taking his time, sensibly. He ought to tell how his son was taken ill, how he suffered, what he said before he died, how he died.... He ought to describe the funeral, and how he went to the hospital to fetch his son's clothes. His daughter Anisya is still in the country.... And he would like to talk about her, too. Yes, he has plenty to talk about now. And his listener should gasp and moan and keen.... It would be even better to talk to women. Though they are foolish, two words will make them blubber.

"I must go out and have a look at the horse," Iona thinks. "There will be time enough for sleep. You will have enough sleep, no fear...."

He gets dressed and goes into the stable where his horse is standing. He thinks about oats, hay, the weather. When he is alone, he dares not think of his son. It is possible to talk about him with someone, but to think of him when one is alone, to evoke his image is unbearably painful.

"You chewing?" Iona asks his mare seeing her shining eyes. "There, chew away, chew away.... If we haven't earned enough for oats, we'll eat hay.... Yes.... I've grown too old to drive. My son had ought to be driving, not me.... He was a real cabby.... He had ought to have lived...."

Iona is silent for a space and then goes on: "That's how it is, old girl.... Kuzma Ionych is gone.... Departed this life.... He went and died to no purpose.... Now let's say you had a little colt, and you were that little colt's own mother. And suddenly, let's say, that same little colt departed this life.... You'd be sorry, wouldn't you?"

The nag chews, listens, and breathes on her master's hands. Iona is carried away and tells her everything.

"Stories are powerful. They are a journey and a joining. In a tale we meet new places, new people, new ideas. And they become our *places,* our *people,* our *ideas."*

Jane Yolen

The Tangerines

BY RYUNOSUKE AKUTAGAWA

TRANSLATED FROM THE JAPANESE BY TAKASHI KOJIMA

The train, the tunnel, the girl, the evening paper full of commonplace events—they were nothing but the symbols of an unintelligible and wearisome life.

One cloudy winter evening I sat in the corner of a second-class car of the Tokyo-Yokosuka train and waited for the starting whistle. In the car there was, surprisingly, no passenger but myself. Looking out on the platform, strangely enough there was not a single person who had come to bid someone good-bye. The only sound was that of a puppy whining sadly from time to time. All of these things seemed wholly suited to my mood. Fatigue and ennui enshrouded me with their dull and heavy shadows, like a gray and shadowy sky. With both hands deep in my pockets, I didn't even feel like taking the evening paper out of my pocket.

After a while I heard the starting whistle. Feeling tired but comfortable, my head leaning against the window frame, I waited for the station to begin moving backward, away from me. Just then I heard the sharp clatter of *geta*[1] and the sharp voice of the guard. The door of my second-class coach clattered open and a girl about thirteen rushed in. At the same time the train, with a jerk, began to move slowly forward. The pillars of the platform, passing one by one, blocked off my vision; a tank car appeared, as though misplaced, and a porter bowed over a tip. All these fell behind me as if with lingering reluctance while the smoke belched from the engine blew against my window. Feeling slightly relieved, I lighted a cigarette, raised my eyes and looked at the girl who was sitting opposite me.

She was a dull-looking country girl but interesting enough to be worthy of my study. I noticed her unoiled hair dressed in a tight butterfly knot. Her chapped cheeks had a slightly disagreeable, but ruddy glow as though she had been rubbing them with her hands. In her lap, over which lay a light green muffler dangling from her neck, lay a large bundle. Her coarse, cold hands, clamped tightly over the bundle, clutched a third-class ticket as though it were her last link with life itself. Her features, coarse in themselves and her clothes, lacking in taste, didn't much appeal to me. She was apparently stupid as well—couldn't tell a second from a third-class coach.

Lighting a cigarette and partly wishing to forget her depressing presence, I casually looked at the evening paper which I had taken from my pocket and spread over my knees. Then the pale twilight which had been falling over my paper was suddenly illumined by a brilliant electric light, and the almost indecipherable letters of several columns flashed into view with unexpected distinctness. The train had just entered one of the many tunnels on the Yokosuka line.

The paper, though illumined by light, merely showed the usual pedestrian events—the peace problem, brides and bridegrooms, bribe cases, obituaries, and so on. The instant we entered the tunnel, I felt, almost as if in hallucination, that the direction of the train had been reversed, while I mechanically ran my eyes from one prosaic column to another.

In the meantime the girl was there, sitting in front of me, appearing to embody all the vulgar realities in the human shape. I was always aware of her. The train, the tunnel, the girl, the evening paper full of commonplace events—they were nothing but the symbols of an unintelligible and wearisome life. Everything was absurd. I dropped the paper I had been reading, and leaning my head against the window frame I closed my eyes as though in another world.

Several minutes passed. Suddenly and unaccountably feeling frightened, I looked around and found that she had moved from the other side to the seat next to mine, and I saw her anxiously trying to open the window. The heavy frame would not move. Her cold, chapped cheeks grew redder than ever and her occasional snifflings were heard above the noise of the train. This was something which could at least claim a bit of my sympathy.

But I could also see that we were near the mouth of another tunnel. The mountain sides overgrown with tall grass bright in the twilight were closing in fast upon us. The girl was still intent upon opening the window which had been closed because we had to pass through tunnels. I didn't know why she wanted it open, and I felt it was merely a whim. So I sat still feeling bitter and watched her cold hands desperately struggling to lift it. Then suddenly with a terrific noise, the train rushed into the tunnel and at the same time the window opened with a crash. Through the square hole of the window, billows of air black with soot began to blanket the entire car. The smoke dashed against my face too suddenly for me to protect myself with a handkerchief, and I, who usually have difficulty in breathing, was almost choked. Her butterfly knot waving in the black streaming air, the girl showed no concern at all for me. Stretching her neck outside the window, she looked straight ahead in the direction the train was going. And my eyes were riveted upon her figure silhouetted in the smoke-dimmed electric light. Had not then the car quickly grown light again, and the refreshing smell of earth, hay, and water flown in to drive off the choking smoke, I should undoubtedly have given her a sharp reprimand to make her close the window, for I had barely stopped coughing by that time.

Now, however, the train had already glided out of the tunnel and was nearing a small crossing on the outskirts of a town hemmed in between hills. Near the crossing stood a dirty cluster of straw-thatched huts and tile-roofed cottages. The white flag of the watchman languidly waved in the dusk. Just after the train had passed out of the tunnel, there appeared at this bleak crossing three ruddy-cheeked little boys, standing closely side by side.

They were all short as though compressed and stunted under the cloudy sky. Their clothes were the same color as the dismal town where they lived. The minute they caught sight of the approaching train, they looked up and raised their hands, and opening their little throats like so many little birds, they yelled out their farewell at the top of their voices.

At that time the young girl who had thrust half of her body out of the train window, stretched out and waved her hands left and right.

Then, as though from the heavenly skies upon the heads of the little children fell five or six tangerines dyed with the warm fiery color of sunshine, which made my heart pound and pause for some seconds.

Breathlessly I watched, for in this instant I understood everything. The girl, who was probably going out to work some place, threw these tangerines which she had held in her lap to her little brothers as both a surprise and a reward for coming to the crossing to wave and shout their good-byes to their big sister leaving home.

The crossing at the outskirts of this lonely town in the dusk of evening, the three little youngsters who called like little birds, and the bright tangerines which fell down over their heads—all this that came and went in the twinkling of an eye was indelibly branded upon my heart.

I felt something like life welling up within me. Deeply impressed, I turned slightly and looked at the young girl as though she were a different person. There she was already back in her own seat which she had first taken opposite mine, burying her cold cheeks in her light green muffler. She was tightly grasping her third-class ticket like a precious treasure in her cold chapped hands upon the large bundle in her lap.

It was at this moment that I completely forgot my intense fatigue and ennui, becoming oblivious to the unintelligible absurdity of my own tiresome, dull life.

NOTE
[1]*geta*: wooden clogs

Island

BY K. SOHAIL

The police threatened him that if he was found again loitering in the city streets, he would be put in the jail. He smiled.

"**A**re your parents alive?"

"Yes."

"When was the last time you met them?"

"Ten years ago."

"Do you have any brothers or sisters?"

"Yes, I do."

"When was the last time you saw them?"

"Seven years ago."

"Where did you see them?"

"In a supermarket."

"Do you have any friends?"

"No."

"Do you have a home?"

"No."

"Where do you live then?"

"On the street."

"Do you have any source of income?"

"Not at all."

"Then how do you live?"

"I just live."

"For how long have you been living like this?"

"For twelve years."

"What do you want in life?"

"Nothing."

"What's your aim in life?"

"I have none."

"Can I arrange welfare for you?"

"No thanks."

"How about a place to live?"

"Don't bother."

"You must need money for food?"

"No. I am fine."

"How can we help you?"

"Don't worry. I will be O.K."

My social worker felt helpless. She did not know what to say.

The police brought him to the hospital. He had been wandering around on the streets for weeks. He had no food; no shelter. He looked like a bagman. The weather too was getting cold. The winter had its first snowfall. The police became worried when they found him one night sleeping in a bus stand. He looked pale and weak. They thought he may freeze to death.

"Admit him doctor and look after him," one of the police officers had suggested.

"Do you want to be admitted?" I asked him.

"No thanks. I am not sick."

I felt helpless too. The social worker called his parents. They came and took him home to look after him.

After a couple of days the police brought him back. We were facing the same dilemma again. The social worker called his sister this time. She came and took him home but he took off after a week.

The police brought him to the hospital once again. They believed he was crazy and should be locked up in a psychiatric hospital for a few months. I did not agree. I thought he was an eccentric and non-conformist. The society and the police could not tolerate him. The social worker this time sent him to a boarding home. The police threatened him that if he was found again loitering in the city streets, he would be put in the jail. He smiled. He didn't care.

A few weeks later, on a Sunday morning, a young man was taking his son for a morning walk in the city park. The child saw something floating in the pond in the middle of the park. He asked his father, "What is that, Daddy?"

The young man recognized the object. It was a dead body. The bloated corpse was floating upside down. He hurriedly called an ambulance from a nearby phone booth. The paramedics came and put the body in a body bag and placed it on a stretcher inside their ambulance. The young man and his son accompanied them to the hospital's emergency section.

While I was examining the body, the child stood there bewildered. He looked at his father and squeezed his hand. "Daddy," he softly asked.

"What is it my son?"

"Our teacher told us that if something is surrounded by water, it is called an island."

"That's true."

"Was this man an island, Dad?"

The young father picked up the child, smiled, and hugged him softly.

Separation

BY BING XIN

TRANSLATED FROM THE CHINESE BY S.R. MUNRO

Amidst the noise of a million exploding firecrackers, I wondered how many thousand smouldering frightened emotions lay concealed in the gloomy black streets and alleys . . .

A monstrous hand wrenched me out of that depressing, painfully close web. I burst out into a long mournful wail.

Opening my eyes, one of my legs was still being held up by that huge hand. I saw my own two, elegantly red, little hands waving and dancing in the space above my head.

Another of those gigantic hands gently held me up under my waist. Smiling, the man belonging to the hand turned and said to a woman who was lying on her back on a portable bed covered in white, "What luck! A chubby little boy!" At the same time he lightly placed me in a little basket covered with white bedding.

I struggled to look outside and saw quite a few nurses wearing their white uniforms and caps frenziedly but silently working around that woman. Her ashen face was covered with sweat. She weakly groaned as if she had just awakened from a nightmare. Her eyelids were red and swollen, and her eyes were vacantly half opened. When she heard the doctor's voice, her eyes rolled and tears flooded out. Now she relaxed completely and with an exhausted smile, she closed her eyes and said, "It's really been hard on all of you!"

I cried loudly, "Mother, it's us that have had it hard. We have just struggled our way out of the jaws of death!"

The nurses in the white uniforms busily but silently rolled mother's bed out of the room; I was picked up as well and carried out. The doctor then beckoned and a man walked across the corridor to him. He had a delighted look on his face as if he had also just thankfully awakened from a bad dream. It seemed as though his hands wanted to pick me up, but yet didn't dare to do so. He stared at me with an astonished yet sympathetic look.

The doctor smiled and said, "Will this one do?"

As if he were embarrassed the man chattered, "His head is so long."

Then I suddenly realized my head hurt like anything, and I cried out loudly again: "Father, you don't know how my skull was crushed. It aches so."

The doctor laughed, "Wonderful! What a noise!"

Standing off to one side, a nurse with a smile on her face came over to get me. We went into a large, very bright room where small white beds were arranged from wall to wall. In each lay a little child. Some of them were peacefully sleeping with their hands pulled up beside their heads. Others wailed: "I'm thirsty!" or "I'm hungry!" or "I'm too hot!" or "I'm wet!"

The nurse who was carrying me to a washing room casually drifted past their beds as if she didn't hear a thing. She laid me down on the porcelain sink beside the basin with my head towards the tap. Then she turned on the faucet which was shaped like a lotus seed pod and poured warm water over my head washing away all of that sticky blood. I shuddered but felt better right away.

Another baby was lying on the other side of the sink being washed by another nurse. He had a round head, big eyes, dark skin, and a strong full chest. He was also awake, looking out the window at the sky not making a sound. By then I had already been picked up. The nurse gently supported my shoulders and dressed me in a long white gown. My little friend had already been dressed as well. Separated by the basin, we faced each other as best we could from our hunched-over positions. The nurse who had bathed me smiled and said to her colleague, "Your baby is so big and strong looking, but he doesn't compare to this fair and delicate one of mine!" At this the other baby raised his head, looked me over more carefully and tenderly smiled.

"Hi, little friend," I timidly said.

"How are you, pal?" he pleasantly responded.

By then both of us had been placed in two adjacent little beds, and the nurses had both left.

"My body is so sore," I said. "This struggle for the past four hours hasn't been easy at all. What about you?"

He laughed and raised his little fist. "Not at all. I was only uncomfortable for half an hour. I didn't suffer at all, and it didn't hurt my mom either."

I silently and dejectedly sighed, then gazed all around. He comforted me saying, "You're exhausted. Go to sleep. I want to rest up a bit, too."

Rousing me from a deep sleep, I was picked up and carried in front of a big glass door. In the corridor outside stood quite a few boys and girls. Each of them had the tip of his nose and both hands pressed against the glass just like a flock of children standing in front of a store window longing for the nicely arranged Christmas presents inside. They smiled happily, each of them prattling away. As if they wanted to apportion me into little pieces, they said my eyebrows looked like my father's sister's, or that my eyes looked like my mother's brother's, or that my nose was like my father's brother's, or that my mouth was like my mother's sister's.

I closed my eyes and really wanted to shake my head at them, but my neck was hurting. I cried loudly, "I'm just me. I don't look like anyone. Let me be!"

The nurse laughed, picked me up and took me back. I could still see them as they kept glancing back at me while they were walking away, laughing and pushing each other as they went.

My little friend had woken up also and called to me, "You're up. Who came to visit you?"

As I was being put down I answered, "I don't know. There were a lot of young people—probably my aunts and uncles. Seems like they all love me."

My pal didn't say anything at first, but then he smiled and said, "You're really lucky. This is already my second day here, and I haven't even seen my father yet."

In my muddled state I didn't have the slightest idea that I had slept so long. My body ached all over, and down below I was wet again. I learned how to cry spasmodically: "I'm wet! I'm wet!" And indeed it wasn't long before a nurse came over to pick me up. I was so happy, but I never guessed that she would give me some water to drink instead!

It was probably around dusk when three or four nurses came bustling in with their stiff white uniforms bristling. In a hubbub they picked us up and changed our wet diapers one by one. My pal was happy too and said, "We're all going to see our mothers. Bye bye."

My little pal was wheeled out with the rest of them on a big ambulatory cart. I was picked up and carried out through the glass door, and then we entered the first room on the right hand side of the corridor.

My mother was lying down on a high bed covered with white sheets. Her eyes were filled with longing and joy when she greeted me. The nurse laid me down on her arm. Mother shyly and modestly untied the front of her nightgown. She seemed to be very young. Her black hair was pulled back into a bun, and her light eyebrows were shaped like the new moon. There was no rouge on her pale white face which was graced with large, very black eyes. She sat on the edge of the bed shadowed under the hazy circle of light like a marble statue.

I opened my mouth and sucked at her breast. Mother snuggled my hair against her cheeks, played with my fingers, and carefully examined me as though she were infinitely pleased and astonished beyond belief. Twenty minutes went by and I still hadn't gotten a drop. I was still hungry, but the tip of my tongue was sore, so I opened my mouth, let the nipple fall out and cried in frustration. Mother was very upset and incessantly rocked and patted me. "Precious," she pleaded, "don't cry. Don't cry!" At the same time she rang the buzzer, and a nurse came in. Mother smiled and said, "It's nothing important, but I don't have any milk, and the child keeps on crying. What shall I do?"

The nurse smiled too and said, "Don't worry. It'll come sooner or later. The baby is still little and doesn't care yet." At the same time she came over and picked me up. Mother slowly let go as though she were unwilling to give me up.

By the time I was brought back to my bed, my little friend was already sleeping sweetly. He smiled from time to time in his dreams as though he were very happy and satisfied. I gazed all around and saw that quite a few of the others were sleeping happily as well. A few were half-awake, listlessly playing and crying a bit. I was awfully hungry and wondered when my mother's milk would finally come. I cared a lot! But no one knew. Looking at all of them sleeping with full tummies, I felt both envious and ashamed, and I began to cry loudly hoping to catch someone's attention. I cried for more than half an hour before a nurse came over, attractively, but foolishly pursed her lips, patted me soothingly, and said, "Really now! Your mommy didn't fill you up? Let's have a drink of water then!" She then stuck the nipple of a water bottle into my mouth; I held it unhappily until I slowly fell asleep.

At bath time the next day my little friend and I were lying on opposite sides of the water basin having a chat. He was completely rested and contented, and when he was picked up to be washed, he rocked his head, half closed his eyes, smiled, and said, "I really had my fill of milk yesterday! My mom's dark round face is really pretty. I'm her fifth child. She told the nurse that this was the first time that she had gone to the hospital to deliver her baby. The Child Welfare Society introduced her to the hospital. My father is very poor. He's a butcher—a pig butcher!" — Right then a drop of boric acid suddenly splashed on his eye.

He was annoyed and cried out a few times. With an effort he opened his eyes and continued, "A butcher! How satisfying: a clean knife goes in and a bloody one comes out. When I grow up, I want to learn how from my father—a pig butcher. Not only will I slaughter pigs, but I'll kill those pig-like people who enjoy the fruits without any labor as well!"

I had been listening to him quietly, but when he said this I hastily shut my eyes and didn't say a word.

My friend went on, "What about you? Did you have enough to eat? What's your mom like?"

I pepped up again, "I didn't get anything to eat... mother's milk hasn't come yet. The nurse said that she would get it in a day or two. My mother is really nice. She can read. The table beside her bed is heaped with books, and there were flower arrangements all over the room."

"How about your dad?"

"My father didn't come. Mother was by herself in the room. She didn't talk to anyone, so I don't know anything about my father."

"That's a first-class room," my friend affirmed. "Wow, one person to a room! The room my mom is in is really jumping. They've got ten beds in there. Quite a few of the kids' moms are in there—they all had enough to eat."

The next day I saw my father. When I was nursing, he leaned over against the edge of mom's pillow. Their faces were close together watching me attentively. Father had a very thin face with a sallow complexion. His eyelashes were long, and he had a bright look in his eyes. His forehead was usually lightly wrinkled as though he loved to meditate.

Father said, "This time I can see it more clearly. The child is really beautiful, just like you."

Mother smiled and gently stroked my face. "He looks like you, too. Such large eyes!"

Father straightened up and then sat down on the chair beside the bed. He took mother's hand and gently patted it. "From now on we won't be lonely anymore. After I come home from classes, I'll help you take care of him and play with him. During vacations we can take him to the mountains and go swimming.—This child will really have to take care of his health. Not like me. Although I'm not sickly, I'm not strong and robust either."

Mother nodded her head and said, "Yes, and he should start taking music and art very early. I'm no good at them myself, and I've always felt my life has been incomplete. In addition..."

Father laughed, "What do you want him to be when he grows up? A writer? A musician?"

"He can be anything—he's a boy," mother replied. "China needs scientific technology. Maybe it would be best if he became a scientist."

At this point I still couldn't get any milk. I was so frustrated that I wanted to cry, but listening to their intensely interesting conversation, I didn't make a sound.

Father said, "We'll have to start saving for his tuition fees. The sooner we get the money together, the better."

Mother went on, "I forgot to tell you... yesterday my brother said that when the boy turns six, he will give him a little bicycle!"

"This child will have everything," father laughingly continued the conversation. "Didn't my sister give him the cradle?"

Mother squeezed me tightly and kissed my hair. "My little precious. You're so lucky. So many people love you. You should be a good boy when you grow up."

Brimming with happiness, I was taken back to my bed not caring about how hungry I was. I raised my head to look at my friend, but he was in deep thought.

I laughingly called him: "Hey friend, I've seen my father. He's real nice too. A teacher. He and mother were just talking about my future education. My father said that he would work very hard to do whatever is best for me. Mother said that it doesn't matter if I don't get any milk from her. When we get home I can have powdered milk. Later I can have orange juice; I can have..." all in one breath.

My little friend smiled. Sympathetically and scornfully he said, "You're so lucky. After I go home I won't get any milk to drink. Today my dad came and told my mom that someone came to hire her as a wet nurse. After one or two days we'll have to leave this place! I'll have to live with my sixty-year-old grandmother. I'll eat rice gruel and stale bread, but I don't care!"

I was speechless. All the joy in my heart vanished, and I felt ashamed.

My friend's eyes gleamed with pride and courage. "You'll always be like a pot of flowers blooming delicately in a greenhouse where the wind and rain won't touch you, and the temperature will always be constant. As for me, I'll be a little blade of grass on the edge of the road, willing to accept being trampled on by others as well as having to brave the storms. You will probably pity me while looking from far off through your glass windows. But above me there will be limitless amounts of air to breathe. The butterflies and crickets will sing and fly around me in their freedom. All the other humble but brave blades of grass won't be able to be burnt nor mowed under. Under the feet of others our green-ness will spread throughout the entire world!"

I was so distressed I wanted to cry. "I don't want to be so delicate!" I said.

My little friend gave a start, then softened up a bit and tried to comfort me. "That's right. Nobody wants to be different from the crowd. But all sorts of things separate us—we'll see about it later!"

The snow outside the window continued to fall. It looked like twisted rolls of cotton fluff and piled up evenly on the green tiles like layers of snowy troughs. Mother and I were to go home for New Year's.

Since my little friend's mom had to start working, they also had to leave before the new year began. We had only another half day to be together. Midst this vast human sea, we would separate from this day on and vanish in the clamor of the boisterous city. When could we ever get together again under the same roof?

We gazed at each other with strong attachment. In the drab night my little friend's face gradually grew bigger in my misty gaze. His strength and resolution were manifested everywhere: by his tightly closed lips, by his strong eyebrows, his far-reaching vision, his slightly jutting chin.... "He will butcher pigs—butcher people?" As I thought, my little hand opened and clenched under the quilt expressing my own insignificance.

From our mothers we all got the word back that it would be tomorrow—the first day of the New Year—that we would go home! My father was afraid that on New Year's Eve there would be too much going on, and that if mother went home she wouldn't be able to get her rest. My little friend's father, on the other hand, had to go out on New Year's Eve in order to avoid his creditors[1], and he was afraid that if his wife went home she would be surrounded by debt collectors. So he didn't let her leave the hospital either. Out of the blue we had another day together!

From midnight on we heard firecrackers continuously exploding both near and far. In the fleecy snow, the coyotes howled a few times as if to announce that another chapter of human gratitude and feuding was over. Tomorrow another episode of putting on a humble and happy facade would begin. Tonight we would try our best to swallow our anxieties and to release our bitterness and tears. Amidst the noise of a million exploding firecrackers, I wondered how many thousand smouldering frightened emotions lay concealed in the gloomy back streets and alleys....

Trembling, I turned to look at my friend. He was biting his bottom lip, not making a sound.—That night was like gently flowing water slowly running away. Close to daylight I vaguely heard my little friend sighing as he lay on his bed.

After daybreak, two nurses came in wearing new year's smiles to give us our baths. One of the nurses opened my little suitcase and dressed me in my small white flannel tights, a long white vest and pajamas. Then on top she put on matching pea green jacket, hat and socks all made of wool. After she had finished dressing me, she picked me up and laughingly said, "Oh, you're so handsome. Look at all the nice things your mother has gotten for you to wear!" I felt very cuddly, but I was so hot. I wanted to cry out of exasperation.

They picked up my little friend too. I was dumbfounded; I nearly didn't recognize him! Outside he was wearing a bulky blue cotton quilted jacket. The sleeves were too big and too long for him. The top part had been mended, and you could see traces of the original stitching. At the bottom was a trim of blue cotton which was faded from washing. His two arms were stretched out. His head and face were buried in a green cotton cowl which was fanned out like a kite! I looked down on the floor and saw piled the two sets of identical white clothing we had been wearing. I suddenly shuddered icily. From now on we would be separated—spiritually and materially separated forever.

He saw me, too. He seemed to be both proud and ashamed at the same time. "You look beautiful," he said. "What gorgeous, warm and soft clothes. My clothes are my armor! I am going into society's battle-field where I'll have to fight others to get enough to eat."

A nurse came in and busily picked up the clothes off the floor and threw them into a crib. Then, just as busily, she picked us up and took us out. When we got to the glass door, I couldn't stop myself from crying aloud. My friend couldn't endure it any longer and cried, too. We waved as though we would never see each other again, and I called, "Little Friend, 'bye. Goodbye." As we each went out our own way, our cries slowly faded away at the ends of the corridor.

Mother was already dressed and standing in the doorway. Father was carrying a small suitcase and was standing beside her. When they saw me coming, mother immediately reached out to take me. She care-fully inspected my face, wiped away my tears, cuddled me, and said, "Precious, don't cry! We're going home. A happy home! Mother and father both love you!"

A wheelchair was brought over. Mother then wrapped me in a green wool blanket and sat down while holding me. Father followed behind. They thanked and said goodbye to the doctor and nurses who saw us out. Then we went down the elevator.

From outside the double glass doors, I saw an automobile parked by the entrance. Father went ahead to open the door, and a gust of wind blew in some snow. Mother quickly covered my face, but I could sense that we got out of the wheelchair, went out the door, and got in the car. Then the door shut with a bang. Mother lifted the blanket away from my face, and I saw that the car was full of flowers. I cuddled against mother's bosom, and both she and father snuggled up to me.

The car turned slowly to go out the driveway. The street was jammed with rickshaws, and while they were chaotically making a path for us, I jerked my head up and saw my intimate acquaintance of the last ten days! He was in his father's arms. His mother was carrying a bundle wrapped with a green cloth. The two of them leaned against each other by the doorway with their backs to us. His father was wearing a wide-brimmed, green felt hat and a long green cotton gown. My friend was resting against his father's shoulder under the brim of the hat. His face was towards me. The snowflakes were falling on his eyebrows and

cheeks. His eyes were tightly closed, but he had a disdainful smile on his face... he was already beginning to enjoy his struggle....

After the car finally made it onto the main street, we just flew along. The snowflakes floated and danced above the road. I could faintly hear the beat of new year's gongs and drums. Mother cuddled me closely and whispered into my ear, "Precious, see how pure and peaceful this world is!"

I cried.

NOTE

[1]Traditionally, all bills were paid before New Year's in order to begin the new year with a clean slate.

"We might compare the novel to a symphony, and a collection of short stories to a good concert recital."

Katherine Anne Porter

His Excellency

BY INDRO MONTANELLI

TRANSLATED FROM THE ITALIAN BY UGUCCIONE RANIERI

Tight-corseted, he wore a monocle and false teeth, and the thought struck me of how convincing, after all, is our racial destiny. What else could a man like that become if not a general?

There it is, lined up with the other sixty-four coffins from the Fossoli concentration camp, and the crowd has sprinkled it, like the others, with flowers. Among all these people gathered here in the silence of the Milan cathedral, surely I am not the only one to know. Yet there has been no protest. Truly, men are as lenient to the dead as they are harsh with the living. The coffin will now pass like the others between the reverent throngs, like the others it will be buried and, on June 22 of each year, will receive its quota of rhetoric spilled over the common grave. Fair enough.... Who are we to judge?

His Excellency, General Della Rovere, army corps commander, intimate friend of Badoglio's and "technical adviser" to General Alexander, was locked up by the Germans in the San Vittore prison of Milan in the spring of 1944 when the Allied armies were still fighting their slow way up the Italian peninsula. He had been captured near Genoa while trying to land at night from an Allied submarine to take command of the resistance movement in the north. A soldier to his finger tips, he had impressed even Franz, the German warder, who would stand at attention when addressing him and had gone so far as to have a cot placed in his cell. So the Italian guard, Ceraso, informed me as he passed my spy hole with a rose in a glass, picked expressly for His Excellency. Later, Ceraso returned to say that the General wished to see me, and letting me out, escorted me to his cell.

"Cavalry officer" was written all over those arched legs, that slight build, and aristocratic profile. Tight-corseted, he wore a monocle and false teeth, and the thought struck me of how convincing, after all, is our racial destiny. What else could a man like that become if not a general? With steely grace he could give an order and make it sound like a plea, and even now, weeks after his capture, his cheeks were clean-shaven, his trousers miraculously pressed, while one could almost detect on his polished shoes a pair of invisible spurs.

"Montanelli, I presume?" he said with a slight drawl, polishing his monocle without giving me his hand. "I already knew of your presence here before landing. Badoglio in person had informed me. His Majesty's Government is following your case with utmost sympathy. Let it be understood, however, that the day you face the firing squad you will have done no more than your duty. Please stand at ease." Only at these last words did I realize that I was standing heels joined, thumbs touching the seams of my trousers just as the drill book says. "We are all on temporary duty here, right?" he continued, cleaning the nail of one little finger with the nail of the other. "An officer is at all times merely on temporary duty, he is a *novio de la muerte*, as the Spaniards say, a bridegroom of death." He smiled at me, paced leisurely up and down the cell flexing his slim, arched legs; then, stopping again before me, cleaned and replaced his monocle. "We two are very near our wedding day," he continued. "My sentence has already been pronounced. And yours?"

"Not yet, sir," I answered, almost mortified.

"It will be," he went on. "You will have the honor of being shot in the chest, I hear. Splendid. There is no better proof of your conduct under interrogation. The Germans are rough in obtaining confessions but chivalrous toward those who abstain. Good. Your orders are to continue. In case of torture, if you feel you must utter a name—I cast no doubt on your spiritual endurance, but there is a limit to the physical—utter mine. I have nothing to lose. Actually, I had nothing to hide even from my old friend, Marshal Kesselring, when he questioned me. I did, however, explain that I hardly expected the British submarine captain to be such a fool as to answer the decoy signals of a German patrol boat. 'You trust the English?' Kesselring smiled. 'Why not? We even trusted the Germans once,' I smiled back. 'Sorry!' he said, 'I have no choice but to shoot you.' 'No hard feelings,' I concluded. But to come back to your case: when you are up for questioning again, stick to your line. After all, we have such a simple duty left: to die like gentlemen. What is your indictment?"

I explained my case fully. His Excellency listened with his eyes to the ground like a confessor, nodding approbation from time to time.

"A clear case," he concluded. "Captured in the performance of duty. It's a soldier's death. They absolutely *must* shoot you in the chest. It's strictly regulations. Let me know how things develop. You can go now."

That was the first day in all the six months since my arrest that I did not think of my wife locked in her cell in another wing of the building. Toward evening I begged Ceraso to sign me up for the barber the next day and in the meanwhile to bring me a comb. And that night, braving the cold, I took my trousers off before lying on my plank and hung them on the window bars hoping they would regain their shape.

On the following days, through my spy hole, I was able to observe His Excellency in his cell just across from mine. One by one, all the prisoners were called to report to him, and all came. In theory, our wing, the dreaded Fifth, was for "solitaries" and so it had been up till that time, but the prestige of His Excellency was obviously so great that the Italian warders felt they could stretch a point. On entering, his guests would stand at attention, even the Communists, and bow stiffly. Later, on leaving, they would walk with a prouder carriage. Number 215, who so often sobbed for his wife and children, after talking with the General fell silent, and even when caught smoking by Franz took his lashes without a whimper. Ceraso told me that almost all, after their talk, had asked, like me, for the barber, a comb, and a little soap. Even the warders now wore their caps straight and tried to speak correct Italian. The wing had never been so quiet, and when Müller came on inspection he praised the new discipline. For the first time, he omitted calling us "anti-Fascist dogs" and "dirty Badoglian traitors," confining himself to an allusion to the "felonious King," at which we all looked at the ceiling pretending not to hear, while His Excellency, who was standing a little forward as befitted his rank, turned deliberately on his heels and re-entered his cell. Müller snorted, but said nothing.

One morning Colonel P. and Colonel F. were taken. Asked if they had a last wish, they mentioned the General, who received them on his threshold, and that was the only time I ever saw him shake hands. Then, caressing with a slow gesture his silvery hair and adjusting his monocle, he smiled and said something to the two officers—something cordial and tender, I am sure. Suddenly, snapping to attention and fixing them coldly in the eyes, he gave them the military salute. P. and F. were pale as chalk, but smiling, and never had they looked so much like colonels as when they moved off, erect, with firm step, between the S.S. men. We heard later that they had both cried, "Long live the King" as they fell.

That same afternoon I was taken down for questioning, and Müller warned me that this was my last chance and that if I did not speak up, etc.... But I hardly heard, nor, though I kept my eyes glued to his, saw him. All I could see were the two pale faces of P. and F. and the marble-like face of His Excellency, and all I could hear was his drawling soft voice... "*novio de la muerte*... performance of duty... death on the field..." Müller gave me up without torture after two hours. Even if he had tortured me, I believe I would not have uttered a word, not even the name of His Excellency, in front of whose cell, on my return, I begged Ceraso to let me stop.

Della Rovere was sitting on the edge of his cot. Putting down his book, he stared at me at length while I stood at attention. Then he said slowly: "Yes, indeed. I expected as much of you," and dismissed me with a gesture. But on the threshold he called me back. "Just a second!" and he rose to his feet. "There is a thing I still wish to say. A—uhm—difficult thing. I am, I wish to say, extremely satisfied with your conduct, Captain Montanelli. And I wish this good warder to listen well, for he will be our only surviving witness. Very, very satisfied.... A jolly good show, sir!" And that night, for the first time, I felt alone in the world, joyously alone with my beautiful bride, Death, forgetful of my wife and my mother, and for once my Country seemed to me a real and an important thing.

I never saw him again, but after the liberation I gathered the details of his end from one of the survivors of Fossoli.

His Excellency appeared very put out when suddenly, together with a crowd of other San Vittore inmates, he was packed into a boxcar train and shipped to the Fossoli concentration camp. During the journey he sat on the kit packs which his fellow prisoners had laid down as a seat for him and refused to rise even when Schultze came in for inspection. Schultze struck him, shrieking: "*Du bist ein Schwein*, Bertoni!"[1] But the General found it superfluous to explain that he was not Bertoni, but Della Rovere, a corps commander, friend of Badoglio's and technical adviser to Alexander. Without a twitch he picked up his monocle, luckily unbroken, replaced it, and remained seated. Schultze went out cursing.

At Fossoli, His Excellency no longer enjoyed the little favors he was used to. He was placed in a common shed and put to work. His companions took turns in sparing him the more humiliating tasks like latrine duty, but never, of his own initiative, did he shirk a job, even though manual labor weighed heavily on him, for he was no longer young. Digging, or carrying bricks, often with a grimace of pain, he would keep a sharp eye open to see that no one gave a poor show, and at day's end he would reprimand those who needed it. To him, they were all officers and gentlemen, and such did they continue to feel under the flash of his monocle and the lash of his words. Desperately, heroically, he struggled to keep his nails spotless and his cheeks shaven. He never complained.

Neither then, nor later, was the motive for the June 22 massacre ever made clear. The order came from Milan, some said as a reprisal for something which had happened in Genoa. Lieutenant Dickermann read out the sixty-five names drawn by lot from those of the four hundred inmates lined up in a square. Among the first was the name Bertoni. No one stepped forward. "Bertoni!" roared Dickermann. "Ber-to-ni!" and he stared at the point where Della Rovere stood. Did Dickermann understand, or did he merely choose to humour a dying man? "*Gut, gut*," he chuckled. "Della Rovere, *wie Sie wollen....* "[2] All held their breath as they watched His Excellency slip his monocle into place and take three slow steps forward. "*General* Della Rovere, please!" he corrected, taking his place by the other doomed men. With the nail of his right forefinger he began to clean the nail of his left—both marvelously steady.

The sixty-five were manacled, blindfolded, and pushed against the wall. Only His Excellency refused to have his eyes covered and was humored. Then the machine guns were set. His Excellency took a step forward. "Hold it! Stop!" cried Dickermann reaching for his revolver. His Excellency took another step. "Gentlemen!" he cried with a voice like a bugle. "In this supreme moment let our thoughts rise..." But Dickermann's "Fire!" and the opening crash of the guns cut him short. They all went down. But the General was the only one who did not squirm on the ground, and his monocle remained miraculously in its place. It was still on when they dropped him into the common trench, and he is still wearing it, I assume, there in his coffin.

That coffin, which today, June 22, anniversary of the massacre, stands before me in the Milan cathedral, does not contain the body of the imaginary General Della Rovere—true enough! Merely the remains of the former jailbird Bertoni, a Genoese, by profession cardsharp and thief, who, when arrested by the Germans for some petty crime, offered to spy for them in prison by impersonating a non-existent general, and succeeded only too well....

Does it really matter? Surely the Cardinal Archbishop did no wrong in blessing this body together with the others?

For, after all, Bertoni, the cardsharp, the thief, the spy, was indeed a general at the hour of death, and undoubtedly he died convinced that he was the friend of Badoglio's and "technical adviser" to Alexander. But for him, I would never have felt a hero for one night in my cell.... And P. and F. would not have walked to the firing squad as colonels should.... Because of him, those who lacked courage found it, and Number 215 stopped whimpering for his wife and children....

Peace to his twisted soul.

NOTES

[1]*Du bist ein Schwein*, Bertoni!: You are a pig, Bertoni!
[2]*wie Sie wollen*: as you wish

THE CLEVER PERSON IV

The Fly

BY MAI VO-DINH

"I want some living thing to be our witness."

Everyone in the village knew the usurer, a rich and smart man. Having accumulated a fortune over the years, he settled down to a life of leisure in his big house surrounded by an immense garden and guarded by a pack of ferocious dogs. But still unsatisfied with what he had acquired, the man went on making money by lending it to people all over the county at exorbitant rates. The usurer reigned supreme in the area, for numerous were those who were in debt to him.

One day, the rich man set out for the house of one of his peasants. Despite repeated reminders, the poor laborer just could not manage to pay off his long-standing debt. Working himself to a shadow, the peasant barely succeeded in making ends meet. The moneylender was therefore determined that if he could not get his money back this time, he would proceed to confiscate some of his debtor's most valuable belongings. But the rich man found no one at the peasant's house but a small boy of eight or nine playing alone in the dirt yard.

"Child, are your parents home?" the rich man asked.

"No, sir," the boy replied, then went on playing with his sticks and stones, paying no attention whatever to the man.

"Then, where are they?" the rich man asked, somewhat irritated, but the little boy went on playing and did not answer.

When the rich man repeated his query, the boy looked up and

answered, with deliberate slowness, "Well, sir, my father has gone to cut living trees and plant dead ones, and my mother is at the marketplace selling the wind and buying the moon."

"What? What in heaven are you talking about?" the rich man commanded. "Quick, tell me where they are, or you will see what this stick can do to you!" The bamboo walking stick in the big man's hand looked indeed menacing.

After repeated questioning, however, the boy only gave the same reply. Exasperated, the rich man told him, "All right, little devil, listen to me! I came here today to take the money your parents owe me. But if you tell me where they really are and what they are doing, I will forget all about the debt. Is that clear to you?"

"Oh, sir, why are you joking with a poor little boy? Do you expect me to believe what you are saying?" For the first time the boy looked interested.

"Well, there is heaven and there is earth to witness my promise," the rich man said, pointing up to the sky and down to the ground.

But the boy only laughed. "Sir, heaven and earth cannot talk and therefore cannot testify. I want some living thing to be our witness."

Catching sight of a fly alighting on a bamboo pole nearby, and laughing inside because he was fooling the boy, the rich man proposed, "There is a fly. He can be our witness. Now, hurry and tell me what you mean when you say that your father is out cutting living trees and planting dead ones, while your mother is at the market selling the wind and buying the moon."

Looking at the fly on the pole, the boy said, "A fly is a good enough witness for me. Well, here it is, sir. My father has simply gone to cut down bamboos and make a fence with them for a man near the river. And my mother... oh, sir, you'll keep your promise, won't you? You will free my parents of all their debts? You really mean it?"

"Yes, yes, I do solemnly swear in front of this fly here." The rich man urged the boy to go on.

"Well, my mother, she has gone to the market to sell fans so she can buy oil for our lamps. Isn't that what you would call selling the wind to buy the moon?"

Shaking his head, the rich man had to admit inwardly that the boy was a clever one. However, he thought, the little genius still had much to learn, believing as he did that a fly could be a witness for anybody. Bidding the boy goodbye, the man told him that he would soon return to make good his promise.

A few days had passed when the moneylender returned. This time he found the poor peasant couple at home, for it was late in the evening. A nasty scene ensued, the rich man claiming his money and the poor peasant apologizing and begging for another delay. Their argument awakened the little boy, who ran to his father and told him, "Father, Father, you don't have to pay your debt. This gentleman here has promised me that he would forget all about the money you owe him."

"Nonsense!" The rich man shook his walking stick at both father and son. "Nonsense! Are you going to stand there and listen to a child's inventions? I never spoke a word to this boy. Now, tell me, are you going to pay or are you not?"

The whole affair ended by being brought before the mandarin who governed the county. Not knowing what to believe, all the poor peasant and his wife could do was to bring their son with them when they went to court. The little boy's insistence about the rich man's promise was their only encouragement.

The mandarin began by asking the boy to relate exactly what had happened between himself and the moneylender. Happily, the boy hastened to tell about the explanations he gave the rich man in exchange for the debt.

"Well," the mandarin said to the boy, "if this man here has indeed made such a promise, we have only your word for it. How do we know that you have not invented the whole story yourself? In a case such as this, you need a witness to confirm it, and you have none." The boy remained calm and declared that naturally there was a witness to their conversation.

"Who is that, child?" the mandarin asked.

"A fly, Your Honor."

"A fly? What do you mean, a fly? Watch out, young man, fantasies are not to be tolerated in this place!" The mandarin's benevolent face suddenly became stern.

"Yes, Your Honor, a fly. A fly which was alighting on this gentleman's nose!" The boy leaped from his seat.

"Insolent little devil, that's a pack of lies!" the rich man roared indignantly, his face like a ripe tomato. "The fly was *not* on my nose; *he was on the housepole*...." But he stopped dead. It was, however, too late.

The majestic mandarin himself could not help bursting out laughing. Then the audience burst out laughing. The boy's parents too, although timidly, laughed. And the boy, and the rich man himself, also laughed. With one hand on his stomach, the mandarin waved the other hand toward the rich man:

"Now, now that's all settled. You have indeed made your promises, dear sir, to the child. *Housepole or no housepole, your conversation did happen after all!* The court says you must keep your promise."

And still chuckling, he dismissed all parties.

The Riddle

RETOLD BY ADELE VERNON

The charcoal maker, who had been looking intently at this finely dressed stranger, suddenly realized that it was THE KING who stood before him.

Once upon a time, long, long ago a king lost his way while hunting in a great forest. The king was cold, tired, and hungry, but there was no one around to help him.

"Oh, where are all my companions?" lamented the king. When suddenly, not far off, he noticed thin spires of smoke drifting up through the tall trees. Guided by the smoke, the king soon came to a clearing in the forest where there lived a poor charcoal maker and his family.

The charcoal maker was busily stacking wood into a mound and didn't hear the king approaching.

"Good day!" greeted the king in a booming voice.

This so startled the charcoal maker that he spun around, sending sticks of wood flying in all directions. His face and hands were covered with soot, and he stepped forward and peered at the king from beneath a mat of reddish hair.

"Ah, my good man," continued the weary king, "could you spare me a drink of water and some food? I have had no refreshment all day."

The charcoal maker, who had been looking intently at this finely dressed stranger, suddenly realized that it was THE KING who stood before him.

"Y... Your Majesty? Oh, dear! C... can it really be you?" stammered the charcoal maker, not quite believing his own eyes. "Yes, of course, Your Majesty. Please, sit down. Here, by the fire."

After making a hasty bow he called excitedly to his wife.

"Anna, Anna! Some water! Some food! Quickly! It is His Majesty, THE KING!"

In the space of a wink, a plump, ruddy-faced woman came scurrying out of the hut, balancing a plate of steaming roasted onions and carrying a jug of cold water.

"Pardon us, Your Majesty. We have so little to offer you," apologized Anna as she set the food down near the king. And with a flustered curtsey, she hurried back to the hut.

The king ate and drank with great gusto.

"Mmmmm, delicious! How hungry and thirsty I was. This fresh cold water is better than wine. You see, I was hunting with my companions when we got separated and I lost my way. They must have returned to the castle thinking that I had gone home."

After his meal, the king looked around at the smoking mounds and wondered about the hard life of a charcoal maker.

"And you, charcoal maker," inquired the king, motioning for him to sit down, "living here in the middle of the forest, far from village or castle, working long hours to make charcoal for others to burn and receiving little thanks for your labor, how much do you earn a day for your work?"

The charcoal maker answered the king cheerfully as he put more wood on the fire, "No more than ten cents a day, Your Majesty. And a great plenty it is, too!"

"What!?" exclaimed the king, unable to hide his surprise. "You can't mean it! How can you live on so little?"

"Not only do I make enough to live on," explained the charcoal maker briskly, "but I also pay back a debt, save for my old age, and still have something left over to throw out the window!"

Amazed, the king leaned forward to look more closely at the sturdy little man sitting before him.

"But it is not possible! How can you do so much with such meagre earnings?"

"It is very simple, Your Majesty," said the charcoal maker with a twinkle in his eye.

"With my earnings I support my family which includes my mother, who took care of me when I was young. Now I am taking care of her. Thus, I am paying back a debt. I also provide for my son, whom I hope will do the same for me when I am old.

"So, I am saving for my old age. Finally, I must provide a dowry for my daughter who will marry some day. And as you know, Your Majesty, money spent on a dowry is as good as throwing it out the window."

The king laughed long and hard at the charcoal maker's riddle. He was delighted with the story but now he was curious to see if such an ingenious man was also honest and trustworthy. So he made a bargain with him.

"Well, charcoal maker, I see that you are both clever and resourceful. I admire you greatly. But I ask you to keep this talk of ours a secret. Do not reveal the answer to this riddle to anyone until you have looked upon my face one hundred times. Agreed?"

The charcoal maker stood up quickly and made a deep bow.

"Yes, of course, Your Majesty. You have my word of honor."

Pleased with this bargain, the king made ready to go.

"Thank you for the delicious meal. Now I must go. Please be good enough to show me the way back to the main road."

"It has been an honor, Your Majesty," answered the charcoal maker, bowing again. "Please come this way."

The next day in the great dining hall of the castle, the king feasted and jested with the members of his court. After the huge meal, he challenged them with the charcoal maker's riddle.

"Now tell me, can any of you solve this riddle? How can a poor charcoal maker, who earns only ten cents a day, make enough to live on, pay back a debt, save for his old age, and even have something left over to throw out the window? Whoever is the first with the answer shall be made First Counsellor of the Kingdom."

Immediately the hall was filled with a great hum buzz as wisemen, courtiers, and scholars talked about the riddle. Many attempted to solve it, but the king, his eyes shining with delight, shook his head—No!—again and again. No one in the whole court could find the answer.

Only one courtier did not participate in the debate. He quietly got up from the table, tied a bag to his belt, and with a cunning smile, slipped out of the palace unnoticed.

After a long ride, he approached the charcoal maker's home.

"I say, you there, charcoal maker," called out the courtier, "I have come a very long way to ask you to solve a simple riddle for me. How can a charcoal maker, such as yourself, who earns only ten cents a day, make enough to live on, pay back a debt, save for his old age, and still have something left over to throw out the window?"

Glancing up from his work at the eager courtier, the charcoal maker slowly shook his head, "Please pardon me, Sir. I am sorry you have made such a long journey, but I can't tell you the answer to the riddle for I have promised not to."

"Hmmm. Yes, of course," smiled the courtier slyly. "But what do you say to these ten gold pieces?" And he pressed them, one by one, in the charcoal maker's hand.

The charcoal maker looked thoughtfully at the coins but shook his head again. "No, Sir. I really cannot break my promise."

"Well, then, how about this?" demanded the courtier impatiently as he counted out more and more shiny coins.

The charcoal maker picked up each coin and studied it carefully. But still he shook his head, no.

Soon there were one hundred coins in front of him.

"Well, have you anything to say to one hundred?" demanded the courtier.

"Hrrhhumm. Well, you see, Sir," said the charcoal maker as he cleared his throat. "It is very simple. With my earnings I support my family which includes my mother, who took care of me when I was young. Now I am taking care of her. Thus, I am paying back a debt. I also provide for my son, whom I hope will do the same for me when I am old. So, I am saving for my old age. Finally, I must provide a dowry for my daughter, and *that* is as good as throwing money out the window!"

The courtier laughed heartily at the charcoal maker's reply.

"Ah, ha. How very clever. Thank you, my good man, thank you, indeed."

Hastily, he mounted his horse and rode off in the direction of the castle, already picturing himself as First Counsellor of the Kingdom.

That evening when the courtier returned to the castle, the king was seated on his throne by a roaring fire. The courtier boldly approached the king and whispered something in his ear. The king's face suddenly turned bright red with angry surprise.

"So you see, Your Majesty," boasted the courtier in a loud voice, "I have guessed the answer to the riddle and I should be made First Counsellor of the Kingdom, as you have promised."

"Yes, yes. I must keep my word, if you did indeed guess the answer to the riddle," replied the disappointed king. "But first I must have a word with the charcoal maker. Have him brought to me at once!"

Before the king finished his dinner, swift riders brought the charcoal maker to him. Dazzled by the splendor of the castle, the charcoal maker approached the king hesitatingly and bowed.

"Your Majesty, you sent for me?"

"You have broken your promise to me and have told the answer to the riddle!" said the king angrily to the poor charcoal maker. "I thought you were as honest as you were clever. I see now, that this is not so. You deserve to be punished, for dishonesty is the very worst of crimes!"

The charcoal maker stood silently for a few moments and then he spoke out bravely.

"Your Majesty, your anger at me is unjust, for I did exactly as you requested. I did not tell the answer to the riddle until I had seen Your Majesty's face one hundred times."

"But that is absolutely impossible!" exploded the king. "You couldn't have!"

"But I did," grinned the charcoal maker, "on each and every one of the hundred coins that the courtier gave to me."

The king looked at the charcoal maker in astonishment, and then burst out laughing, as did everyone in the court.

"Yes, yes, you are right. I see that you are even more clever than I thought. And still you kept your promise. I praise you, and curse the courtier in front of the whole court. And I give you three bags of gold. One for your debt, one for your old age, and one to throw out the window."

Polyphemus the Cyclops

BY HOMER

RETOLD BY BARBARA LEONIE PICARD

He was as tall as three men and broad, with but one eye in the middle of his forehead; and as soon as Odysseus and his men caught sight of him, they knew that they had been unwise to wait.

The next land that they reached was the country of the Cyclopes, a simple, savage folk, of more than human size, who never tilled their land, or built ships or houses, or traded with other nations. Instead they lived in caves in the rocks and spent their time pasturing their flocks on their rich green fields.

Just off the mainland lay a wooded island, the home of many wild goats, and to this island the twelve ships came on a misty night. The men disembarked and slept; and in the morning, when the mist had cleared, they saw opposite them the land of the Cyclopes and were surprised, for in the fog they had not imagined the mainland to be so close.

All that day they rested from their labours on the sea and feasted on the flesh of the island goats. Keeping a careful watch upon the land, Odysseus was just able to make out the huge flocks of sheep and the cattle of the Cyclopes browsing in the fields, and the smoke from the fires of the herdsmen. "Tomorrow," he said, "I shall go with one ship to the mainland to see who lives in that rich country. It may well be a friendly folk who will give us welcome hospitality after our days at sea."

Accordingly, in the morning Odysseus sailed to the mainland and beached his ship on the shore below a rocky cliff which towered above their heads, with shrubs growing among the rocks and little yellow wall-flowers springing from every cleft.

Close by, halfway up the cliff and approached by a zigzag pathway, was the opening of a wide cave, half hidden by laurel bushes and surrounded by a wall of huge stones. It was plain to see that the cave was someone's home, and picking out twelve of his best men, Odysseus set off up the cliff carrying a skin of the finest wine he had on board, as a gift for whoever might live there.

Beyond the wall they found a courtyard with pens for sheep and goats; though the pens were empty when they saw them, for the flocks were out at pasture with their owner.

"There is no one here," said Odysseus. "Let us wait in the cave for the shepherd to return." And they passed beneath the glossy foliage of the overhanging laurels and went inside.

Within, the light was dim, but when their eyes grew used to it, they saw that the huge cave held many pens of lambs and kids, all separated according to their ages. There were, too, great pails of milk, and cheeses stacked in baskets hanging from the roof. But, for all this abundance of good food, the cave did not seem a friendly place, and Odysseus' men urged him to let them take as many cheeses and lambs as they could carry and return at once to the ship. But he would not hear of this. "We could not rob a stranger in his absence," he said. "Besides, when he returns it may please him to give us far more gifts than thirteen men can carry off, and it would be folly to miss the chance of filling our ship with savoury cheeses and tender kids which we might share with our comrades waiting on the island."

So they remained in the cave, and towards evening the herdsman returned with his flocks. He was as tall as three men and broad, with but one eye in the middle of his forehead; and as soon as Odysseus and his men caught sight of him, they knew that they had been unwise to wait.

He came to the entrance of the cave and flung inside a huge bundle of logs, large branches lopped from tall pines and oaks, as faggots for his fire; and in terror the Greeks fled to the darkest corner of the cave and hid themselves. The monster penned his rams and goats in the courtyard and drove the ewes and she-goats into the cave for milking, blocking the entrance with a great stone. And even his sheep and goats were larger than any Odysseus had ever seen before.

When the milking was over, the monster penned the ewes with their lambs and the goats with their kids, and set himself to make a fire from the wood he had brought home. As soon as he had a blaze, he was able to see, by the light of the leaping flames, Odysseus and his men, crouching in the very farthest corner. "Who are you, strangers?" he asked in a voice like thunder.

For all his terror Odysseus stepped forward and answered boldly enough. "We are Greeks, sailing home to Ithaca from the war with Troy. The winds have carried us somewhat from our course, and we have come to you in hope that you may be our host until we can set sail once more."

The giant roared, "I am Polyphemus the Cyclops, and I entertain no guests unless it pleases me. But tell me this, where have you beached your ship? Is she close by?"

Odysseus suspected the question and guessed the Cyclops meant harm to his ship and the men guarding her, and he answered cunningly, "Our ship was wrecked upon your shore, and only I and these twelve men escaped alive from the sea."

But Polyphemus gave no word of sympathy in reply. Instead, he seized a man in each hand, and dashing out their brains against the rocky floor, he tore them in pieces and ate them for his supper before the eyes of their horrified comrades. Then after drinking several large pailfuls of milk, he lay down by the fire to sleep.

Odysseus would have drawn his sword and crept upon him while he slept and killed him, but that he knew it would be impossible for him and his men to move away by themselves the great stone that blocked the opening of the cave. So, terrified, they waited all night, whispering together and trying to devise some means of outwitting the cruel monster.

At dawn Polyphemus rekindled the fire and milked his ewes and goats again. That done, he snatched up two more of Odysseus' men and ate them as a wild beast might have done. Then he rolled aside the great stone from the mouth of the cave and drove out his flocks; and replacing the stone once more, he went towards the mountain pastures, whistling cheerfully at the thought of the good supper which awaited his return.

Odysseus and the eight men left to him sat down beside the fire to think how they might escape the fate which would surely be theirs unless they could find a way to leave the cave; and at last a plan came to Odysseus. In the cave there lay a long pole of green olive-wood, drying so that it might serve the Cyclops for a staff. From this pole Odysseus hacked off with his sword a piece the length of a tall man, and set his companions to sharpen one end into a point and harden it in the fire.

"Tonight," he said, "when the monster sleeps, we will heat the wood red-hot and with it put out his single eye."

When the point of the stake was hard and sharp, they hid it and then chose by lot the four men who should help Odysseus use it in the night.

When evening came the Cyclops returned with his flocks, and this time he drove all the sheep into the cave, rams and ewes alike, and penned them safely. When he had milked the ewes and goats, he thought of his own supper and seized two more men. While he sat by the fire eating them, Odysseus poured out a huge bowlful of the wine he had brought with him, and coming forward, offered it to Polyphemus. "Such wine as this our ship held before it was wrecked upon your shores," he said. "Come, taste of it and tell me if you think it is not good."

The Cyclops took the wooden bowl and drained it at one draught. He held it out to Odysseus. "Give me more," he said.

Odysseus filled it a second time, and again the monster drank. "Give me yet more of your wine, stranger," he demanded, "and tell me your name, that I may give you a gift in return."

A third time Odysseus filled the bowl and the Cyclops drank. "My name is No-one," said Odysseus. "Tell me now what gift you will give to No-one in exchange for his good wine."

"I will eat you last of all your comrades. A few more hours of life, that shall be my gift to you." And with a mighty laugh that echoed through the cave Polyphemus lay down beside the fire; and made drowsy by the wine, he fell deeply asleep at once.

Odysseus thrust the stake into the embers and held it there until it was red-hot; then taking it, he and the four men on whom the lot had fallen drove it deep into the Cyclops' eye.

With screams and with shouts of rage, Polyphemus awoke and pulled the stake from the socket of his eye, and wildly flinging his arms about and stumbling around the cave, he tried to catch Odysseus and his friends, who crouched trembling against the wall.

The neighbouring Cyclopes who dwelt in caverns nearby heard his cries, and coming to his cave, stood outside the great stone and called to him. "What ails you, Polyphemus? Why do you wake us with your cries? Does someone steal your sheep or kill you?"

"Good neighbours," said Polyphemus, "it is the cunning wiles of No-one that are killing me."

"If no one is killing you," answered the neighbours, "you must be sick, and illness comes from the gods, and we can be of no help to you. You have woken us in vain. May your sickness have left you by the morning." And they returned to their own homes.

But the Cyclops groped his way to the entrance of the cave and pushed away the great stone, and sitting down in the doorway, waited to catch any of the men who might try to pass him; so that they saw that there was no escape for them that way.

At the far end of the cave Odysseus and his companions made whispered plans; and taking reeds from Polyphemus' bed, Odysseus bound together eighteen of the finest rams in threes, with one of his six men tied beneath each middle ram. Then he himself laid hold of the largest ram of all, a great creature with a splendid fleece, and lay underneath it, clinging on and hidden by the shaggy wool that hung down from its broad sides.

By that time it was dawn, and the rams were eager to be grazing in the rich pastures. Bleating, they moved together to the entrance of the cave, where Polyphemus felt across the back of each one as it came to him, before passing it through the courtyard. But he never thought to feel beneath the animals, so the six men went safely out. Last of all to come was the leader of the flock, walking slowly under the weight of Odysseus, clinging to its fleece.

As Polyphemus felt its back he spoke to it. "My good ram, you are ever the foremost of the flock, leading the others to their grazing ground. Why are you last today? Are you grieved for your master, blinded by wicked No-one, and would stay to comfort him? I would that you could speak and tell me where he hides, that wretch who took away my sight. But go, dear ram, join your companions in the fields." And Polyphemus moved his hand aside and the ram stepped through the opening into the sunlight, bearing Odysseus.

Once outside the courtyard, Odysseus freed himself from his hiding-place and went to release his companions. Then hastily they drove the sheep down to the ship and their comrades waiting on the shore. With no delay they stowed the flock on board and set out to row back to the island where the fleet was moored.

A little way from the shore Odysseus stood up in the ship and shouted with all his might, "Now indeed, wicked Cyclops, do you know what ills your cruelty to helpless strangers has brought to you."

Polyphemus heard him and came out from his cave in fury, and breaking off a huge piece of rock, he flung it into the sea in the direction of Odysseus' voice. It fell in the water by the bows, and the great waves made by its fall washed the ship back towards the shore; but Odysseus seized a long pole and pushed off again, and his men fell to rowing hard once more.

Again Odysseus stood up to shout his taunts to the Cyclops, and though his men tried to restrain him, for they feared another rock might be cast at them, he called out, "Polyphemus, if anyone should ever ask you how you lost your sight, you may tell him that Odysseus, king of Ithaca, put out your eye."

And Polyphemus cried out with a loud voice, "Alas, it was foretold that great grief would come to me through Odysseus, king of Ithaca, but I had thought he would be a fine big man, a worthy enemy for me, not a tiny weakling like yourself. But evil will come to you as well from this, for Poseidon, god of the sea whereon you sail, is my father, and he will avenge my eye." And then he held out his hands over the water and prayed to his father for vengeance. "Great Poseidon, lord of all the seas, grant your son this one request. May Odysseus and his men never reach their home in Ithaca. But if, in spite of all his misdeeds, it is the will of the gods that Odysseus should gain the shores of his own land, let it be alone and friendless, and may he find sorrow awaiting him in his house."

And again Polyphemus tore off and hurled into the sea a rock. But this time it fell to the stern of the ship and sent her rushing forward to the island.

Once safely with the men from his other ships, Odysseus divided the sheep among them, a fair share to each. But his companions allotted him the fine ram by the help of which he had escaped, as an extra gift, because he was their leader and because he had saved six of his men from the Cyclops.

The Great Beyond

BY CYPRIAN EKWENSI

It was clear now. The voice was coming from inside the coffin.

He had always said that on the day of his death he would come back—if only to have his last laugh: for Ikolo was a man who loved to laugh and to make others laugh. No one ever took him seriously. Certainly not the mourners who now followed the coffin along Molomo Street. They were too wrapped in grief to think of the ridiculous.

You could always tell the sort of man who had died by the trail following the hearse. A medical man would have a large proportion of the mourners in the khaki uniform of the Health Department, their brass buttons shining; a popular man would attract all sorts of cars from smoke-screen machines to the long, sleek, and silent throbbers; and for a freemason—the lodge members in their terrible regalia would monopolize all rituals. But Ikolo's funeral was something different. You could not tell that he was very popular by the length of the procession. Funeral processions had been known to stretch all the way down Molomo Street and far into Jideh Street and beyond. Perhaps it was the rain that kept the mourners away.

The rain was a nuisance that afternoon; since morning it had looked threatening; by afternoon the sky would have clouded over and a half-hearted drizzle would spray the entire city. But when it actually did rain, the showers were enough to soak a shirt. Many people said that when a person of some importance dies the weather changes. Judging by that, Ikolo must have been important.

By the time the procession was well under way, the hearse-bearers were wiping their faces with their sticky hands. They were not quite as fortunate as the men in raincoats and the women whose umbrellas formed an intermediate sky of all colours. The singing too was disturbed. Those in front were on the first line of the second verse, while those at the back were dragging and weeping away at the last line of the first verse. The onlookers who lined the route appeared embarrassed by this lack of coordination, but what does a dead man care about burials? He's dead, and it is up to the living to do him proud or just give him the usual six feet. In some cases, I'm told, he doesn't even get the six feet.

Now there was a very affected group a few inches from the coffin. They had kept abreast of it, listening to the grinding iron wheels of the hearse, and watching the pastor's well-fed face as he intoned the hymn. In fact, you did not need to look a second time to know that these people were Ikolo's aunts and nephews, to say nothing of his mother-in-law, his sisters, and uncles.

It must have been his mother-in-law who first heard the curious sound. When the rain is falling and a crowd is singing and the hard wheels of a hearse are grinding the road, it is rather difficult to hear anything else. But one of the women stopped her singing and pinched the other on the arm.

"Did you hear anything?" she whispered.

"Please!" said the other, and she burst out weeping.

She was tall and her nice black eyes were now red. Presently she, too, raised her cloth to wipe away a tear, and then stopped. Everybody in front stopped suddenly as a muffled voice said thickly:

"Jokeh! Jokeh!"

The hearse-bearers stopped. There was a violent thundering—like someone trying to force a door open.

"Jokeh... Jokeh...."

It was clear now. The voice was coming from inside the coffin. The hearse-bearers chewed their lips fearfully not knowing what was expected of them. Already they had forsaken the handles of the carriage, and were looking for a suitable place of safety. All along Molomo Street, the funeral procession had stopped. Everyone was tense.

"Are they repairing the coffin?"... "What's gone wrong?"... "What are they waiting for?"

Then the voice came even louder. "Jokeh... Jokeh... Open!" At once pandemonium broke loose.

"The dead man is awake!" shouted the hearse-bearers and tore into the Town Council buildings like people possessed. When everyone around you is fleeing from danger it is impossible not to follow the mob.

The instinct of self-preservation cannot be disregarded so lightly. Perhaps that was why the pastor himself advanced a few paces in the direction of his home (which, incidentally, was not too far away), but then he suddenly seemed to remember his duty. By the time he came back to the coffin, the beating was unmistakable. The dead man was thundering hard against the wooden walls of his prison.

"The Lord bless his soul!" cried the pastor, muttering a quick prayer.

He was a sorry sight. Alone in the rain, with no-one brave enough to help him, he accepted his responsibility with the true spirit of a man who has faith in himself and faith in the things beyond his understanding. He called for a carpenter, but could you see a living soul anywhere along Molomo Street?

"Lord keep him alive," he panted.

He was across the street in a moment. Doors were banged in his face. He knew why. Had he not often told these same people in his sermons that there was no faith in them?

"Open the door! I want a hammer and pincers!"

You never know how brave somebody really is until something like this happens. Now, as the pastor stood neglected yet hammering hopefully on a door, a little boy—not more than fourteen—stepped out. He had barely a pair of shorts on, and the rain was dancing off his smooth body as if he were a duck. He went straight up to the pastor and said: "Please, sir, I have the tools."

The pastor looked at him, and a smile of pity and admiration spread across his face. He did not know of course that the father of the boy, Raifu, was an undertaker. Their shop overlooked Molomo Street, and many people said that father and son slept and cooked in a coffin. Little Raifu led the way through the rain, and the pastor rolled up his sleeves. He did not handle the tools much because Raifu knew just a little more about coffins than he did. What seemed to disturb them both was the fact that they were alone in the rain; and apart from that, the man in the coffin was rather impatient to get out.

At last the lid creaked open, and there was Ikolo. His face was much too young. He gave a huge sneeze, as if to clear the stale air from his lungs; and the pastor could actually see him licking the raindrops from his lips with some relish, as if they brought life to his weary body. And now his eyes were dancing with delight, just as they had often done when he had told a funny story. What he had to be so pleased about, when everyone else was so frightened, was hard to tell. He sat up in his forty-pound suit—his best, they say, and the one he had ordered Jokeh to dress him in, in case of death—and then he beckoned, to no one in particular. All at once, the crowd began to converge on the hearse.

"Jokeh…," he said again. "I want Jokeh."

The pastor stood aside, and with halting steps, Jokeh, the tall black girl with the red eyes, approached her late husband. He looked at her for perhaps half an hour, during which time he said not a word. You cannot blame the rest of the onlookers for retreating to a safe distance. The pastor watched too, but he was barely an inch from Jokeh, and she was resting on his arm. He held the umbrella which she had dropped in her fear and kept muttering encouraging words to her.

"I... I have understood," Jokeh said, still looking at her husband.

"But he has said nothing!" the pastor replied.

Jokeh's eyes were fixed. She seemed to be listening to something which the pastor himself—for all his daily devotion to the Great Beyond—could not hear. Then, quite suddenly, Jokeh sprang forward. She caught her husband before he toppled over sideways, and with great care laid him down in the coffin. She took the hammer and nails from Raifu, and with her own hands nailed down the lid. Then she threw herself upon the coffin, weeping, and had to be torn away. Raifu and a few men pulled the hearse into the cemetery at the end of Molomo Street. The pastor read his piece and the men lowered Ikolo into his cold six feet of earth.

Jokeh did not talk to the pastor on their way home. She seemed to have changed completely. Nobody came to visit her after this strange funeral: perhaps they were afraid of the cowardly way in which they had all behaved.

Exactly two weeks after her husband's death, Jokeh called on a man who lived in Patey Street. She had never seen this man before and did not know that he existed. She entered the compound, went straight up to his door, and knocked. She found him counting out some money on the floor and handing it to another man, who appeared to be a trader.

"Welcome, madam," the strange man said.

"Thank you," Jokeh said. She sat down and arranged her dress.

"Just hold on," the man said. He finished counting the money, then climbed onto one of the little stools in the room. "I hope there is nothing?"

Jokeh said, "No, there is nothing... but my husband said I should come and collect the money you owe him!"

The man's throat seemed to contract. "But your husband, he's dead—he promised not to tell anyone about...."

"The money is just forty-five pounds, ten shillings and two pence ha'penny."

"That's a lie!"

"Attend to me, I'm a busy woman...."

The stranger wiped his brow. He turned to the trader and said: "Give her the bag." He watched Jokeh wrap the bag into the folds of her cloth. As she rose to go, he said: "Your husband was to call for this money today, but as he was dead...."

"*Odabo-O!*" said Jokeh and went out of the room.

She went straight to the pastor and gave him all the money. "My husband said no one should touch this money but the poor and needy—the cripples and beggars of the city. It is to be given to them on a Friday to be chosen by you."

"I do not understand this," the pastor said. "I mean no harm to your husband's memory... but was he all that religious?"

"I do not understand it myself," Jokeh said. "But remember he loved to pull people's legs. You see, when my husband looked at me like that, something seemed to happen to me. I was looking at things, pictures before my eyes... just like in a cinema. He did not talk to me, but every wish of his I saw before me. It was happening, and the wonderful thing is I haven't forgotten the slightest detail. I remember all he wanted me to do." She worked her hands nervously together. "Since that day, I have promised to be good. He told me not to marry for at least three months, and to watch carefully the new suitor who is promising me heaven and earth just now."

The pastor started. "How did he know?"

Jokeh shook her shoulders. "Who knows? You see he told me that he went on a long journey beyond death. There was a very great hall... an endless hall, white, without limit of length or breadth. Just a hall with white clouds; and in the midst of that cloud was some Great Power. This Power sent him back to make amends for all he had done wrong. Did you not see?—I saw just when he was called back once again."

Jokeh's eyes were twinkling. She, too, seemed to have become younger, even younger than Ikolo. The pastor looked at her and shook his head sadly.

"All my life," he said, "I have tried to do just what you did that day in the rain...."

"Me? What did I do?"

"You contacted someone who had been there... to the Great Beyond, and who came back to tell."

Jokeh said: "I am awaiting my turn anxiously; I want to go and join him. But I must first prepare my soul."

"Yes," said the pastor, "prepare your soul."

There Is Always Hope

ISTVÁN ÖRKÉNY

TRANSLATED FROM THE HUNGARIAN BY MIKLÓS HERNÁDI

"A little unusual, but it can be done."

"**B**ut then graves are never cheap," the clerk said, "let alone along the main walk."

"No need for it to be along the main walk," the interested party said. "What's important is that it should be concreted."

"Concreted?" The clerk was astonished. "A little unusual, but it can be done."

He put the typewritten price list aside and made a quick calculation on a pad. A concreted grave, no tombstone—the total would come to quite a sum, even on a side lot. The interested party declared that he didn't mind.

He thought for a moment.

"Furthermore," he said, "we shall want a pipe too."

"What kind of a pipe?" the clerk in the black suit asked.

"I wouldn't know myself. A chimney-like affair. Something like a chimney-stack. Like the ones on a ship. Or in a wine cellar."

The engineer whom they called over from the construction department was a bit slow. He got them to explain the whole business twice, but even then he was full of doubts.

"What, if I may ask, do you want this pipe to be made of?" he inquired.

"It's your business to know that," the interested party said, losing his temper.

"Will slate do?" the engineer asked. "Or shall we line it with bricks? Or would you prefer some kind of metal?"

"What would you suggest?" the interested party asked.

"I don't know what this is all about," said the engineer, "but slate would be the obvious choice."

"Let it be slate then," said the interested party looking dreamily at the obtuse engineer. "Then," he added, "we shall want electricity too."

"Electricity?" They both stared at him. "Whatever for?"

"A good question," the interested party said getting angry. "So that it won't be dark in there, that's why."

"You can be more careless, you can put more trash in a novel and be excused for it. In a short story that's next to the poem, almost every word has got to be almost exactly right. In the novel you can be careless but in the short story you can't."
William Faulkner

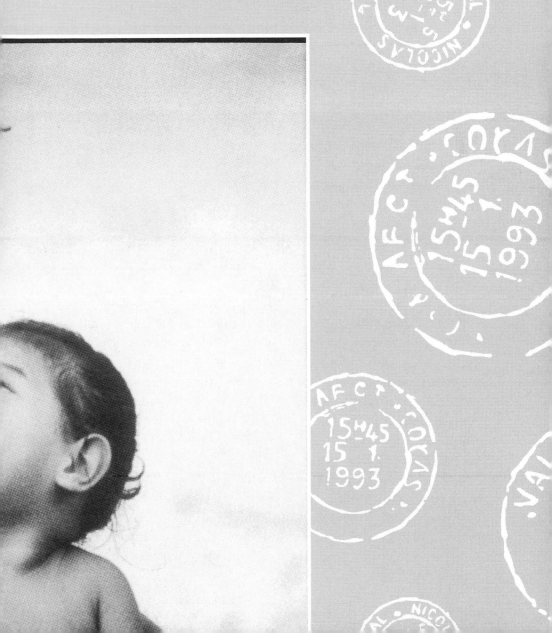

RELATIONSHIPS V

All Is Calm

BY ANN WALSH

"Leave me alone. Don't touch me. Help, help me someone!" I couldn't believe it. She was calling for help as if I were trying to kidnap her—me, her own granddaughter!

I don't know how it happened, but I was the only one who could do it, and it was turning out to be worse than I thought it would be. I mean, I love my Grandma; everyone loves their grandmother, right? But my Gran had become, well, strange isn't quite the word. Mom said it was Alzheimer's and she cried when she told me. It didn't mean much to me at the time, but believe me, as the year went by I learned more than I ever wanted to know about the disease.

It makes people forget. Not just ordinary forgetting—the square roots of numbers or your last boyfriend's phone number—but serious blanking out, like the names of your children, where you live, what you do in a bathroom, and whether your bra goes on before or after you put on your blouse. My Gran didn't do those things yet, but chances were she *would* as the disease took her farther and farther away from the person she once had been. She still had good days, times when she seemed so normal, so like her old self that it made it worse when she went off into whatever strange place the Alzheimer's was taking her mind. She had always been a bit "odd"—actually "ditsy" was the word my father used—but she had been kind and funny and caring and clean. Now— well, sometimes she was really different, weird even, and I was on a bus with her at four o'clock on a Wednesday afternoon hoping that today would be one of her good days.

I was the only one who could do it, take Gran to the doctor's appointment. Mom was away at a conference, my brother had to get his braces adjusted, and Dad couldn't get off work in time. "Katie," Mom said before she left, "Katie, she *has* to go. It took us months to get this appointment, and this specialist is the one who can help us get Gran into a home—he has to classify her condition as serious so that we can get her into a place where she'll be looked after properly. I can't do it any more; I just can't. She's only lived with us a year, but I can't handle her anymore."

I thought Mom was going to cry again when she said that. She'd been doing a lot of crying lately, so I put my arm around her and hugged her and said all the right things about how I didn't mind at all, and sure, it was just a short bus trip, and no, Gran wouldn't embarrass me and we'd manage just fine.

Sure. We were managing. Barely.

It started when I got home from school. Mom had left a note, reminding Gran of the appointment, and Dad had phoned her at noon reminding her again—but she hadn't picked up the phone, and I heard his anxious voice when I checked the answering machine. At three-thirty, an hour before we had to be at the doctor's, Gran was sitting at the kitchen table in her nightgown writing Christmas cards. At least she *thought* she was writing them. She'd taken the box of cards out of the drawer where Mom had stored them until next November, and she'd written her own address on every envelope—no name, just the address. She was singing to herself when I got home, singing Christmas carols and stuffing blank cards into envelopes—in March!

It took a while, but I got her dressed, and we got out of the house and down to the bus stop in record time. The bus came along right away, and everything was going to be okay, and I was sort of proud of myself—and then she started singing again. "Silent night, Holy night, All is calm...." Gran has a loud voice, loud and friendly, and the kind of voice you wanted to hear singing happy birthday to you when you were nine, but on a crowded bus it didn't sound friendly but just plain strange.

People turned around to stare at us, and I said, "Gran, it's not Christmas. Don't sing those songs now."

She looked at me, and the singing stopped. Her mouth stayed open for a while, sort of caught in the "mother and child," and then her face crumpled and she began to cry.

Out loud. Cry as if I had kicked her, or told her her puppy had been run over. "Don't cry, Gran," I said quickly. "Listen, you can sing all you want to once we get home—really."

She clutched at my hand, and suddenly the tears were gone. "We'll go carol singing," she said. "All of us. I'll make hot chocolate, and we'll all go out in the snow and sing."

"Sure, Gran," I said, trying to untangle my hands from hers. "Sure, when Christmas comes we'll all go carol singing."

She smiled at me, and I gave up trying to get my hand away from hers and just held it and squeezed it. Gran always had a nice smile. She looked at you when she smiled, too, right in the eyes, and you always knew that smile was for you and not for anyone else.

"Where are we going?" she asked loudly. "Why are we going this way? We'll get lost."

"It's the way to the doctor's office, Gran." I spoke really softly, hoping she'd get the idea and lower her voice, too. Again heads were turning, as people craned their necks for a look at my... for a look at the crazy old lady who used to be my Grandma. I tried not to meet anyone's eyes. "Shhh, Gran. We won't get lost," I reassured her.

It didn't make any difference. "Stop the bus, stop it, right now! We're lost!" she yelled. She tried to stand up, but the bus lurched away from a stop, and she sort of fell backwards into her seat.

"Sit down... everything's going to be all right," I said. And then, just like the sun coming out, she smiled at me and, as if everything was normal and fine, she said, "Isn't it a lovely day, Katherine? It's so nice to spend some time with you, dear. Shall we go and have tea cakes after our appointment? You always liked those sticky buns they make at the Tea Shoppe."

She had come back again. Just like that. One moment there was this crazy old lady sitting beside me, and the next moment my grandmother was back. I don't know why, but suddenly I wanted to cry too.

"Sure," I said. "We'll go for tea and goodies." We sat there, silently, for the rest of the trip.

Then it was our stop, and we had to get off. "Come on, Gran," I told her. "We're here."

She turned to me, and her face changed again, and she grabbed onto the seat in front of her and said, "I'm not moving. You're just trying to trick me."

"Gran," I urged, hoping that she hadn't gone too far away into the craziness of the disease again, "Gran, come on. The bus is stopping." I took her arm and tried to gently pull her to her feet, but she just clutched the handrail tighter.

"Leave me alone," she said, her voice now louder than it had been when she was singing carols. "I don't know who you are. I don't go places with strangers."

"Come on, Gran. It's me, Katie... Katherine. We're going to see the doctor. This is where his office is. Come *on*, Gran." The bus had stopped now, and the other people who were getting off had already left. I stood up and tried to pull her to her feet.

"Leave me alone. Don't touch me. Help, help me someone!" I couldn't believe it. She was calling for help as if I were trying to kidnap her—me, her own granddaughter!

"Gran," I said. "Please come with me. You know who I am... you've just forgotten for a moment. Please, get off the bus."

"Everything all right back there?" called the driver, and I could see him turning around and halfway rising from his seat. "I've got a schedule to keep, miss. You'll have to get her off right now because I can't wait any longer."

"I'm never going anywhere with *you*," Gran said to me. "I hate you. You're a nasty little girl, and I don't know why you want me to go with you." The doors of the bus closed, and the driver pulled slowly ahead and I stood there in the aisle and wondered what on earth I could do. One thing I knew I mustn't do, though, was get angry. It wasn't my Gran talking. It was the disease, the Alzheimer's. I must remember that; Mom had told us over and over that Gran didn't mean to be cruel or to say horrible things to us, but the disease took over her voice as it took over her mind, and she couldn't always control the words that she said.

It's the disease speaking, I told myself, only the disease, not my Gran. Fine. But the stupid disease wasn't going to let her get off the bus, and what could I do about it? I put my arm around her shoulder, "Gran, Gran... please, try to remember. It's me, Katie."

The bus began to slow again, approaching the next stop. I didn't hear him come up behind me, but suddenly he was there. "Hi," he said, and then stood beside me, smiling down at my grandmother. "I have to get off at this stop," he told her. "Can I help you? Would you like to come with me?"

Gran was silent for a moment, and I was, too. I knew this guy, Kevin; he was in several of my classes this semester. He was tall, blond, and into sports, not a type I hang around with. He always seemed to be clowning around with a group of kids, mainly girls, and I had figured he wasn't worth the effort of getting to know—just a jock who hung around with airheads. "It's okay," I said stiffly. "We'll manage."

But Gran was smiling up at him and taking the arm he offered. "What a nice young man," she said. "Yes, please, do help me. I think I'm on the wrong bus."

Kevin helped her out of her seat, then down the stairwell, and out the doors of the bus. He held out his hand as she stepped down to the curb, and she took it and smiled at him, as gracious as the Queen Mother. "I think your doctor's office is one block back," he said. "Would you like me to walk with you and Katie?"

"Katie?" said Gran, and for a minute I thought she'd forgotten me again, but then she noticed me and the glazed look went from her eyes and she, my Gran, not the crazy old lady, was back again. "Why, Katie, come on. We don't want to be late for the doctor, and then we're going for tea. Perhaps your young man would like to join us?" She slung her handbag over her shoulder and straightened the scarf around the neck of her coat and strode off down the sidewalk, heading in the right direction, walking tall and proud and normally.

"Thanks, Kevin," I said. "I'm sorry...." And the tears that I'd been fighting with for almost the whole bus trip won the fight, and I began to bawl.

"I know," he said. "It's really hard. Go ahead and cry. I'll keep an eye on her." He gestured to my grandmother, who had stopped in front of a grocery store and was staring at a crate of oranges as if she had never seen that fruit before. Well, in the world she lived in these days, perhaps there weren't any oranges. Or any apples or bananas or grand-daughters.

"I'm okay," I said, and blew my nose. "Thanks again for your help.

You were really great with her. I don't know what I would have done if you hadn't helped get her off the bus." Then it struck me. Here was this guy I barely knew, big-shot jock and classroom clown—what was he doing helping out with my ditsy grandmother?

It's almost as if Kevin read my thoughts. He grinned at me. "Yeah," he said. "Didn't you know that your grandma is my type?"

I grinned back. "No. But then, I guess I don't know you well enough to know what your type is, do I?"

"We'll work on that," he said. "I think we've a lot in common, more than you realize."

"A lot in common...?" I began, then I saw him looking down the street at my Gran and I remembered how patient and good he'd been with her, how he'd gotten her off the bus when I couldn't, and suddenly I understood.

"Your grandmother, too?" I asked. Your grandmother has Alzheimer's?"

"My father," he said, and he began walking towards Gran. "The doctors say it's 'early onset,' which means it starts when someone's younger. He just turned forty-six."

"Oh," I said. "I'm sorry." And I was. Sorry for Kevin and what he had to go through as his father went away to that special hell where people with Alzheimer's live; sorry for my family and me for what we had to go through with Gran; sorry for the embarrassment and pain and ugliness that was ahead and couldn't be avoided.

I was sorry for us all, but I knew we'd get through it, we'd survive. But my Gran and Kevin's father, they wouldn't get through it. They *wouldn't* survive except as lonely shadows of themselves in a world where nothing made sense and no one was familiar.

I went up to my Gran, who was still staring at the oranges, and right there, in the middle of the sidewalk with people all around us and Kevin staring at me, I gave her a hug. "I love you, Gran," I said. "I'll always love you."

She looked me right in the eyes and smiled. Then, from somewhere far, far away she said, "I love you too, Mary."

Dear Daddy

BY LEE MARACLE

I started to grow up the other day, daddy. I realized that even when you were home you weren't really there.

I am going to be fourteen next month. I am almost grown up now, so I thought you might like to know what kind of a child I am before I am not one anymore. I know you don't know very much about me because I could never tell you—you weren't there to tell. Oh, I understand you tried to be there, daddy, but it just couldn't happen. I know it wasn't your fault. Still, I thought you might want this letter to help you see the kind of girl I have been without you.

I am not very tall, about five feet, my hair is long and mommy says I am pretty—but that's how love-eyes see. I am honey-brown, amber coloured. I never see girls like me on billboards, but I don't mind, most of them aren't modest.

Do you remember when I was three? No? Well me and you got lost. We were out with your friends. The big people, you, Mary, and her man, were drinking. You got drunk, you argued with the taxi driver and he threw us out and then you punched him. Sister and I and Mary were scared. We all took off and then you and I played that game. Stupid game. We were walking in front of Mary and sister—at least we thought we were in front—and you said "let's hide." They disappeared. We couldn't find them. It got cold and dark and you kept asking me where our street was. I knew the name but couldn't read the signs. We both started to cry. It was the first time I made you cry.

Mommy was trying to have another baby and wasn't happy with sister and me—maybe that was why she wanted a new one. We were both bad. She yelled, "Go to bed," a lot and then she would talk through her teeth. "You are going to go to bed, damn it," and she would spank us with the wooden spoon. We were scared when she was so mad. All that hate in her eyes. We would beg her not to hit us, especially me, because sister would always get in bed before she came with the spoon but I would get hit.

"Bend over," she would yell. I would dance up and down and around begging "Please, please, no, mommy, no-o, no-o, no-o."

"If you don't bend over I am going to hit you anywhere I can." Then I would run all over the room, over the bed and around the chair trying to get away from her. She hit me all over. All the while I would beg "Mommy, I'll be good, mommy, I love you, mommy, please, no, no, no." I didn't mean to be bad. I just couldn't get into bed, so busy was I with trying to get away from the spoon. Finally, I would fall on the bed screaming, she hitting me all over until she got tired. You don't remember, daddy, because you weren't there. I think mommy thought you weren't there because of her. Was it us, daddy? Was it because you didn't like us to be bad?

Sister told mommy she hated her. I know why. Mommy cried and cried. That was the end of the winter she hit us. She still yelled at us, but when she started yelling she would suddenly stop and go to her room, like she thought she was bad. Sometimes she yelled at you. Once she threw milk on you. Yelling like she was full of hate. I know you don't remember, but I can see her now, yelling at your lifeless form on the couch, your old newspaper covering up your face and your feet.

Then she had her baby and he took up most of her time. She started to leave us alone more. He was so tiny and kind of helpless looking. He couldn't laugh or play or anything. Mommy laughed more. Just once, though, I saw her lying down looking up at the ceiling like she was dead. She couldn't hear me when I asked her as nice as I could about supper for sister and me, so I learned to cook.

We both were going to school then and I wasn't so lonely. Before the baby I had to go to kindergarten for awhile. The kids called me names and I got into fights and mommy said I didn't have to go anymore. She had such a faraway sadness in her eyes, and then she hugged both sister and me for a long time. She didn't make a sound, but I could feel the wet against my hair from her tears. After, she made tea and told us little funny stories about four bratty little kids, and we all laughed.

Sister quit kindergarten too. The teacher made her sit in a corner every day for three weeks because she didn't have carrots and celery, just peanut butter—sister liked peanut butter. It got on the carpet and sister got into trouble. Mommy went to the school and the teacher started to yell at her. Mommy squared off, hands on her hips, and bellowed right back. You remember, mommy has a big voice for such a little person. The teacher started to talk nice, but sister still refused to go to school and mommy took her home. Even after the teacher said sorry, sister never went back. I was lonely again.

Mommy yelled at other people, once at a guy driving a car that almost ran us over. He got out of the car, but she wasn't scared. I think she could have beat him up, but he got back in the car. Another time someone pushed her and the baby; she hollered and pushed right back. She handed me the baby first, of course. I wonder if these men are ashamed to be so afraid of such a small woman.

It was around then that I learned about "can't afford this and that." We were on welfare, you see, daddy, and mommy was sneaking and going to school. Welfare wasn't supposed to find out or mommy would get into deep trouble. We were kind of proud of her, going to school, looking after us and trying to fix everything so she could get a good job and me and sister and baby would never have to have "fast days" again. Did I forget about "fast days"? Every end of the month we would run out of things like food and mommy talked about the old days when our "people"—she always says "our people"—used to fast and clean out their system. We didn't mind.

The welfare found out about school and mommy got cut off. She looked thinner and sadder. She just said she would have to find a job sooner than she wanted to, and she did.

The people next door moved away. We were the last kids on the block and we had no one to play with after school except each other. It was hard, now that mommy was working. I had to get sister ready for school and she wouldn't listen too well to me. I'd have to say over and over, "Come on now, eat your cereal, c'mon now, put your boots on," and like that until finally she'd be ready. She still sang then, daddy, like a little bird. I forgave her not getting ready because she sang to me the whole time I was cooking mush and putting her socks and shoes on. Mommy kept warning her, "You are old enough to remember this. When you are seventeen, little lady, you will be embarrassed at not dressing yourself when you were seven years old."

Work must have been good for mom because although she always seemed to be hurrying, she laughed and treated us better. She stopped being so sad and she never looked out the window for you anymore. I asked her if she was ever going to bring home a boyfriend. "What for?" she said. "I got all the friends here I need. I sure don't need another round of misery." I didn't understand her. I thought she meant she didn't miss you, daddy, and I was scared. How could she not miss you? Sometimes I had bad dreams. I would dream the welfare took us away and no one missed us, not even mommy. Daddy where were you?

We put holes in our ceiling with our umbrellas and then we were scared of the mice falling through the holes. We had it coming, I guess—we were naughty to put those holes in the ceiling. Anyway, mommy said, "It's your own damn fault, now go to bed." Not loud, she said it kind of cool. It took me such a long time to stop crying and finally fall asleep. I knew better than to make noise—just tears trailing down my cheeks and sister's soft deep breathing, the dark and my crazy imagination working overtime, whispering evil about you and the mice.

Morning always came though. I don't remember when I first noticed that. One morning mommy was singing in the kitchen. I realized it was the first time I had heard her sing in a long time.

"Do I look any browner?" she asked.

"No-o," I answered soft and slow, wondering what the heck she was up to.

"I am an Indian now." She said it as though it were something you could become, and I began to think she was really losing it. She went through a whole bunch of explaining about Bill C-31[1]. I hear that line a lot since she got her "status back." Bill C-31. You know when you are ten, Bill C-31 sounds like the name of some kind old man who runs about fixing things for Native women. What did it all mean? Well, it meant mommy could go to school and we never had "fast days" again.

Finishing her degree was a lot of pain for her. She wasn't young and learning didn't come so easy as it used to, she said. She wept through math, physics and chemistry, and didn't do too bad in English. When she was almost a teacher she told us that as soon as she got her degree we would move out of the city. Then you wouldn't know where we were, daddy. Didn't you want to know, daddy, or was it all too painful being married to my mom?

Baby knew by then that you weren't coming back. He still looked out the window every now and again and asked if you are at "wirk" and when were you coming home, but not even he believed his question anymore. We all thought if we were good you would just walk right in the door again. I think about that now—the long periods of time between your coming home, mommy telling us you were out working, and eventually we would learn that you were just gone, "pulling a disappearing act." You laughed when you said that. It wasn't funny, daddy.

I started to grow up the other day, daddy. I realized that even when you were home you weren't really there. You were a body on the couch. I know now that you and mommy had not slept together since the baby, but you took three years, three painful years of going and coming—us not knowing when or if you were going to return—to actually leave. Every old Ford baby saw, he would run after it hollering, "Daddy, daddy, come home," and he would cry. Mommy would bite her lip and we would all go home and hug each other. She played "Pretty Brown" hundreds of times for us the first couple of years after you went. And sister, she stopped singing. It was the one thing you really loved, we all loved. I didn't dare ask her about it. She didn't need to feel bad about not doing it on top of losing the joyful reason she did it for in the first place. Daddy, she sang because it was the one sure-fire way of making you smile. Daddy, I never saw you laugh and I would like to see you bend your head back the way mommy sometimes does and really let out a gut-busting laugh.

Time muddled along for us over the years and I am sitting here at the window of our own home (mommy bought it not so long ago) watching the ground break up and spring struggle to push back winter. There is a lonely little crocus looking up at me from her purple and yellow blossom, winking, as I write this letter. Time closed in on me like a fine, fine rain. The world got smaller and I don't remember when it happened. I peeked at the world through a thin veil full of small holes. The veil lifted, and I realized flowers bloom in spring, die before fall; trees shed leaves every autumn to sleep during winter, and somehow this all has to do with the greatness of the world. I can touch the greatness, feel it, and as I write this letter the unhappy feelings that were so large when I started have grown small.

I realized just now that despite all the lonely nights of tears and missing you, in the day we laughed, we ran, we jumped, we did school-work, and it was only in those few moments just before sleep that we thought of you and missed you. We carried on living. All this time I had written sad feelings onto my dreams just before I slept, when really, daddy, I grew up without you. I don't suppose you ever had to deal with missing us. I know why you were always on the couch buried under a newspaper at nine o'clock at night. Mommy still won't talk about it, but I know, and it's OK. You see, daddy, you are the one to be pitied. I don't think you can laugh at your own folly, overcome weakness or see a little crocus on the lawn and imagine it winking at you.

love always,

your daughter

NOTE

[1]Bill C-31 was passed by the Canadian legislature in 1985 to reinstate Native women who had lost their status by marrying non-Natives.

The Two Friends

RETOLD BY PINHAS SADEH

TRANSLATED FROM THE HEBREW BY HILLEL HALKIN

"It's asking too much of me to believe that, having eluded my grasp, you'll come back for the sole purpose of being killed."

In a city lived two friends whose wondrous love for each other was proverbial. Once there was a war between two kingdoms, and each of the friends was taken captive by the army of a different king. After a while, when one of them was freed, he went to the capital of the other kingdom to visit his beloved friend. The king there heard that a man had arrived from the land of his enemies, took him for a spy, and ordered him arrested and put to death. At once the king's men seized him and dragged him to the place of execution.

As he was being led away to his death, the condemned man asked to be brought before the king, because he had something to tell him. This wish being granted, he threw himself at the king's feet and begged for a stay of the sentence.

"What good will that do you?" asked the king.

"Your Majesty," pleaded the man, "in the town that I came from I'm a well-known merchant; all my goods and money, however, are in the hands of shopkeepers to whom I have given credit, and I have no written receipts. If you kill me now, my wife and children will be left hungry and penniless, because they do not know who owes me what and have no way of proving it. Therefore, I beg you, Your Majesty, have pity and let me go home before my execution in order to recover my assets, so that my family will have something to live on when I'm gone."

"But how do I know you'll return?" asked the king. "It's asking too much of me to believe that, having eluded my grasp, you'll come back for the sole purpose of being killed."

"Your Majesty," said the man, "I have a friend in this city. I'm sure he will agree to stand hostage for me."

At once the king sent for the man's friend, who was brought before him. "Are you willing to agree," the king asked him, "that if this man, who has been condemned to death and now wants time to set his affairs in order, does not return to be executed by a set date, you will die in his place?"

"Your Majesty," said the friend, "I will stand hostage for him. If he is not back by the date you set, I will die in his place."

Whereupon the king gave the condemned man a month and had his friend held in prison until then. "I would like," he thought, "to see this wonder, of a man laying down his life for a friend!" And when thirty days had passed with still no sign of the condemned and the sun was about to set, he ordered the hostage taken from prison and put to death.

Just as the sword was being put to the hostage's throat, a cry went up in the city that the condemned man had returned. He reported at once to the king and then hurried to the place of execution, where he seized the sword that was already on his friend's throat and placed it on his own. Then the two began to wrestle for it, each demanding to be killed, while the king sat looking out his window and marveling at such love, which surpassed anything he had ever seen before. So astounded was he and all his court that he ordered the sword put aside and the two men pardoned, after which he gave each a generous gift. "I have never," he declared, "seen such love between friends and I would like to ask to be your friend too." A request which they were only too glad to grant!

Young Man's Folly

BY SUSAN MICHALICKA

It was like the news. You knew it was bad, so you just let the details wash over you.

Who knows what makes people love each other? My parents were married a little over a decade, but I could never understand their love for each other, or the nature of their love for me.

Maybe you know my Dad. He reads the local news on television every night at six o'clock. Whenever we went out together, complete strangers would stop him and talk to him as if he were their closest friend. It used to really tick me off, but Mom always laughed and explained it was his voice people warmed to. So strong and reassuring. You can listen to him for a half an hour and feel just great, she'd say. Only later you'd realize he told you about swarmings in the mall, a car accident on the 401, and gunmen in the neighborhood milk store.

I think it was because of his voice that my mother didn't hear him say he was going to leave us. It was in code, at first. He said he hated living in our house in the suburbs. The neighbors were boring. It was too far to drive to work; traffic was too heavy. But Mom works for a government department where someone is always complaining to her about something. To her, I guess it just sounded like Dad was being polite.

Then he started to complain about her. He hated what she'd done to the house, filling it with crafts and quilts from her night-school courses; she was so out of it, he'd complain. And didn't she think she was packing on the beef a little bit? Her hair was turning gray—why didn't she touch it up a tad? She's really starting to look like her mother, he'd say shaking his head, as if he was surprised she wasn't growing more and more like Christie Brinkley every day.

I began to look at her differently, too. Because Dad is on television, he seems to have arrested development. His hair, his voice, his face never changed. Viewers demanded consistency in someone who was delivering bad news, and Dad supplied it. But Mom did seem different from the photos taken before I was born. She had no girlishness left. Her hands were continually chapped from her sewing. She seemed solid. Dependable. Like someone who always had a Kleenex when you needed it.

Eventually, Dad decided that he could remember his own Kleenex. Or get someone who looked more like Erica, his production assistant, to give him what he needed. Because one summer Saturday, he came into the kitchen to tell us he wasn't staying for breakfast. He needed to find himself, and Erica would be picking him up in a few minutes to drive him there.

I'm a little embarrassed to say that, for an otherwise pulled-together guy, I made quite a spectacle of myself, wailing and begging him not to go. He said all the things the psychologists say will make kids feel better, but don't. He said it was him, not us. He needed more space, but I wondered about that. It seemed to me that there was a lot less space in Erica's apartment downtown than here at home with us. But when he skipped down the driveway and threw his duffle bag into the back seat of Erica's convertible, he called to me that he'd see me soon. I waved and said okay, as if it really was.

I turned to Mom and asked her for something I could use to wipe my face, which was tear-streaked and matted with snot. She looked confused momentarily, and then told me just to use my pyjama sleeve. She'd do a wash later. Thanks for nothing, I said, and left to find my own Kleenex.

That was the beginning of our life together—Mom and me. Our lives looked the same. I went to school, signing up for basketball after classes. She went to work and closed herself in her sewing room in the evening, just as she'd always had. But everything felt different. Maybe if she'd changed, Dad would have stayed. I picked up the litany of suggestions I'd heard from Dad. Couldn't you have lost some weight? Do you really prefer gray hair? The neighbors picked up the chant; after all they'd been deprived of a local celebrity in their midst and in exchange had one more single parent who'd be a problem to seat at Home & School Association banquets. What happened? they'd ask. What did you do to deserve this? Neither I, nor they, ever listened for her answer.

Dad didn't, as he'd promised over his shoulder that morning, see me soon. It was hard to get a hold of him while he was busy searching for himself. He didn't find himself with Erica, or with Barbara the weather girl, or even with Jennifer the summer student from journalism school, but the effort took most of his time. I'd call him just to listen to the message on his answering machine, but he'd often forget to return my calls. I missed him a lot.

Luckily, I could always watch him on the six o'clock news. In his rush to leave, he hadn't taken many of his clothes. I took one of his old tweed sports jackets and put it on every night to hear his voice. "Good

evening," he'd say and tell me stories about life in the city. I could breathe in and smell him from the jacket. It was almost as if he was holding me in his arms as he did when I was young and telling me a bedtime story. Now though, it was rapes and murders. Scandal at city hall. Impending strikes. A stagnant economy. The weather for tomorrow (always frosty, if delivered by Barbara) and a final, "until tomorrow." I'd wipe my eyes on the sleeve, switch off the set and run upstairs to have dinner with Mom.

One day, Mom needed to know the weather and came downstairs before the news had finished. I don't know how long she'd been there, but when I took off the jacket I saw her leaning in the doorway, watching. "Anything new today?" she asked.

"Angry residents are fighting a mall expansion in the west end, and transit fares are going up," I replied.

As I pushed past her to go to the stairs, I heard her ask very quietly, "Why the jacket? Are you cold?"

"I need him here." I shouted it, though I didn't need to. In fact, I think she already knew what I wanted to say before I spoke.

We didn't speak of my ritual again. Month after month, I watched the news, Mom held dinner until half past six. But eventually, the jacket smelled like me—a combination of a kid's sweat and tears. I went to Dad's closet to get a replacement.

It had been cleared out. There had been at least thirty or forty shirts, mostly Oxford cloth and tightly woven cottons that photograph well on camera. Masculine colors, as Dad always called them; soft blues and greens and grays were the only colors he wore. You could still faintly smell his aftershave in the closet. They were gone. I blamed Mom.

That night after dinner I told her I wanted to go and live with Dad. We argued about it for some time; the food went cold. But in the end, she called him up. I could hear her talking to him in that quiet, reliable voice she uses at the office when she's dealing with someone who didn't fill out the forms correctly and is now facing deportation or something equally disastrous. Eventually she hung up.

"What did he say?" I demanded, "When can I go?"

"He'll meet you at McDonald's after school," she replied. "He'll talk to you about it then."

Instead of taking my gym stuff to school the next day, I packed some clothes in my duffle bag. I didn't expect to come back again and I was looking forward to my new life with Dad. Just us guys. I skipped the last period so I would be sure to be ready when he came.

He arrived late. And he came with Jennifer, who bought us fries and Cokes, while Dad and I found a booth. Before I could speak, Dad put his arm around me and told me that I wouldn't be coming with him. He told me all about the changes in his life. He and Jennifer were having such a great time—they were planning to travel to California for a while. Things were so great for him, and basically, this crazy idea of mine, it just wasn't going to work.

He kept talking, but I didn't hear it all. It was like the news. You knew it was bad, so you just let the details wash over you. I watched him talk and looked at him with Jennifer. He looked kind of stupid, wearing some sort of Hammer pants and oversized shirt that might have looked okay on some boy in Grade Thirteen, but bizarre on a father. He still looked like he did on television, but the skin around his eyes was kind of creepy. And with his arm around me, I noticed that he smelled different. Sort of like fires. And Jennifer's perfume.

I finished my drink quickly, thankful that he had to be back in the studio for the news. I decided to walk home, hoping that it would give me extra time to figure out what I'd say to Mom. By the time I did get home, though, I still hadn't thought of anything. We ate in silence.

As she cleared the dishes, Mom said she was sorry if I was disappointed.

"How did you know?" I asked her. She said she'd heard it in his voice on the telephone. But, she said she had something for me that she hoped would cheer me up. It was in my bedroom.

When I switched on the light in my room, there on the bed was a new quilt. I was used to her quilting projects, of course, but this one looked significantly different. The colors—soft blues, greens, and grays in finely woven cottons—looked odd in such a traditional design. I guess she recognized the quizzical look on my face.

"I made it from his shirts," she said. "After I saw you with the jacket, I thought it would be a comfort to have something of his."

I went to the bed hoping she wouldn't see the look on my face. What if it smelled like him? Or what I remembered of him? It would haunt my dreams. I picked up the quilt and buried my face in it.

It smelled of my mother's hands. Of the hand cream she used to soften her skin, of the water and steam she used to iron out the creases of my father's shirts. It smelled of the months of work she must have put into this thoughtful act, trying to give an ungrateful son the comfort sought from someone else.

"It's beautiful," I said truthfully. "I like the pattern very much. What's it called?"

My mother laughed. I hardly remembered how great her laugh could sound. It came from deep in her chest, near her heart. It's an old pattern," she said. "It's called Young Man's Folly. I thought it fit."

I didn't know if her laugh was at Dad's expense, or mine. But you know, whenever I slept wrapped in its folds, I always felt surrounded by love.

"A country may have great corporations, but if it has no literature it is a country that has no soul. It is a shopkeeper's society. The new nationalists, it seems to me, are concerned only with who is minding the store."
Morley Callaghan

Beauty and the Beast

BY MADAME LEPRINCE DE BEAUMONT

RETOLD BY MICHAEL FOSS

The days sped by with music and magical entertainments. And every evening, at supper, the Beast came, snorting and twisting his ugly great head.

In a far country, there was a merchant who had once been rich, but fell on hard times. His children, used to the best things, did not like their new life in a poor cottage. They had grown selfish and spoilt, and they complained bitterly. All except one.

She was the youngest, and she was neither selfish nor spoilt. In their little cottage she did the housework while the others complained. And because she was so willing and kind and pretty her father called her Beauty.

Then the merchant heard that a ship which he had thought was lost had now returned. Thinking that his fortune was saved, he prepared to go to the city and asked the children, just as he used to do, what presents he could bring them. The brothers and sisters wanted many expensive and foolish things, but Beauty asked for no present, except to see her father safe home.

"Oh, do accept something," her father said. And at last she asked for just one rose. In the city, the arrival of the lost ship led to bitter arguments. The quarrel was taken to court, but after six months, while the lawyers grew rich, nothing was settled. In mid-winter, the merchant sadly set out for home, as poor as he had ever been. As he went, the snow was falling. In the gloom of the forest he could not find the path and the wolves howled. His horse stumbled, blinded by the weather.

In the night, the merchant almost gave up hope, for it seemed that death was coming to gather him. But the next morning, suddenly he found himself in a strange land of sunlight. Instead of snow-covered forest paths, he saw an avenue of orange-trees leading through gardens to a castle with towers that reached into the sky. He rode to the door and called but there was no answer. He stabled his horse and entered the castle, going through rooms full of light and treasures and silence. In a far room he found food ready. Then, tired out by his journey, he slept.

When he awoke he was still alone. In the great, silent rooms he could find no-one. He walked through the castle and through the gardens, seeing wonderful things on every side, and soon he began to think of his lost wealth and of his family. How happy they would be in this place! And since there seemed to be no one here, why should he not fetch them? Yes, he would do it. So he hurried to the stables, but as he passed through a pathway of roses he remembered his promise to his youngest, dearest child. He stopped and picked a single red rose.

At once, there was a terrible noise and a monstrous Beast stood in the path.

"Did I not," the frightful thing roared, "give you the freedom of my castle? How dare you steal my rose. I have a mind to kill you right now."

The merchant fell on his knees, begging for mercy. He explained his sad story, telling the Beast that the rose was for his daughter Beauty who was so good and kind. The Beast listened, grinding his ugly teeth. But when he spoke again he was not quite so fierce.

"Your life will be saved," said the Beast, "if one of your daughters will offer to live with me here. Go now, and let them choose. Return at the end of the month. And do not think you can escape my power."

The horse seemed to know the way without any guide, but the merchant rode with a heavy heart. At the cottage, his children, who had feared that their father was dead, kissed him and laughed with joy. But when they heard what the Beast had said, they were angry and blamed Beauty for wanting the rose. Now they would have to fly to a far land, beyond the reach of the Beast.

But Beauty said: "Dear father, it is my fault. Come, let us go to the castle. I will stay with the Beast."

Sadly the merchant agreed, and sadly they returned to the strange castle, standing above the forest so shining and mysterious. They went through the rich, empty rooms and again found a meal made ready. When they were eating they heard a roaring of wind. The door burst open and the Beast came in like thunder.

"Well, Beauty," he bellowed, "have you chosen to stay?"

His looks were terrible to her eyes, but she answered quietly that she would stay.

"Very well, but your father must leave. He may take two trunks of jewels for his family but he must never return. Choose what you like, then wave your father goodbye."

With many tears she kissed her father goodbye. Then, worn out by sorrow, and by fear for the future, she fell on her bed and slept. She dreamed. She found herself in a golden country of meadows and woods. As she wandered there, a handsome Prince appeared and spoke to her in a tender and loving way, begging her to be kind to him.

"Dear Prince," she sighed, "what can I do to help you?"

"Be grateful for what you are given," he replied, "but do not believe all you see. Above all, do not leave me. Rescue me from my cruel suffering."

Then the Prince faded away and his place in the dream was taken by a tall, lovely lady, who commanded Beauty: "Do not sigh for the past. Have faith and do not believe in appearances only. Great things await you in the future."

Thus began her life in the castle. Each day, she wandered through the rooms and the gardens. She met no one. Hidden hands prepared everything she might need. The days sped by with music and magical entertainments. And every evening, at supper, the Beast came, snorting and twisting his ugly great head.

"Well, Beauty," he roared, "are you going to marry me?"

But Beauty shook with fright and tried to creep away. And when the Beast had gone she went quickly to bed and entered the land of dreams where her Prince was waiting.

"Do not be so cruel," the Prince would beg, "I love you but you are so stubborn. Help me out of my misery." He had a crown in his hands, which he offered her, kneeling and weeping at her feet.

But what did this dreaming mean? Beauty did not know. Her days were full of wonders. The sun shone always, and the birds sang. Bands of pretty apes were her servants. But each evening came the Beast, with his grim looks and his terrible question. And each night, in sleep, her Prince sighed for his freedom.

As the days passed, slowly she began to feel sorry for the Beast. He was kind, in his rough way, and gave her everything. Surely his ugliness was not his fault. But she was lonely, too. She saw no one but the Beast. She missed her family. She began to sleep badly. Her dreams were full of worry. Her Prince seemed close to despair.

Then, one night, she dreamed that the Prince ran at the Beast with a dagger, meaning to kill him. Beauty stepped between them, pleading for the Beast, saying that the terrible monster was her friend and protector. The Prince disappeared and at once the tall lady was standing in his place.

"You will soon be happy," she told Beauty, "but only if you do not believe in appearances."

Next morning, waking tired and sad and lonely, she decided to ask the Beast for permission to see her family just once more.

When the Beast heard this he fell to the ground and groaned. But he said he could not deny anything to his Beauty. She could go, and take four chests of treasure with her. But if she did not return after two months, her Beast would die.

Her family were amazed to see her. Her father laughed and cried to have his favourite daughter back. And the four chests of treasure made even her brothers and sisters forget their troubles. They all begged her not to go back to the castle, and for a while she was so happy with her family that she never thought of the Beast.

Two months went by without her notice. Then, one night, she had another dream. She dreamed that she saw the Beast at the point of death. At once, she awoke. She remembered a ring that the Beast had given her, and turning it on her finger she was carried in a flash to the castle. She ran through the great, silent rooms but there was no sign of the monster. She dashed into the gardens and the park, calling his name, running here and there. At last, when night had fallen, she stumbled on his still body in the moonlight.

"Dear Beast," she cried, "are you dead? Oh, please forgive me. I never realized before that I love you. Now I fear I have killed you."

But his heart was still beating and her presence began to revive him. In a while he was able to stagger to the castle. As he lay on a sofa, she heard him whisper in his sad, growling voice.

"Beauty, have you come back to me? Will you marry me now?"

And she answered at once: "Yes, dear Beast."

Then there was a blaze of lights, and loud music, and the Beast vanished. Instead, before her stood the Prince of her dreams, with the tall lady beside him. Beauty and the Prince took hands, and the lady smiled and blessed them.

"You have rescued my son," she told Beauty, "from the evil magic that has imprisoned him for so long in the hideous body of the Beast. When you chose him freely, you released the Prince from the spell. Now you will marry him. No longer will you be Beauty and the Beast, but the Prince and Princess of all this great and lovely land."

The Shining Mountain

BY ALISON FELL

Pangma-La woke up frightened and wanting her mother, but she said nothing, for she was afraid her father would be disappointed in her.

Once there was a Scottish girl with a strange name and a father who was always on television. The girl was called Pangma-La, and of course she was teased about it. At first she cried, but her father scolded her.

"Pangma-La," he said, "I called you after a shining mountain so that you would stand tall and be proud. Pangma-La," he said, "Scotland has enough ordinary Morags and Janets already."

And he pinned a picture of the Shining Mountain on her wall, and told her that one day they would climb it together.

For Pangma-La's father was a famous mountaineer. She would come home from an ordinary school day and there he would be on the BBC news, planting the Union Jack on a far, far mountain peak. She would sit on an ordinary bus and hear people say, "Now there's a hard man, there's a hero."

So Pangma-La dried her tears and vowed never to be ordinary and disappoint him.

As the years passed and Pangma-La grew bigger, her father taught her to balance finely on the high tops of walls, and shin up sheer rocks by toe- and finger-holds. Her mother shook her head and fussed.

"Pangma-La," she said, "you'll tear your good jumper. Pangma-La," she said, "you'll fall and hurt yourself."

But her father only laughed and said, "Let her be, she's tough and hard as nails," and Pangma-La was proud.

At last it was time to set out for the Shining Mountain. Pangma-La and her father took off in a white plane. Below them the houses and cars and her mother waving were small and bright as Smarties. Then the earth disappeared and they were high in the crystal blue sky where the sun hurts your eyes.

Pangma-La fell asleep and dreamt a bad dream. She was a white swan flying high above the Shining Mountain, with no father or mother anywhere. She was tired, she wanted to land on the top of the mountain and rest her wings. But the mountain turned its back on her, saying, Pangma-La, you cannot land here and you cannot rest. You must fly on until your white wings freeze and you tumble down to the hard ground.

Pangma-La woke up frightened and wanting her mother, but she said nothing, for she was afraid her father would be disappointed in her.

When the plane landed, Pangma-La and her father set out for the mountains. The villagers, hearing that the young girl was called after their shining mountain, smiled and gave her sherbet and figs. But then Pangma-La and her father came to the last village, where the trees stopped and the snows began. There Sherpa men crowded round, offering to carry their loads at a price.

"My daughter and I do not need porters," Pangma-La's father said proudly. "We are strong and we will climb the mountain alone."

The Sherpa men were angry.

"The mountain goddess will send winds to tear at you," they said, "and spindrift snow to sting your face, and avalanche to toss and tumble you."

But Pangma-La's father turned away and laughed. "Only weak men believe in old wives' tales," he said scornfully.

Above them the mountain rose like a tall white tower. At first Pangma-La climbed happily, smelling the clear air, while up ahead her father's feet made deep blue prints in the snow.

But soon she began to grow weary.

Just then an old Sherpa woman appeared, in a ragged brown cloak.

"Let me carry your heavy sack, daughter," said the woman, but

Pangma-La shook her head, for she was afraid that her father would be disappointed in her. That night under the bright stars she told him about the Sherpa woman, but her father looked at her strangely.

"I saw no woman," he said. And he made Pangma-La promise that she would speak to no one, no matter what they asked or what help they offered.

On the second day, Pangma-La set out boldly and well. Then a strong wind blew up to tear at her, and the going was hard. She began to feel weak and ill under the weight of the rucksack, but she would not stop, for her father would be disappointed in her.

Just then the Sherpa woman appeared, and pulled a handful of swan's feathers from under her ragged cloak.

"Take out your heavy things from the sack, daughter," she said, "and fill it with this swan's down. Then you will get to the top of the mountain, and your father will never tell the difference."

Pangma-La thought of her promise, but she had such a bad sick feeling everywhere in her, that she did what the woman asked. The Sherpa woman carried the heavy things under her ragged cloak, and Pangma-La carried a light rucksack full of swan's down, and her father never told the difference. And at sunset, the woman gave back her heavy things, and Pangma-La lay down to sleep.

On the third day, she set off with a weary feeling already in her bones. Spindrift snow blew up to sting her face, and just when she was sure she could go no further, the Sherpa woman appeared.

"Take off your heavy, heavy clothes, daughter, and I will cover you with swan's feathers, and you will get to the top of the mountain."

And so Pangma-La did, and once again, as the sun went down, the woman gave her back the heavy clothes, and her father never told the difference.

On the fourth day, the roar of an avalanche thundered past them, and this time Pangma-La's father walked beside her.

Oh, father, she thought to herself, my boots are too big and I can't fill them, and I want to go home to my mother more than anything in the world. And a tear escaped and ran down her nose.

"Pangma-La," her father scolded, "Look at the mountain I named you for, is it not beautiful?" Pangma-La felt so ill she could hardly bear to look up at it, so crystal-cold and merciless above her. She hung her head, ashamed.

"Yes father," she said, and the tear froze to an icicle on her face.

Her father climbed on and on, and Pangma-La tried hard to keep up with him. Soon her legs could not go another step, and a dizziness took her, and she fell down in the snow.

Just then the Sherpa woman appeared, kneeling over her.

"Give me your heavy, heavy heart, daughter," she said, "and I will fill you with swan's down. Then you will get to the top of the mountain, and your father will never tell the difference."

So Pangma-La gave up her heart, and the lungs which panted and hurt, and the bones which weighed like iron, and flew easily to the top of the mountain in all her light swan's feathers.

But this time when it came to sunset the Sherpa woman did not give back Pangma-La's heavy, heavy heart, and Pangma-La's father stood at the top of the Shining Mountain, calling wildly for his daughter, but she was nowhere to be seen.

Then the Sherpa woman appeared in her ragged cloak.

"Here is your Pangma-La," she said, pointing to the white swan which fluttered beside her, "but now she is my daughter for ever and always."

Pangma-La's father cried out in anger and cursed the hag for her cruel spell. He raised his ice-axe to strike the woman down, but just then a peal of thunder shook the mountain and threw him to the ground.

And there in front of him stood no hag, but the mountain goddess herself, tall and straight, with skin of darkest gleaming gold, and eyes yellow and far-seeing as a snow leopard. She wore a cloak of swan's feathers, and blue lightning-fire danced at her finger ends.

"You wanted your daughter to get to the top of the mountain," said the goddess, "and I have given you your heart's desire. You named your daughter after me, to be strong and light as the gods, and feel no human pain, and weep no human tears. And I have given you your heart's desire."

Then Pangma-La's father saw that his daughter had given her life away just to please him, and he cursed himself and his heart's desire, and ran to the edge of the mountain to cast himself off.

But the goddess barred his way easily with a bolt of blue lightning.

"Not so hasty to make an end of it, brave hero," she said. She brought Pangma-La's heavy sack and heavy clothes from under her cloak and gave them to him. "First you must feel the weight of your heavy, heavy burden," she said. Then she brought out Pangma-La's heart, and gave it to him. "And now you must feel the weight of your heavy, heavy heart," she said.

At this Pangma-La's father fell on his knees and for the first time wept hot tears like any human.

The mountain goddess, seeing this, was satisfied.

"You have learned your lesson," she said, and was gone in a swirl of swan's feathers.

Pangma-La's father looked down to see his daughter alive and heavy and human in his arms.

Feeling the wet drops on her face, Pangma-La opened her eyes. When she saw that her father the hero was crying she was no longer ashamed, and a great weight lifted from her. She jumped up and pulled him strongly to his feet. Then, skidding and sliding, Pangma-La and her father ran all the way to the bottom of the Shining Mountain, while the snow flew up behind them like sherbet or swan's feathers, and never again was Pangma-La afraid that her father would be disappointed in her.

POLITICS AND POWER VI

There Is a Nut on the Roof

BY AZIZ NESIN

TRANSLATED FROM THE TURKISH BY GÖNÜL SUVEREN

"He won't come down no-matter what you do. Once a person goes nutty enough to climb on the roof he will never come."

The whole neighborhood was in a state of excitement. "There is a nut on the roof."

The street from one end to the other was full of people curious to see the lunatic.

First from the local station, then from police headquarters, cops came in cars. Fire engines followed them. The mother of the nut was imploring her son, "Come down, my boy. Please come down, son."

The lunatic was saying that if he was not made sheriff he would throw himself down.

The firemen opened their nets in case he did. Nine firemen were bathed in sweat while running around the building holding out the net. In a half-imploring, half-threatening tone the police sergeant was trying to lure the nut down.

"Make me sheriff and I'll come down, or else I will throw myself down."

All the imploring and threats were of no use.

"Come on, friend…. Why don't you come down!"

"Hey, look… Instead of making me come down, why don't you come up!"

Someone from the crowd had a suggestion. "Let's tell him that we made him sheriff."

Another one contradicted him. "How is that possible? Can you get a sheriff from a loony?"

"Good God! We are not really going to make him sheriff."

An old man leaning on his cane said, "That's impossible. In jest or otherwise, that's impossible."

"But maybe he'll come down."

"No, he won't. I know these people. Once they go up, they never come down."

"If he would only come down.… The rest is easy."

"He won't come down."

Someone down below shouted, "Hey, we made you sheriff. Come down."

The nut started dancing and shouting. "I won't come down! If you won't make me a member of the City Council, I won't come down."

The old man said, "You see, didn't I tell you."

"Let's do what he says."

"He won't come down no matter what you do. Once a person goes nutty enough to climb on the roof he will never come."

The sergeant shouted, "All right. We made you a member of the City Council. Don't keep all of us waiting down here. Come down."

The nut just kept on dancing. "I won't come down.… Make me the mayor, then I'll come down."

The old man said, "You see, it's too late. Now he will never come down."

The first chief, who was sweating profusely, said, "What if we said we made him Mayor." Then he cupped his hands to his mouth and shouted, "OK, son, come down. We made you Mayor, come down and take over your office."

The nut, dancing like mad, shouted back: "I won't come down. What am I to do among people who elect a nut for Mayor?… I won't come down."

"All right, then. What do you want?"

"I will come down only if you make me a cabinet member."

After a short discussion the people down below shouted:

"All right, we made you a cabinet member. Now come down. You see, you're holding everybody up."

The nut thumbed his nose at them. "I won't come down among people who make a cabinet member of a nut."

"Come on, brother. Don't be so difficult. You see, we made you a cabinet member and all the other cabinet members are waiting for you. Come on down."

"Who are you kidding? I'll come down and you'll put me in the nuthouse. I won't come down."

The old man said: "Don't make yourself hoarse. I know these nuts well. If you were made a cabinet member, you wouldn't want to come down either."

By now the nut was shouting frantically: "If you don't make me the Prime Minister, I will throw myself down."

"All right," they shouted back, "we made you Prime Minister."

The old man said, "He won't come down."

The nut started to dance again. After a while he shouted: "Make me the King. Otherwise I'll throw myself down."

What the old man said was coming true. They consulted him. "What do you think? Shall we make him King?"

The old man said, "It's too late now. You have to do what he tells you. He was made the Prime Minister already."

"All right," they shouted, "we made you King. Come down now."

The dancing nut shouted back, "I won't."

"Well, what else do you want? We made you King, too."

"I won't come down. Make me the Emperor or else I jump."

They asked the old man, "Would he really jump?"

The old man told them he would.

"All right," they shouted, "we made you Emperor. Now come down."

The nut answered right back. "What has an Emperor like me to do among stupid jerks like you?"

"Well, what is it that you want, then? Tell us, we'll do it. Why don't you come down?"

"Am I the Emperor?" the nut asked.

"You are the Emperor!" they shouted from below.

"If I am the Emperor, I come down when I like. I am not coming down."

The police sergeant was getting mad. "Let him jump," he thought. "There will be one nut less." That was true, but it would have caused him problems later.... The Fire Chief turned to the old man.

"What are we to do now?" he asked. "Won't this nut come down ever?"

"He will."

"How?"

"Let me bring him down."

Everyone was curious as to how the old man was going to bring the nut down. The old man addressed the nut, who was on the seventh floor: "Your Highness, the Emperor. Would you like to go up to the sixth floor?"

The nut answered in all seriousness. "All right." He then went through the roof opening, came down the steps to the sixth floor and looked out the sixth floor window to the crowd below.

The old man asked again, "Would your Highness like to go up to the fifth floor?"

The nut answered that he would.

Everyone was dumbfounded. The old man addressed the nut, who this time was looking out of the fourth floor window: "Would My Reverend Emperor like to go up to the third floor?"

The nut answered, "Certainly."

He was now looking out of the third floor window. He was no longer dancing madly as he had on the roof. He had assumed the seriousness of a Real King.

"Would His Excellency like to go up to the second floor?"

"I would."

He had come down to the second floor.

"Would Your Excellency come up to the first floor?"

The nut had come down to the street; he was among the crowd. He went directly to the old man and put his hand on his shoulder: "God, it is only too evident you are a nut too. Only a nut understands a nut," he said, and then turning to the police sergeant addressed him: "All right, now you tie me up and send me to the nuthouse.... But did you learn something about how to treat a nut?"

While the nut was taken away, the crowd gathered around the old man: "Hey, pop," they asked, "how did you do it?"

The old man shook his head. "It is not easy to be in politics for forty years," he said, and added yearningly: "If only my legs had the strength, I also would climb up on the roof, and no one could bring me down."

"The short story is a demanding literary form. Its brevity and intensity can win general readers who have little time or patience for longer works. Its most skillful writers must, however, exercise the greatest selectivity and precision."

Nancy Sullivan

Las Mantillas

BY LAURIE CHANNER

Rosa and the other women picked up their candles and photos and walked to their homes as revolution rained down on the capital.

Rosa arrived at the square as always, just as dawn turned the night into gray. She took up her usual position at the bottom of the wide steps of the Presidential Palace. The uniformed guards on the top step paid no attention to her.

A young man in dusty, ragged clothes melted out of the building's shadow. "*Señora*, you must go," he had told Rosa. "You and the other *mantillas*. You are in great danger."

They were *las mantillas* because they arrived at the square each morning in the lace shawls they wore to cover their heads at early Mass. They carried candles blessed by the priests in their parishes and photographs of their husbands, sons, and brothers who had disappeared at the hands of *los uniformes*. They stood their photos and candles on the steps of the Presidential Palace where the government officials could not miss them as they arrived each morning.

"We will not leave until the government acknowledges our loved ones," Rosa answered. It was an automatic reply, but no less passionate for having been repeated thousands of times since the *mantillas* had started coming to the square.

"No, *madre*," he said, using the word with heartfelt respect. "You don't understand. You must go. There will be fighting soon in this square. We are coming down from the hills."

"The rebels—?"

"Quiet!" The young man drew her aside. "A coup is coming. We do not want you *mantillas* to be hurt. You must all stay out of the square today."

The thought of a coup brought a surge of excitement, and fear. The overthrow of the government of *los uniformes* had been long awaited, but if it failed, more lives would be lost.

"We must stay," Rosa had told the young man. "If we leave the square, *los uniformes* will know that something is wrong."

He knew she was right. He went away. Rosa spoke quietly to several of the other women. They, too, were anxious, and more fearful of the failure of a rebel attack than for their own safety.

In the heat of the afternoon, the man returned. "My people are very concerned that the *mantillas* are not hurt. We respect your cause too much to allow it. You must leave."

"And we respect your cause," Rosa replied. "We will stay rather than betray your intentions to *los uniformes*."

"Mother of God, you are stubborn!" he exclaimed.

"Stubbornness is our trademark," Rosa said. "Without it, the government would have had us disperse long ago." She made a gesture that included the dozens of women coming into the plaza to walk or kneel in front of the Presidential Palace with their candles and photographs, praying that God might let *los uniformes* see the evil of their ways and return their loved ones to them.

The young man squinted in the sun, looking at the distant brown hills where his compatriots waited. Then he turned to Rosa. "They have told me, if you would not go, that there is only one option. *Las mantillas* must not be endangered. We will come into the capital when the women return home tonight."

And so it happened. But Rosa and several of the other *mantillas* stayed in the square, adding prayers for the success of the revolution to those for their lost relatives. Their candles and their courage flickered in the growing dusk after most of the women had gone home to take care of what family remained waiting there.

They waited until the sound of gunfire could be heard in the

streets near Government Square. Then, shaking, but serene, Rosa and the other women picked up their candles and photos and walked to their homes as revolution rained down on the capital.

Two days later, the square at dawn, though quiet, showed evidence of the struggle that had taken place. The facade of the Presidential Palace was pockmarked with scars from the shooting. Damage and debris from mortars were apparent around the square. Lights burned in the Presidential Palace where the rebels were now forming a new government.

Rosa adjusted her lace veil, knelt, and set her candle and the photograph of her smiling son, Eduardo, on her makeshift altar.

She stayed alone, her candle flame burning paler and paler against the growing light of day, until a foreign journalist approached. He waited until she looked up from her prayers before he spoke to her.

"May I speak with you, *Señora?*" he asked. Rosa nodded, her hands still folded. "You are one of the *mantillas* aren't you?" His accent was British. "Don't you know there's been an uprising?" he asked, puzzled. "The dictatorship's been overthrown. Why do you still demonstrate?"

"It is not a protest," Rosa replied. "It is a prayer that we may know the fates of our family. We don't want the new government, in their youth and exuberance, to forget that we are still here, and still waiting to hear."

The journalist moved off. Later that morning, Rosa saw a television crew on the edge of the square point its camera briefly in her direction. As the day wore on, with the streets safe again, a number of the other women came to join her. By evening, thousands of people had thronged to the square to show support for the rebels. Impromptu celebrations sprang up when the rebel leaders took to the balcony to greet them. In the midst of the jubilation, Luisa Delgado, a neighbor of Rosa's whose husband had been taken eight months before, came running over to her.

"Rosa," she gasped, "look!" She carried a large plastic sack, and opened it for Rosa to see. It was filled with strips of paper. She closed it up again quickly as several nearby revellers reached for it. "No!" she cried. "These are not streamers!"

She pulled the bag closed and drew Rosa aside. "Rosa, it's government paper! Shredded documents! A woman gave me the bag. She said her children found it in an alley."

"An alley?" Rosa looked into the bag. She fingered the paper inside. Yes, it was office paper, with typewriting on it. But from *los uniformes?* A second later, at the sight of the military seal, she gasped and made the sign of the cross.

"And look, Rosa!" Luisa added. "It looks like names. Lists of names. Rosa, they might be our *desaparecidos!* My husband, your son! Rosa, what shall we do?"

Rosa closed the bag again. "We will take it home," she said quietly.

They worked all night, at Rosa's kitchen table. Word spread among *las mantillas,* and many came to help.

Hands red and gnarled by years of housework sorted through the fragile strips, and eyes strained from decades of sewing and mending squinted to read the fragments of words printed on them.

One thin piece at a time, scrap by scrap, by the end of the night they had reassembled a mere half-page, but enough to confirm Luisa's suspicion.

With the dawn, the women put on their shawls and went to early Mass to give thanks. Then they returned to Rosa's kitchen table, the first morning in so many months that *las mantillas* had not assembled in Government Square.

As the hours passed, a picture of undeniable evil came to light. What emerged from the plastic sack, the same kind they all used in their own homes for trash, was a computer printout, a catalog of kidnappings, imprisonment, torture, and killing.

The lives of so many men and women, so many loved ones, reduced to bare entries. "Detained," followed by a date; "interrogated," another date, or more often, a series of dates; and then, too many times, "executed."

The shocked silence they worked in was shattered by a cry several hours into the morning. Angel Benitez had found her brother's name. The import of their find made the rest of the women more determined to get through the awful task. Even if the loved one was dead, to know was better than to be always wondering. They set their jaws and worked on, reclaiming memories from the trash of *los uniformes,* each hoping, yet dreading to find the names that went with the photos they had carried daily to the square.

As the piecing went on, Rosa had to send some of the women away, there were so many wanting to help and so many others who stood by anxiously awaiting news of their relatives. Because of the huge number of names coming out on the printout, the women decided that in the end, they would turn whatever they had over to the free press. Once the decision had been made, Rosa went next door to see Luisa.

"Is it my Marco?" Luisa's face went pale as she answered the door.

"No, we haven't found his name yet," Rosa said. "I came to ask about the woman who gave you the bag. She's a hero. I think people should know her name."

"I don't know her," Luisa said. "She was small and frightened. I think she is missing someone, too."

"Did she wear *la mantilla* at the square?"

"No," said Luisa, "but she may have been afraid to. I was for a long time."

"Maybe she will come to the square again," Rosa said. "If you see her, tell her we are very grateful."

For days they worked, and through the nights, piecing together shattered lives. They had many full pages of names now.

The women drank coffee as they worked, and listened to Rosa's radio for broadcasts from the new government. Details of the fighting began to come out, and the news that the previous president, and many of his top advisers were being held by the revolutionary council.

At last the announcement came that the new government was attempting to find and free political prisoners from secret jails all over the country. Their cells would be needed for their torturers, the new president said.

The women in Rosa's kitchen embraced each other and worked on with new hope that there might be happy reunions for some of the names on the printout of *los uniformes*.

Those women who were not in Rosa's kitchen began to appear again in Government Square to show their faith in the new regime. They sang hymns and laid flowers on the steps of the Presidential Palace.

On the sixth day of democracy, Rosa's kitchen became very still. Rosa's Eduardo had been found on the list. Executed. Rosa quietly put her black lace *mantilla* over her hair, lit her candle, and went to the square.

It was nearly dusk. She placed her candle carefully on the bottom step, as she had done many hundreds of times before. Tears rolled down her cheeks as she knelt, her hands folded, and her mind numb. The flame grew brighter as night folded over the capital.

Occasionally, men passed her, coming up and down the steps. "God be with you, woman," one or two murmured in passing. One stopped long enough to say, "We will make them pay, *mantilla*." Rosa looked up at the sound of the familiar voice and recognized the young man who had come to her in the square the day of the *coup*. He raised his fist in the revolutionary salute before continuing on.

As he moved away, Rosa became aware of someone nearby. A petite woman stood beside the great stone lion at the bottom of the stairs a few yards away. She looked young, but like so many of the women Rosa knew, wore an expression of deep worry and strain that would age her in a very short time. A candle, unlit, hung from the hand at her side, while her other hand clutched a white lace *mantilla* around her shoulders.

Rosa knew it had to be Luisa's woman with the plastic sack. She gestured for the woman to join her. The woman hesitated, then came over as Rosa stood to receive her.

Luisa was right, the woman looked terribly frightened. "Welcome," said Rosa. "I am Rosa."

"Teresa," said the woman. "Do you know those men? Those rebels?" She looked up the steps toward the massive doors to the Presidential Palace. "Will they be good men?"

"I think they will be better than *los uniformes*," Rosa said. "They care for the people. They went out of their way to keep us from harm."

Teresa looked up the steps for a long minute before turning back to Rosa. "And what of their prisoners? The secret police, the torturers...."

"Who can say?" Rosa replied. "'They will pay,' one man said to me. I hope it will mean trials, with judges and evidence that will prove their guilt, the kind of trials they did not dare give our children and husbands, because it would have proved their innocence."

Tears welled up in Teresa's eyes. "I gave some paper to one of the women in the square...," she said. "Could it be used as evidence?"

"Perhaps," Rosa said.

"My husband—" Teresa started, then began to cry.

"He is missing?" Rosa put an arm around her.

"Please—" the women pulled away. Her words came out in a rush. "I'm not one of you! The papers belonged to my husband. He took them from the ministry to our house, hoping to buy his safety with them if the rebels took power. When they came, he telephoned me and told me to hide them away from the house until he was ready to bargain with them. That was the first time I realized what the documents were, and what he had done in the name of the government. I couldn't keep the papers after that, so I gave them to *las mantillas*."

Rosa tried to suppress her horror. "And now your husband's in prison?"

Teresa nodded, tears streaming down her cheeks. "Forgive me. I do not belong here." She took the lace from her shoulders and laid it and the candle on the step. "I only took these up so that I could find out if the documents were being used as I hoped."

"They are," Rosa said. "They are putting hearts at ease and souls at rest. I think *las mantillas* would not mind if you stayed."

"You would," Teresa said, "because I still hope my husband will live. It may be wrong, without him I am alone. I know you all wish him to suffer the fates of your *desaparecidos*."

Rosa looked at Teresa's dark head, bowed down in shame. "If the new regime only means more torture and execution, we have gained nothing," Rosa said at last. "I am here praying for my Eduardo's soul. If you wish to pray for your husband's, there is enough room on these steps."

Teresa knelt, clasping her hands tightly together. Quiet sobs shook her shoulders. Rosa picked up Teresa's candle and lit it from her own. Then she placed the white *mantilla* over Teresa's hair and knelt beside her.

The Fish Who Chose a Magnificent Leader

BY ALAN NEIDLE

They followed him across broad reaches of ocean, through beautiful warm tropical waters, and through stormy icy seas. There seemed no limit to how far they could go.

Once upon a time, the ordinary fish in the ocean decided that they should have a leader. The field was narrowed to two candidates: a handsome athletic sailfish and an old sea turtle. A few of the fish thought the turtle should be chosen because his experience over many years gave him wisdom and a sober sense of caution about the great dangers which infested the oceans. He would have sea smarts. But the overwhelming majority of the fish thought the turtle was ugly. And it would be just plain boring to trail after him as he paddled through the oceans.

Almost everyone preferred the sailfish. They admired his magnificent style. With his long sharp sword sticking straight out from his head he could cut through the water faster than any other fish. Even more wonderful, he could leap out of the water, extend the huge sail-like fins on the top of his body and fly through the air above the waves. It would be exhilarating to follow such a leader through the oceans. All of the fish would feel good about themselves.

After the sailfish became leader, life did, indeed, become more exciting for most of the fish. They followed him across broad reaches of ocean, through beautiful warm tropical waters, and through stormy icy seas. There seemed no limit to how far they could go. And frequently their pride swelled as they looked up and saw on the surface of the water the shadow of their leader flying above the waves.

But it was not equally satisfactory for all the fish. Some, no matter how hard they tried, could not swim fast enough to keep up. These dropouts, abandoned in the great ocean, were easy prey for the sharks.

And sometimes the sailfish led his followers through dangerous waters. Once, in tropical seas, he led the fish into a school of barracuda. These savage hunters tore to pieces a great many of the little fish. Of course, the leader was perfectly safe. He had spent most of the time sailing above the water.

Most fish were at first reluctant to blame their leader. He was, after all, doing what they had elected him to do. He was cutting a magnificent figure, and it was not his fault if the older fish were not as strong or as swift as he was.

Then, one day, while the fish were following their handsome leader through cold northern waters, they suddenly found themselves face to face with a school of killer whales. There was no escape for thousands of fish, who were devoured.

"What's going on?" complained some of the fish who had been lucky enough to survive. "Does our leader know where he's taking us? Does he have any plan for all these excursions?" There were no answers.

"Does he have any idea what's going on below the surface while he's flying high?" asked one of the fish. Still there were no answers.

"And what I want to know," demanded yet another fish, "is whether he really cares about us." Nobody spoke.

"It's time we found the turtle who wanted to be our leader," suggested one of the fish. "He's like us. You can be sure *he* won't fly."

All the fish agreed. They abandoned their magnificent leader. In his place they appointed the turtle.

The sailfish hardly noticed that his followers were gone. He just went on flying safely above the waves.

The Censors

BY LUISA VALENZUELA

TRANSLATED FROM THE SPANISH BY DAVID UNGER

. . . he was shocked by the subtle and conniving ways employed by people to pass on subversive messages . . .

Poor Juan! One day they caught him with his guard down before he could even realize that what he had taken as a stroke of luck was really one of fate's dirty tricks. These things happen the minute you're careless and you let down your guard, as one often does. Juancito let happiness—a feeling you can't trust—get the better of him when he received from a confidential source Mariana's new address in Paris and he knew that she hadn't forgotten him. Without thinking twice, he sat down at his table and wrote her a letter. *The* letter that keeps his mind off his job during the day and won't let him sleep at night (what had he scrawled, what had he put on that sheet of paper he sent to Mariana?).

Juan knows there won't be a problem with the letter's contents, that it's irreproachable, harmless. But what about the rest? He knows that they examine, sniff, feel, and read between the lines of each and every letter, and check it's tiniest comma and most accidental stain. He knows that all letters pass from hand to hand and go through all sorts of tests in the huge censorship offices and that, in the end, very few continue on their way. Usually it takes months, even years, if there aren't any snags; all this time the freedom, maybe even the life, of both sender and receiver is in jeopardy. And that's why Juan's so down in the dumps:

thinking that something might happen to Mariana because of his letter. Of all people, Mariana, who must finally feel safe there where she always dreamed she'd live. But he knows that the *Censor's Secret Command* operates all over the world and cashes in on the discount in air rates; there's nothing to stop them from going as far as that hidden Paris neighborhood, kidnapping Mariana, and returning to their cozy homes, certain of having fulfilled their noble mission.

Well, you've got to beat them to the punch, do what everyone tries to do, sabotage the machinery, throw sand in its gears, get to the bottom of the problem so as to stop it.

This was Juan's sound plan when he, like many others, applied for a censor's job—not because he had a calling or needed a job: no, he applied simply to intercept his own letter, a consoling but unoriginal idea. He was hired immediately, for each day more and more censors are needed and no one would bother to check on his references.

Ulterior motives couldn't be overlooked by the *Censorship Division*, but they needn't be too strict with those who applied. They knew how hard it would be for those poor guys to find the letter they wanted and even if they did, what's a letter or two when the new censor would snap up so many others? That's how Juan managed to join the *Post Office's Censorship Division*, with a certain goal in mind.

The building had a festive air on the outside which contrasted with its inner staidness. Little by little, Juan was absorbed by his job and he felt at peace since he was doing everything he could to get his letter for Mariana. He didn't even worry when, in his first month, he was sent to *Section K* where envelopes are very carefully screened for explosives.

It's true that on the third day, a fellow worker had his right hand blown off by a letter, but the division chief claimed it was sheer negligence on the victim's part. Juan and the other employees were allowed to go back to their work, albeit feeling less secure. After work, one of them tried to organize a strike to demand higher wages for unhealthy work, but Juan didn't join in; after thinking it over, he reported him to his superiors and thus got promoted.

You don't form a habit by doing something once, he told himself as he left his boss's office. And when he was transferred to *Section J*, where letters are carefully checked for poison dust, he felt he had climbed a rung in the ladder.

By working hard, he quickly reached *Section E* where the work was more interesting, for he could now read and analyze the letters' contents. Here he could even hope to get hold of his letter which, judging by the time that had elapsed, had gone through the other sections and was probably floating around in this one.

Soon his work became so absorbing that his noble mission blurred in his mind. Day after day he crossed out whole paragraphs in red ink, pitilessly chucking many letters into the censored basket. These were horrible days when he was shocked by the subtle and conniving ways employed by people to pass on subversive messages; his instincts were so sharp that he found behind a simple "the weather's unsettled" or "prices continue to soar" the wavering hand of someone secretly scheming to overthrow the Government.

His zeal brought him swift promotion. We don't know if this made him happy. Very few letters reached him in *Section B*—only a handful passed the other hurdles—so he read them over and over again, passed them under a magnifying glass, searched for microprint with an electronic microscope, and tuned his sense of smell so that he was beat by the time he made it home. He'd barely manage to warm up his soup, eat some fruit, and fall into bed, satisfied with having done his duty. Only his darling mother worried, but she couldn't get him back on the right road. She'd say, though it wasn't always true: Lola called, she's at the bar with the girls, they miss you, they're waiting for you. Or else she'd leave a bottle of red wine on the table. But Juan wouldn't overdo it: any distraction could make him lose his edge and the perfect censor had to be alert, keen, attentive, and sharp to nab cheats. He had a truly patriotic task, both self-denying and uplifting.

His basket for censored letters became the best fed as well as the most cunning basket in the whole *Censorship Division*. He was about to congratulate himself for having finally discovered his true mission, when his letter to Mariana reached his hands. Naturally, he censored it without regret. And just as naturally, he couldn't stop them from executing him the following morning, another victim of his devotion to his work.

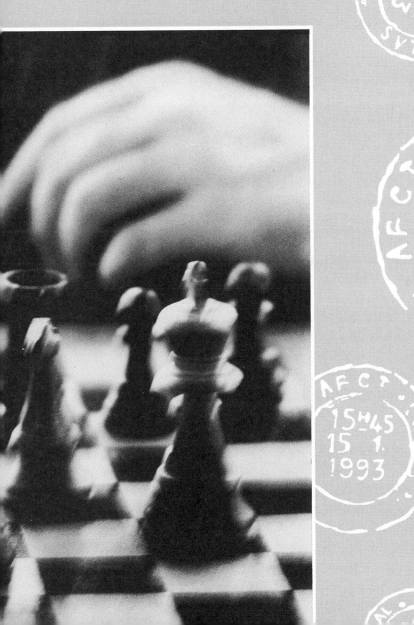

DECISIONS VII

A Rupee Earned

BY I.F. BULATKIN

The father took the coin from his son, turned it over again and again in his hand, then threw it into the fire.

Once upon a time, in a land to the north, there lived a blacksmith who had worked hard all his life to provide for the needs of his family. So diligently had he labored and so carefully had he saved that his wife and his children never knew want, and he even managed to put by a small store of wealth.

But unlike his father, the son of this industrious man was such a lazybones that in the whole wide world there was none to equal him. Although he was healthy and strong he did not know how to do anything but eat, drink, and sleep in the shade. In all the twenty years of his life he had not earned a single anna, and he never gave a thought to the fact that he was living on his father's bread.

Now the time came when the blacksmith grew old and no longer had the strength to raise a spark from his anvil. Finally the old man took to his bed, and when he realized that death was near, he called his son to his side.

"I do not know why you are so lazy," the aged blacksmith lamented. "You cannot take after me, for I have been on friendly terms with work my whole life long. Little by little I acquired my household goods by toil and honest sweat. How can it be that a son of mine cannot earn even one rupee?"

"Well, to earn just a rupee is not such a magnificent thing," the youth replied.

"My son," said the father, "show me that you can earn one rupee and all that I own will be yours when I die. Yes, you must prove to me now that you can earn something by the labor of your hands; otherwise, when I am gone you will not receive a rusty horseshoe nail. That is my will."

Now the blacksmith's son wanted very much to come into this inheritance, but he was so lazy he hated to bestir himself to perform the small task his father required. Besides, he did not know how. What a cruel thing, to have to earn a whole rupee when he had never earned a single anna since the day he was born! But a paternal word is a stone mountain, and as a stone mountain is not removed, a paternal word is not changed. His father had spoken.

The doting mother of this good-for-nothing youth could not bear to see him suffer. When she found a convenient moment, she said to him:

"Listen, little son, here is a rupee for you. Go and amuse yourself today, but when you come home in the evening, pretend you are returning from work and tell your father that you have earned the money."

The youth was so lazy he did not want to bother himself even this much, but he knew that something had to be done. So he took his mother's rupee, and with a bit of bread and cheese and a leather bag of wine he went off into the mountains. All day long he ate and drank and counted the birds in the sky. Then at nightfall he returned home and gave his father the rupee, saying:

"Here, Father, take it. It wasn't easy for me to earn this rupee. I cannot straighten my back, I worked so hard."

The father took the coin, looked at it from both sides, and tossed it from palm to palm. Then he threw it into the fire.

"No," he said, "you did not earn that rupee."

With a shrug of his shoulders the son replied: "Well, you don't have to believe me." And he went off to bed.

The next day the worried mother gave her son a second rupee, but this time she instructed him:

"Sleep all day if you wish, little son, but before you come home in the evening, run one mile. You will perspire, you will be tired, and then your father will believe that you have been at work, and that you did his bidding and earned the money by your labor."

The lazybones cared for his legs, but he cared still more to inherit his father's fortune. So he took his mother's rupee, and with food and drink he set out for the mountains as before. From dawn to dusk he ate and drank and warmed himself in the sun, but when it came time to go home he ran a mile, and then for good measure he ran another.

And when he arrived at the threshold he was so tired he could hardly draw a breath. Perspiration poured from him in streams. He toppled onto a bench and held out the rupee.

"It surely was hard for me to earn this rupee!" he gasped. "I worked like an ox the livelong day. I am falling over my feet with fatigue."

The father took the coin from his son, turned it over again and again in his hand, then threw it into the fire.

"No," he said, "you are deceiving me, my son. This rupee was given to you. It was useless for you to run from the mountains."

What could the lazy youth say? "You don't wish to believe me," he shrugged, smiling. "To be sure, it's not true." And forthwith he lay down by the fire and went to sleep.

The good-for-nothing youth dreamed sweet dreams, but sleep did not come to his dear mother. She realized now that in deceiving her husband they only lost their hard-earned money, and she also knew that all this brought no profit to her son.

So the next day she instructed differently:

"Come now, little son. If you want to inherit your father's property, you must take yourself off and really go to work. If you only earn one or two annas a day, in a week you can make a whole rupee."

It seemed there was nothing else to do; the time had come to obey. The lazybones worked for a whole week. He carried something for one man; he helped with something for another. One man gave him one anna; another gave him two. Bit by bit he accumulated a whole rupee.

Then he went to his father and poured a handful of coins before him. Again the old man turned over the money, weighed it in his hand, and held some pieces up to the light. Then he said:

"No, my son. You have deceived me again. You did not earn this money." And he seized all the coins and threw them into the fire like so much rubbish.

But this time the son was in a frenzy. He hurled himself into the fireplace, separated the burning coals with his bare hands, and snatched the money out of the very fire itself. "Why did you do that?" he cried. "I haven't straightened up my back for a whole week and you want to burn my money in the fire!"

The father looked at his son and said:

"Now I believe that you earned this rupee yourself. Someone else's money you do not care about—that is cheap. But the money you earn by your own labor—ah, that you make a big fuss over! So it is, my son. Remember my words: As long as you work, you will have money and contentment, and all things will be yours. But if you will not work, another person's money cannot help you, for someone else's rupee is not worth one anna."

Then the father willed all his property to his son and went to the land from which no man ever returns.

A True Money Tree

BY M.A. JAGENDORF
AND VIRGINIA WENG

Good Life came to his brother in his little hut and said, "Brother, did our father give you some treasure we don't know about?"

In years gone by, there lived an old Chinese man by the name of Li. He had two sons, Long Life and Good Life.

Long Life's mother had died when he was a young boy, and Li had been lonely without a wife in the house. So he had married again, and when she gave him a son, he named him Good Life, for life in his house was good. But alas! The new wife did not like Long Life, so she made him do all the hard work in the house and in the fields and garden. But Long Life was an obedient son and did not complain. He did all that had to be done while his stepmother and brother looked on.

When he was seventeen years old, his father died, and his life with his stepmother was made even harder than it had been before. Although he did all the work in the house and fields, he was scolded all the time. No matter how much he tried to please his stepmother, she was always finding fault with him. She was always thinking of ways to get rid of him.

So one day she said, "You are old enough to be on your own now. We should divide the land your father left. Your brother is still young, and he can stay with me. We should each live in our own home, then there will be no quarrel between us."

Long Life agreed to this and left the division of property to his stepmother. She took the house and the best fields around it for herself and her son. To Long Life she gave a barren piece of land on a hill far from the village.

Long Life did not complain. He built himself a little hut and began clearing the land and plowing and planting on it. He cut some firewood, and little by little he grew enough food to support himself nicely.

With Long Life gone from the house and land where he had done all the work, there was no one to do it. Good Life and his mother were lazy and careless, so they became poorer and poorer. One day the mother said to her son, "Look we have a fine house and good land, and your brother lives in a hut on a piece of barren and hilly land, but he is getting richer and we are getting poorer. I am sure your father left him something of which we did not get our share. Son, go to your brother and make him tell you the truth, and ask him why he is getting rich and we are becoming poor. Tell him if he got something from his father we don't know about, he must give us at least half of it."

Good Life came to his brother in his little hut and said, "Brother, did our father give you some treasure we don't know about? We have fine land and you have a rocky barren piece—how is it that you are doing so well and we so poorly? You have plenty of everything and we have nothing. Did our father leave something you are hiding from us? We want our share of it."

"Brother, you are right. Our wise father left me a wonderful treasure—a money tree. It has two trunks and there are five branches on each trunk. All my food and clothing depend on that wonderful tree. From that tree I will always get enough money to live in good health and pleasure.... It—"

Good Life broke in, "Where is that tree? Where are you hiding it?"

"I am not hiding it. It is with me all the time on my little piece of land, in my garden, and I am always there working at it. It gives me food, drink, and clothes and anything else I need, and if you—"

Before he could finish his words, Good Life rushed out and ran to his home. "Mother, Mother," he cried, "you were right. My father left a money tree that will give us money for all we need, but Long Life took it. He told me. It will give money for food, clothes, and everything else we need."

"I knew we were cheated," she cried. "Run to Long Life's orchard and dig up that money tree and plant it in our garden. It should be here."

Good Life did not need any coaxing. He found a spade and ran to Long Life's garden. He searched for a long time until he found a tree with two trunks and ten branches. He worked hard digging it up. Then he dragged it to his mother's garden and there he dug a deep hole and planted the tree, watering it well. Day after day he watered the tree and shook it hard—but no money fell from it.

Then Good Life went back to his brother in anger and cried, "I took a tree with two trunks and ten branches from your garden, and planted it in our garden, watered it and took care of it, but no money falls from it. Did you tell me the truth?"

"Dear brother, I told you the truth—but you did not wait to hear the end of what I had to say. My money tree can never be stolen. It is my two arms and hands. The arms are the trunks and the fingers are the branches. Use them for planting trees and crops and to do all other work. Then money will come from them, and that will get you every-thing you need. My arms and hands are my fortune and I call them my money tree. You have a money tree, too. Put it to work as I do, and you will have all the money you need to buy whatever you want."

Good Life went home to his mother. On the way he had been thinking of his brother's words. "Mother," he said, "now I have the true money tree and..." He put his hands to work and soon he and his mother reaped money from that tree for food and everything else, just as his brother did.

Haute Cuisine

BY AMPARO DÁVILA

TRANSLATED FROM THE SPANISH BY ALBERTO MANGUEL

From my room in the attic I could hear them shriek.

When I hear the rain lashing against my window, their cries come back to me once again, those cries that used to stick to my skin like leeches. Their pitch would increase as the pot heated up and the water began to boil. And I also see their eyes, small, beady and black, popping from their sockets when they were cooked.

They were born during the rainy season, in the vegetable gardens. Hidden among the leaves, gripping onto the stalks, or lurking in the wet grass. From there they were torn off to be sold, and at a good price, too. Three for five cents usually, and when there were many, at fifteen cents a dozen.

At home we used to buy about two pesos' worth every week, being as it was the established Sunday dish, and even more often than that if we had guests. My family would only serve it to distinguished or well-loved visitors. "Nowhere else do they prepare them as well," my mother used to say, so proudly, when complimented on her cooking.

I remember the gloomy kitchen and the pot in which they were cooked—a pot fashioned and burnished by an old French chef—the wooden spoon dusky with age, and the cook, a fat, ruthless woman, unmoved by their suffering. The heart-rending cries did not affect her; she would carry on fanning the fire, blowing on the coals as if nothing were happening. From my room in the attic I could hear them shriek. It was always raining, and their cries would mix with the patter of the rain. They took ages to die. To me, it seemed as if their agony would go on forever. I would stay in my room, my head buried beneath my pillow, but even beneath the pillow I could hear them. Sometimes I would wake up at midnight and go on hearing them. I never knew whether they were still alive, or whether their cries had stayed on inside me, inside my head, inside my ears, inside and outside, hammering away, tearing me apart.

Sometimes I would see hundreds of little eyes glued to the dripping window-panes. Hundreds of black, round eyes. Shining eyes, wet with tears, begging for mercy. But there was no mercy in our house. No one felt moved by our cruelty. Their eyes and their cries would follow me—as they follow me even today—everywhere I went.

A few times they sent me out to buy them. I would always return empty-handed, swearing that I had not found any. One day they began to suspect, and I was never sent again. The cook would go instead. She would return with a pailful, and I would look at her full of contempt as one would look at the cruelest executioner. She would wrinkle her pug nose and snort superciliously.

Preparing them was a complicated task and took time. First she would put them in a box lined with grass, and give them a certain rare herb that they would eat—seemingly with pleasure—and that acted as a purgative. There they would spend the first day. On the following morning she would bathe them carefully so as not to harm them, she would dry them, and she would place them in the pot full of cold water, spices, aromatic herbs, salt and vinegar.

When the water began to heat they would start shrieking, shrieking, shrieking…. They would shriek like newborn babies, like squashed mice, like bats, like strangled kittens, like hysterical women.

On that occasion—my last day at home—the banquet was long and exquisite.

Cane Is Bitter

BY SAMUEL SELVON

Though Romesh never spoke of the great things he was learning, or tried to show off his knowledge, the very way he bore himself now, the way he watched the cane moving in the wind was alien to their feelings.

In February they began to reap the cane in the undulating fields at Cross Crossing estate in the southern part of Trinidad. "Crop time coming, boy—plenty work for everybody," men in the village told one another. They set about sharpening their cutlasses on grinding stones, ceasing only when they tested the blades with their thumbnails and a faint ping! quivered in the air. Or they swung the cutlass at a drooping leaf and cleaved it. But the best test was when it could shave the hairs off your leg.

Everyone was happy in Cross Crossing as work loomed up in the way of their idleness, for after the planting of the cane there was hardly any work until the crop season. They laughed and talked more and the children were given more liberty than usual, so they ran about the barracks and played hide-and-seek in those cane fields which had not yet been fired to make the reaping easier. In the evening, when the dry trash was burnt away from the stalks of sweet juice, they ran about clutching the black straw which rose on the wind; people miles away knew when crop season was on, for the burnt trash was blown a great distance away. The children smeared one another on the face and laughed at the black streaks. It wouldn't matter now if their exertions made them hungry, there would be money to buy flour and rice when the men worked in the fields, cutting and carting the cane to the weighing bridge.

In a muddy pond about two hundred yards east of the settlement, under the shade of spreading *laginette* trees, women washed clothes and men bathed mules and donkeys and hog-cattle. The women beat the clothes with stones to get them clean, squatting by the banks, their skirts drawn tight against the back of their thighs, their saris retaining grace of arrangement on their shoulders even in that awkward position. Naked children splashed about in the pond, hitting the water with their hands and shouting when the water shot up in the air at different angles, and trying to make brief rainbows in the sunlight with the spray. Rays of the morning sun came slantways from halfway up in the sky, casting the shadow of trees on the pond, and playing on the brown bodies of the children.

Ramlal came to the pond and sat on the western bank, so that he squinted into the sunlight. He dipped his cutlass in the water and began to sharpen it on the end of a rock on which his wife Rookmin was beating clothes. He was a big man, and in earlier days was reckoned handsome. But work in the fields had not only tanned his skin to a deep brown but actually changed his features. His nose had a slight hump just above the nostrils, and the squint in his eyes was there even in the night, as if he was peering all the time, though his eyesight was remarkable. His teeth were stained brown with tobacco, so brown that when he laughed it blended with the color of his face, and you only saw the lips stretched wide and heard the rumble in his throat.

Rookmin was frail but strong as most East Indian women. She was not beautiful, but it was difficult to take any one feature of her face and say it was ugly. Though she was only thirty-six, hard work and the bearing of five children had taken toll. Her eyes were black and deceptive, and perhaps she might have been unfaithful to Ramlal if the idea had ever occurred to her. But like most of the Indians in the country districts, half her desires and emotions were never given a chance to live, her life dedicated to wresting an existence for herself and her family. But as if she knew the light she threw from her eyes, she had a habit of shutting them whenever she was emotional. Her breasts sagged from years of suckling. Her hands were wrinkled and calloused. The toes of her feet were spread wide from walking without any footwear whatsoever; she never had need for a pair of shoes because she never left the village.

She watched Ramlal out of the corner of her eye as he sharpened the cutlass, sliding the blade to and fro on the rock. She knew he had something on his mind, the way he had come silently and sat near her, pretending that he could add to the keenness of his razor-sharp cutlass. She waited for him to speak, in an Oriental respectfulness. But from the attitude of both of them, it wasn't possible to tell that they were about to converse, or even that they were man and wife. Rookmin went on washing clothes, turning the garments over and over as she pounded them on a flat stone, and Ramlal squinted his eyes and looked at the sun.

At last, after five minutes or so, Ramlal spoke.

"Well, that boy Romesh coming home tomorrow. Is six months since last he come home. This time, I make up my mind, he not going back."

Rookmin went on scrubbing, she did not even look up.

"You see how city life change the boy. When he was here the last time, you see how he was talking about funny things?"

Rookmin held up a tattered white shirt and looked at the sun through it.

"But you think he will agree to what we going to do?" she asked. "He must be learning all sorts of new things, and this time might be worse than last time. Suppose he want to take Creole wife?"

"But you mad or what? That could never happen. Ain't we make all arrangement with Sampath for Doolsie to married him? Anyway," he went on, "is all your damn fault in the first place, wanting to send him for education in the city. You see what it cause? The boy come like a stranger as soon as he start to learn all those funny things they teach you in school, talking about poetry and books and them funny things. I did never want to send him for education, but is you who make me do it."

"Education is a good thing," Rookmin said, without intonation. "One day he might come lawyer or doctor, and all of we would live in a big house in the town, and have servants to look after we."

"That is only foolish talk," Ramlal said. "You think he would remember we when he come a big man? And besides, by that time you and me both dead. And besides, the wedding done plan and everything already."

"Well, if he married Doolsie everything might work out."

"How you mean if? I had enough of all this business. He have to do what I say, else I put him out and he never come here again. Doolsie father offering big dowry, and afterwards the both of them could settle on the estate and he could forget all that business."

Rookmin was silent. Ramlal kept testing the blade with his nail, as if he were fascinated by the pinging sound, as if he were trying to pick out a tune.

But in fact he was thinking, thinking about the last time his son Romesh had come home....

It was only his brothers and sisters, all younger than himself, who looked at Romesh with wonder, wanting to ask him questions about the world outside the cane fields and the village. Their eyes expressed their thoughts, but out of some curious embarrassment they said nothing. In a way, this brother was a stranger, someone who lived far away in the city, only coming home once or twice a year to visit them. They were noticing a change, a distant look in his eyes. Silently, they drew aside from him, united in their lack of understanding. Though Romesh never spoke of the great things he was learning, or tried to show off his knowledge, the very way he bore himself now, the way he watched the cane moving in the wind was alien to their feelings. When they opened the books he had brought, eager to see the pictures, there were only pages and pages of words, and they couldn't read. They watched him in the night, crouching in the corner, the book on the floor near to the candle, reading. That alone made him different, set him apart. They thought he was going to be a pundit, or a priest, or something extraordinary. Once his sister had asked, "What do you read so much about, *bhai?*" and Romesh looked at her with a strange look and said, "To tell you, you wouldn't understand. But have patience, a time will come soon, I hope, when all of you will learn to read and write." Then Hari, his brother, said, "Why do you feel we will not understand? What is wrong with our brains? Do you think because you go to school in the city that you are better than us? Because you get the best clothes to wear, and shoes to put on your feet, because you get favor from *bap* and *mai?*" Romesh said quickly, "*Bhai*, it is not that. It is only that I have left our village, and have learned about many things which you do not know about. The whole world goes ahead in all fields, in politics, in science, in art. Even now the governments in the West Indies are talking about federating the islands, and then what will happen to the Indians in this island? But we must not quarrel, soon all of us will have a chance." But Hari was not impressed. He turned to his father and mother and said, "See how he has changed. He don't want to play no games anymore, he don't want to work in the fields, he is too much of a big shot to use a cutlass. His brothers and sisters are fools, he don't want to talk to them because they won't understand. He don't even want to eat we food again, this morning I see he ain't touch the *baghi*. No. We have to get chicken for him, and the cream from all the cows in the village. Yes, that is what. And who it is does sweat for him to get pretty shirt to wear in Port of Spain?" He held up one of the girl's arms and spanned it with his fingers. "Look how thin she is. All that is for you to be a big man, and now you scorning your own family?" Romesh got up from the floor and faced them. His eyes burned fiercely, and he looked like the pictures of Indian gods the children had seen in the village hall. "You are all wrong!" he cried in a ringing voice. "Surely you, *bap*, and you, *mai*, the years must have taught you that you must make a different life for your children, that you must free them from ignorance and the wasting away of their lives? Do you want them to suffer as you have?" Rookmin looked like she was going to say something, but instead she shut her eyes tight. Ramlal said, "Who tell you we suffer? We bring children in the world and we happy." But Romesh went on, "And what will the children do? Grow up in the village here, without learning to read and write? There are schools in San Fernando; surely you can send them there to learn about different things besides driving a mule and using a cutlass? Oh *bap*, we are such a backward people, all the others move forward to better lives, and we lag behind believing that what is to be, will be. All over Trinidad, in the country districts, our people toil on the land and reap the cane. For years it has been so, years in the same place, learning nothing new, accepting our fate like animals. Political men come from India and give speeches in the city. They speak of better things, they tell us to unite and strive for a greater goal. And what does it mean to you? Nothing. You are content to go hungry, to see your children run about naked, emaciated, grow up dull and stupid, slaves to your own indifference. You do not even pretend an interest in the Legislative Council. I remember why you voted for Pragsingh last year; it was because he gave you ten dollars—did I not see it for myself? It were better that we returned to India than stay in the West Indies and live such a low form of existence." The family watched Romesh wide-eyed. Ramlal sucked his clay pipe noisily. Rookmin held her youngest daughter in her lap, picking her head for lice, and now and then shutting her eyes so the others wouldn't see what she was thinking. "There is only one solution," Romesh went on, "we must educate the children, open up new worlds in their minds, stretch the horizon of their thoughts…" Suddenly he stopped. He realized that for some time now they weren't listening, his words didn't make any sense to them. Perhaps he was going about this the wrong way; he would have to find some other way of explaining how he felt. And was he sufficiently equipped in himself to propose vast changes in the lives of the people? It seemed to him then how small he was, how there were so many things he didn't know. All the books he'd read, the knowledge he'd lapped up hungrily in the city listening to the politicians making speeches in the square—all these he mustered to his assistance. But it was as if his brain was too small, it was like putting your mouth in the sea and trying to drink all the water. Wearily, like an old man who had tried to prove his point merely by repeating, "I am old, I should know," Romesh sat down on the floor, and there was silence in the hut, a great silence, as if the words he'd spoken had fled the place and gone outside with the wind and the cane.

And so after he had gone back to the city his parents discussed the boy, and concluded that the only thing to save his senses was to marry him off. "You know he like Sampath daughter from long time, and she is a hard-working girl. She go make good wife for him," Rookmin had said. Ramlal had seen Sampath and everything was fixed. Everybody in the village knew of the impending wedding.…

Romesh came home the next day. He had some magazines and books under his arm, and a suitcase in his hand. There was no reception for him; everyone who could work was out in the fields.

He was as tall as the canes on either side of the path on which he walked. He sniffed the smell of burning cane, but he wasn't overjoyful at coming home. He had prepared for this, prepared for the land on which he had toiled as a child, the thatched huts, the children running naked in the sun. He knew that these were things not easily forgotten which he had to forget. But he saw how waves of wind rippled over the seas of cane and he wondered vaguely about big things like happiness and love and poetry, and how they could fit into the poor, toiling lives the villagers led.

Romesh met his sisters at home. They greeted him shyly but he held them in his arms and cried, "*Beti*, do you not know your own brother?" And they laughed and hung their heads on his shoulder.

"Everybody gone to work," one girl said, "and we cooking food to carry. Pa and Ma was looking out since early this morning. They say to tell you if you come to come in the fields."

Romesh looked around the hut in which he had grown up. It seemed to him that if he had come back home after ten years, there would still be the old table in the centre of the room, its feet sunk in the earthen floor, the black pots and pans hanging on nails near the window. Nothing would change. They would plant the cane, and when it grew and filled with sweet juice cut it down for the factory. The children would waste away their lives working with their parents. No schooling, no education, no widening of experience. It was the same thing the man had lectured about in the public library three nights before in Port of Spain. The most they would learn would be to wield a cutlass expertly, or drive the mule cart to the railway lines swiftly so that before the sun went down they would have worked sufficiently to earn more than their neighbors.

With a sigh like an aged man Romesh opened his suitcase and took out a pair of shorts and a polo shirt. He put these on and put the suitcase away in a corner. He wondered where would be a safe place to put his books. He opened the suitcase again and put them in.

It was as if, seeing the room in which he had argued and quarreled with the family on his last visit, he lost any happiness he might have had coming back this time. A feeling of depression overcame him.

It lasted as he talked with his sisters as they prepared food to take to the fields. Romesh listened how they stumbled with words, how they found it difficult to express themselves. He thought how regretful it was that they couldn't go to school. He widened the thought and embraced all the children in the village, growing up with such little care, running naked in the mud with a piece of *roti* in their hands, missing out on all the things that life should stand for.

But when the food was ready and they set off for the fields, with the sun in their eyes making them blind, he felt better. He would try to be happy with them, while he was here. No more preaching. No more voicing of opinion on this or that.

Other girls joined his sisters as they walked, all carrying food. When they saw Romesh they blushed and tittered, and he wondered what they were whispering about among themselves.

There were no effusive greetings. Sweating as they were, their clothes black with the soot of burnt canes, their bodies caught in the motions of their work, they just shouted out, and Romesh shouted back. Then Ramlal dropped the reins and jumped down from his cart. He curved his hand like a boomerang and swept it over his face. The soot from his sleeves smeared his face as he wiped away the sweat.

Rookmin came up and opened tired arms to Romesh. "*Beta*," she cried as she felt his strong head on her breast. She would have liked to stay like that, drawing his strength and vitality into her weakened body, and closing her eyes so her emotions wouldn't show.

"*Beta*," his father said, "you getting big, you looking strong." They sat down to eat on the grass. Romesh was the only one who appeared cool, the others were flushed, the veins standing out on their foreheads and arms.

Romesh asked if it was a good crop.

"Yes, *beta*," Ramlal said, "is a good crop, and plenty work for everybody. But this year harder than last year, because rain begin to fall early, and if we don't hurry up with the work, it will be too much trouble for all of us. The overseer come yesterday, and he say a big bonus for the man who do the most work. So everybody working hard for that bonus. Two of my mules sick, but I have to work them, I can't help. We trying to get the bonus."

After eating, Ramlal fished a cigarette butt from his pocket and lit it carefully. First greetings over, he had nothing more to tell his son, for the time being anyway.

Romesh knew they were all remembering the last visit, and the things he had said then. This time he wasn't going to say anything; he was just going to have a holiday and enjoy it, and return to school in the city refreshed.

He said, "Hari, I bet I could cut more canes than you."

Hari laughed. "Even though I work the whole morning already, is a good bet. You must be forget to use *poya*, your hands so soft and white now."

That is the way life is, Ramlal thought as Romesh took his cutlass. Education, school, chut! It was only work put a *roti* in your belly, only work that brought money. The marriage would change Romesh. And he felt a pride in his heart as his son spat on the blade.

The young men went to a patch of burnt canes. The girls came too, standing by to pile the fallen stalks of sweet juice into heaps, so that they could be loaded quickly and easily on to the carts and raced to the weighing bridge.

Cane fell as if a machine were at work. The blades swung in the air, glistened for a moment in the sunlight, and descended on the stalks near the roots. Though the work had been started as a test of speed, neither of them moved ahead of the other. Sometimes Romesh paused until Hari came abreast, and sometimes Hari waited a few canes for Romesh. Once they looked at each other and laughed, the sweat on their faces getting into their mouths. There was no more enmity on Hari's part; seeing his brother like this, working, was like the old days when they worked side by side at all the chores which filled the day.

Everybody turned to in the field, striving to outwork the others, for each wanted the bonus as desperately as his neighbor. Sometimes the women and the girls laughed or made jokes to one another, but the men worked silently. And the crane on the weighing bridge creaked and took load after load. The laborer manipulating it grumbled: there was no bonus for him, though his wage was more than that of the cane cutters. When the sun set all stopped work as if by signal. And in Ramlal's hut that night there was laughter and song. Everything was all right, they thought. Romesh was his natural self again, the way he swung that cutlass! His younger sisters and brother had never really held anything against him, and now that Hari seemed pleased, they dropped all embarrassment and made fun. "See *bhai*, I make *meetai* especially for you," his sister said, offering the sweetmeat.

"He work hard, he deserve it," Hari agreed, and he looked at his brother almost with admiration.

Afterward, when Ramlal was smoking and Rookmin was searching in the youngest girl's head for lice ("put pitch oil, that will kill them,"

Ramlal advised), Romesh said he was going to pay Doolsie a visit.

There was a sudden silence. Rookmin shut her eyes, the children stopped playing, and Ramlal coughed over his pipe.

"Well, what is the matter?" Romesh asked, looking at their faces.

"Well, now," Ramlal began, and stopped to clear his throat. "Well now, you know that is our custom, that a man shouldn't go to pay visit to the girl he getting married...."

"What!" Romesh looked from face to face. The children shuffled their feet and began to be embarrassed at the stranger's presence once more.

Ramlal spoke angrily. "Remember this is your father's house! Remember the smaller ones! Careful what you say, you must give respect! You not expect to get married one day, eh? Is a good match we make, boy. You will get good dowry, and you could live in the village and forget them funny things you learning in the city."

"So it has all been arranged," Romesh said slowly. "That is why everybody looked at me in such a strange way in the fields. My life already planned for me, my path pointed out—cane, labor, boy children, and the familiar village of Cross Crossing." His voice had dropped lower, as if he had been speaking to himself, but it rose again as he addressed his mother. "And you, *mai*, you have helped them do this to me? You whose idea it was to give me an education?"

Rookmin shut her eyes and spoke. "Is the way of our people, is we custom from long time. And you is Indian? The city fool your brains, but you will get back accustom after you married and have children."

Ramlal got up from where he was squatting on the floor and faced Romesh. "You have to do what we say," he said loudly. "Ever since you in the city, we notice how you change. You forgetting custom and how we Indian people does live. And too besides, money getting short. We want help on the estate. The garden want attention, and nobody here to see about the cattle and them. And no work after crop, too besides."

"Then I can go to school in San Fernando," Romesh said desperately. "If there is no money to pay the bus, I will walk. The government schools are free; you do not have to pay to learn."

"You will married and have boy children," Ramlal said, "and you will stop answering your *bap*...."

"Hai, Hai!" drivers urged their carts in the morning sun, and whips cracked crisply on the air. Dew still clung to the grass as workers took to the fields to do as much as they could before the heat of the sun began to tell.

Romesh was still asleep when the others left. No one woke him; they moved about the hut in silence. No one spoke. The boys went to harness the mules, one of the girls to milk the cows, and the other was busy in the kitchen.

When Romesh got up he opened his eyes in full awareness. He could have started the argument again as if no time had elapsed, the night had made no difference.

He went into the kitchen to wash his face. He gargled noisily, scraped his tongue with his teeth. Then he remembered the toothbrush and toothpaste in his suitcase. As he cleaned his teeth his sister stood watching him. She never used a toothbrush; they broke a twig and chewed it to clean their mouths.

"You going to go away, *bhai?*" she asked him timidly.

He nodded, with froth in his mouth.

"If you stay, you could teach we what you know," the girl said.

Romesh washed his mouth and said, "*Baihin*, there are many things I have yet to learn."

"But what will happen to us?"

"Don't ask me questions, little sister," he said crossly.

After he had eaten he left the hut and sulked about the village, walking slowly with his hands in his pockets. He wasn't quite sure what he was going to do. He kept telling himself that he would go away and never return, but bonds he had refused to think about surrounded him. The smell of burnt cane was strong on the wind. He went to the pond where he and Hari used to bathe the mules. What to do? His mind was in a turmoil.

Suddenly he turned and went home. He got his cutlass—it was sharp and clean, even though unused for such a long time. Ramlal never allowed any of his tools to get rusty.

He went out into the fields, swinging the cutlass in the air, as if with each stroke he swept a problem away.

Hari said, "Is time you come. Other people start work long time; we have to work extra to catch up with them."

There was no friendliness in his voice now.

Romesh said nothing, but he hacked savagely at the canes, and in half an hour he was bathed in sweat and his skin scratched from contact with the cane.

Ramlal came up in the mule cart and called out, "Work faster! We a whole cartload behind!" Then he saw Romesh and he came down from the cart and walked rapidly across. "So you come! Is a good thing you make up your mind!"

Romesh wiped his face. "I am not going to stay, *bap*." It was funny how the decision came; he hadn't known himself what he was going to do. "I will help with the crop; you shall get the bonus if I have to work alone in the night. But I am not going to get married. I am going away after the crop."

"You are mad, you will do as I say." Ramlal spoke loudly, and other workers in the field stopped to listen.

The decision was so clear in Romesh's mind that he did not say anything more. He swung the cutlass tirelessly at the cane and knew that when the crop was finished, it would be time to leave his family and the village. His mind got that far, and he didn't worry about after that....

As the wind whispered in the cane, it carried the news of Romesh's revolt against his parents' wishes, against tradition and custom.

Doolsie, working a short distance away, turned her brown face from the wind. But women and girls working near her whispered among themselves and laughed. Then one of the bolder women, already married, said, "Well girl, is a good thing in a way. Some of these men too bad. They does beat their wife too much—look at Dulcie husband, he does be drunk all the time, and she does catch hell with him."

But Doolsie bundled the canes together and kept silent.

"She too young yet," another said. "Look, she breasts not even form yet!"

Doolsie did not have any memories to share with Romesh, and her mind was young enough to bend under any weight. But the way her friends were laughing made her angry, and in her mind she too revolted against the marriage.

"All you too stupid!" she said, lifting her head with a childish pride so that her sari fell on her shoulder. "You wouldn't say Romesh is the only boy in the village! And too besides, I wasn't going to married him if he think he too great for me."

The wind rustled through the cane. Overhead, the sun burned like a furnace.

"Should a writer, then, write about home? It is both natural and sensible that the place where we have our roots should become the setting, the first and primary proving ground of our fiction."

Eudora Welty

The Departure of the Giants

BY HAROLD COURLANDER

The chief of the giants returned to his tribe. He told the people of the blessings God had given them, and they were happy.

Before the first Mensa, Habab, Beni-Amer, and Cunama people arrived, a tribe of giants was living in the land. It is said by some that God created the giants first, and that later he made people in the size they are today. The giants were truly giants. They used water skins made of whole elephant hides. Their spears were as tall as euphorbia trees, and the stones they threw from their slings were not pebbles but large boulders. They roasted whole cows over their fires for a single meal, and drank milk from great wooden tubs. When other tribes came into the country looking for water for their cattle and goats, the giants killed them or drove them away. Many courageous Mensa, Beni-Amer, and Habab warriors died trying to hold watering places against the giants.

Today the giants are gone, but you may still see the great stones they used for foundations of their houses, and here or there people find the remains of the enormous tombs in which the giants were buried. This story is about how the giants finally disappeared. It is told by the old people of the tribes.

God concluded that things were not peaceful because of the giants. The world was out of balance. So he sent for the chief of the giants and said to him, "It is time for your tribe to leave the world."

The chief of the giants said, "Master, how have we offended you that we should have to leave?"

God replied, "Your tribe has been too hard with the small people. You have forgotten that water holes were given to all the tribes for their cattle. You drive the people away, though they have done you no harm."

The chief of the giants said, "Master, all tribes guard their wells. All tribes fight to protect their land. What have we done that is different?"

God said, "Because you are so large and the others so small, everything is out of balance. Your tribe consumes everything. While you eat a whole cow for your dinner, the other tribes stand on a hilltop watching you swallow down enough to keep them alive for a month."

The giant chief said, "Master, it was you who created us as we are. Is the fault ours?"

God said, "No, the fault is not yours, yet I have to send your tribe out of this world. Therefore I will be as kind as I can. I will give you a choice. I will let you choose how to depart. You may disappear with my curse or my blessings."

The chief of the giants said, "Who would want to receive God's curse? If we must go, send us on our way with your blessings."

God answered, "Good. Let it be that way. I will lay blessings on you. Because sons are a blessing to all families, henceforth all your children to come will be sons. Because cows are a blessing on account of the calves they bear and the milk they give, henceforth all calves that are born will be females."

The chief of the giants returned to his tribe. He told the people of the blessings God had given them, and they were happy. Things came to pass as God had promised. Women gave birth only to sons, and cows gave birth only to female calves. The sons grew up. It was time for them to marry, but there were no young women to be their wives. The female calves matured, but there were no bulls for them to mate with. So in time no more children were born to the giants, and no more calves were born to the cattle. People grew old and died. Cattle grew old and died. The tribe of giants withered.

At last the chief called a council of the old people who were still alive. He said to them, "As all men can see, we are dying out from our blessings. Let us not linger here any more, waiting for the end. Let every person build a tomb for himself and cover it with a roof of stones. Let each one enter his tomb and close up the entrance. In this way we will finally depart from the world."

So every person built himself a tomb and covered it with a roof of stones, after which he entered, closed up the opening, and remained there until he died. Thus the giants perished and disappeared from the face of the land.

The roofs of the tombs fell long ago, and all that remain are piles of stones. Because they remember what happened to the giants, people of the tribes sometimes say when life seems too generous to them:

"Take care, let us not die from blessings like the giants did."

The Other Face

BY SALMA SHALLASH

When he saw me his face revealed total astonishment.

I got up early. On my way to the bathroom I looked at myself in the mirror. I was horrified by my appearance. My hair was disheveled and my face stripped of makeup. It looked quite different from yesterday. I thought of Fu'ad, my fiancé, and it struck me that the faces we show each other aren't the real us. They are artificial faces, masks. A few days ago I learned that my friend at the office had gotten divorced after two years of marriage. I asked in amazement how she could be divorced when she had married for love. They told me there had been differences and problems. I scrutinized my face in the mirror. There's no way around it, I told myself. When a couple gets married both the bride and groom are going to be surprised by the sight of each other's true face. During the engagement we show each other a different face. We behave in a studied, calculated way. If we could see each other as we really are before the union, there would be no end of problems.... Fu'ad is in for a shock after we get married. He will see a different woman from the one he loves and plans to marry.

Suddenly I had a crazy idea. I quickly put on an ordinary housedress, went out to the street, and jumped into the first taxi I found.

I knocked on Fu'ad's door, then put my hand on the buzzer and held it there. I heard his voice shouting from inside, "Yes.... Coming." When he saw me his face revealed total astonishment. He asked me why

I had come at such an early hour, and looked all the more bewildered as he studied my appearance. He seemed to be seeing me for the first time. He looked comical too. He wore baggy pajamas, and a cap on his head to keep down his curly hair. He had not yet shaved, and his eyelids were still puffed up with sleep. Eyeing me uneasily, he said, "Your visit has taken me by surprise."

I said, "I wanted to safeguard the future of our marriage by letting each of us see the other's real face so that we won't have a shock when we get married."

Most people were satisfied by the sensible reason Fu'ad gave to my family when he broke off the engagement: that he would be traveling overseas on a scholarship and might not return.

But I keep wondering whether what I did was naïve, or absolutely the right thing.

"Each reader brings to each work of literature only what is within oneself."
Marcel Proust

The Visitation

BY FERNANDO SORRENTINO

How could I help but notice this man? He was a beggar or a tramp, a scarecrow draped in shreds and patches.

In 1965, when I was twenty-three, I was training as a teacher of Spanish language and literature. Very early one morning at the beginning of spring I was studying in my room in our fifth-floor flat in the only apartment building on the block.

Feeling just a bit lazy, every now and again I let my eyes stray beyond the window. I could see the street and, on the opposite side, old don Cesáreo's well-kept garden. His house stood on the corner of a site that formed an irregular pentagon.

Next to don Cesáreo's was a beautiful house belonging to the Bernasconis, a wonderful family who were always doing good and kindly things. They had three daughters, and I was in love with Adriana, the eldest. That was why from time to time I glanced at the opposite side of the street—more out of a sentimental habit than because I expected to see her at such an early hour.

As usual, don Cesáreo was tending and watering his beloved garden, which was divided from the street by a low iron fence and three stone steps.

The street was so deserted that my attention was forcibly drawn to a man who appeared on the next block, heading our way on the same side as the houses of don Cesáreo and the Bernasconis. How could I help but notice this man? He was a beggar or a tramp, a scarecrow draped in shreds and patches.

Bearded and thin, he wore a battered yellowish straw hat and, despite the heat, was wrapped in a bedraggled greyish overcoat. He was carrying a huge, filthy bag, and I assumed it held the small coins and scraps of food he managed to beg.

I couldn't take my eyes off him. The tramp stopped in front of don Cesáreo's house and asked him something over the fence. Don Cesáreo was a bad-tempered old codger. Without replying, he waved the beggar away. But the beggar, in a voice too low for me to hear, seemed insistent. Then I distinctly heard don Cesáreo shout out, "Clear off once and for all and stop bothering me."

The tramp, however, kept on, and even went up the three steps and pushed open the iron gate a few inches. At this point, losing the last shred of his small supply of patience, don Cesáreo gave the man a shove.

Slipping, the beggar grabbed at the fence but missed it and fell to the ground. In that instant, his legs flew up in the air, and I heard the sharp crack of his skull striking the wet step.

Don Cesáreo ran onto the pavement, leaned over the beggar, and felt his chest. Then, in a fright, he took the body by the feet and dragged it to the kerb. After that he went into his house and closed the door, convinced there had been no witnesses to his accidental crime.

Only I had seen it. Soon a man came along and stopped by the dead beggar. Then more and more people gathered, and at last the police came. Putting the tramp in an ambulance, they took him away.

That was it; the matter was never spoken of again.

For my part, I took care not to say a word. Maybe I was wrong, but why should I tell on an old man who had never done me any harm? After all, he hadn't intended to kill the tramp, and it didn't seem right to me that a court case should embitter the last years of don Cesáreo's life. The best thing, I thought, was to leave him alone with his conscience.

Little by little I began to forget the episode, but every time I saw don Cesáreo it felt strange to realize that he was unaware that I was the only person in the world who knew his terrible secret. From then on, for some reason I avoided him and never dared speak to him again.

In 1969, when I was twenty-six, I was working as a teacher of Spanish language and literature. Adriana Bernasconi had married not me but someone else who may not have loved and deserved her as much as I.

At the time, Adriana, who was pregnant, was very nearly due. She still lived in the same house, and every day she grew more beautiful. Very early one oppressive summer morning I found myself teaching a special class in grammar to some secondary-school children who were preparing for their exams and, as usual, from time to time I cast a rather melancholy glance across the road.

All at once my heart literally did a flip-flop, and I thought I was seeing things.

From exactly the same direction as four years before came the tramp don Cesáreo had killed—the same ragged clothes, the greyish overcoat, the battered straw hat, the filthy bag.

Forgetting my pupils, I rushed to the window. The tramp had begun to slow his step, as if he had reached his destination.

He's come back to life, I thought, and he's going to take revenge on don Cesáreo.

But the beggar passed the old man's gate and walked on. Stopping at Adriana Bernasconi's front door, he turned the knob and went inside.

"I'll be back in a moment," I told my students, and half out of my mind with anxiety, I went down in the lift, dashed across the street, and burst into Adriana's house.

"Hello!" her mother said, standing by the door as if about to go out. "What a surprise to see you here!"

She had never looked on me in anything but a kindly way. She embraced and kissed me, and I did not quite understand what was going on. Then it dawned on me that Adriana had just become a mother and that they were all beside themselves with excitement. What else could I do but shake hands with my victorious rival?

I did not know how to put it to him, and I wondered whether it might not be better to keep quiet. Then I hit on a compromise. Casually I said, "As a matter of fact, I let myself in without ringing the bell because I thought I saw a tramp come in with a big dirty bag and I was afraid he meant to rob you."

They all gaped at me. What tramp? What bag? Robbery? They had been in the living room the whole time and had no idea what I was talking about.

"I must have made a mistake," I said.

Then they invited me into the room where Adriana and her baby were. I never know what to say on these occasions. I congratulated her, I kissed her, I admired the baby, and I asked what they were going to name him. Gustavo, I was told, after his father; I would have preferred Fernando but I said nothing.

Back home I thought, That was the tramp old don Cesáreo killed, I'm sure of it. It's not revenge he's come back for but to be reborn as Adriana's son.

Two or three days later, however, this hypothesis struck me as ridiculous, and I put it out of my mind.

And would have forgotten it forever had something not come up in 1979 that brought it all back.

Having grown older and feeling less and less in control of things, I tried to focus my attention on a book I was reading beside the window, while letting my glance stray.

Gustavo, Adriana's son, was playing on the roof terrace of their house. Surely, at his age, the game he was playing was rather infantile, and I felt that the boy had inherited his father's scant intelligence and that, had he been my son, he would certainly have found a less foolish way of amusing himself.

He had placed a line of empty tin cans on the parapet and was trying to knock them off by throwing stones at them from a distance of ten or twelve feet. Of course, nearly all the pebbles were falling down into don Cesáreo's garden next door. I could see that the old man, who wasn't there just then, would work himself into a fit the moment he found that some of his flowers had been damaged.

At that very instant, don Cesáreo came out into the garden. He was, in point of fact, extremely old and he shuffled along putting one foot very carefully in front of the other. Slowly, timidly, he made his way to the garden gate and prepared to go down the three steps to the pavement.

At the same time, Gustavo—who couldn't see the old man—at last managed to hit one of the tin cans, which, bouncing off two or three ledges as it went, fell with a clatter into don Cesáreo's garden. Startled, don Cesáreo, who was halfway down the steps, made a sudden movement, slipped head over heels, and cracked his skull against the lowest step.

I took all this in, but the boy had not seen the old man nor had the old man seen the boy. For some reason, at that point Gustavo left the terrace. In a matter of seconds, a crowd of people surrounded don Cesáreo's body; an accidental fall, obviously, had been the cause of his death.

The next day I got up very early and immediately stationed myself at the window. In the pentagonal house, don Cesáreo's wake was in full swing. On the pavement out in front, a small knot of people stood smoking and talking.

A moment later, in disgust and dismay, they drew aside when a beggar came out of Adriana Bernasconi's house, again dressed in rags, overcoat, straw hat, and carrying a bag. He made his way through the circle of bystanders and slowly vanished into the distance the same way he had come from twice before.

At midday, sadly but with no surprise, I learned that Gustavo's bed had been found empty that morning. The whole Bernasconi family launched a forlorn search, which, to this day, they continue in obstinate hope. I never had the courage to tell them to call it off.

"Unlike the novel, a short story may be, for all purposes essential."
Jorge Luis Borges

The Fortunate One

BY SUNITI NAMJOSHI

"For all these gifts we hold you responsible."

Once upon a time the gods decided to be lavish in their blessings. "We will make you a queen," they told the little girl. "Thank you," she said, a bit startled, but not really knowing what else to say. She supposed that being a queen was probably a good thing. "And we will give you a king who is a genuinely good person, and who will help you with everything." She said "thank you" again. A helpful partner was almost certainly a good thing; being a queen might be difficult and she could do with some help. "And we will give you five children who will prosper reasonably and seventeen grandchildren to go with them." The little girl looked doubtful. Seventeen grandchildren was rather a lot; but she decided that on the whole they'd turn out to be nice.

"Have we left out anything?" the gods murmured among themselves. "Oh yes, you will have excellent health and a long life." "And you will also be intelligent and beautiful." This last was an afterthought. The little girl shuffled her feet, thinking she was being dismissed at last; but the gods weren't done with her. "There's one more thing," they informed the child. "For all these gifts we hold you responsible. Do you agree?" For the first time the little girl felt apprehensive: what did it mean to be held responsible? But since there wasn't very much she could say to the gods, she said, "Yes."

Well, everything turned out as they had said it would. And when her long life came to an end, she knew she would have to face the gods. So she prepared an apologetic speech in advance. The gods summoned her. She dared not look at them. She launched into her speech. "I tried to be a responsible queen, but in time somehow the kingdom dissolved. And even the money trickled away. As for the children, they are all right, but not as prosperous as I once was. Both beauty and good health, and even my power over words, faded at the last. And now of my long life nothing is left. I could not preserve any of your gifts. I ask your pardon." She was certain that the gods were displeased with her.

But the gods merely said, "So you think you were a failure?"

"Yes," she answered humbly. "You gave me wealth and power, and I lost it all."

"And you thought we expected you to keep it forever? Had you power over time?"

"No," she faltered.

"You were only expected to try to grow to your full stature. And from that responsibility as a queen or a mother or an ordinary woman you didn't abdicate. Come, do you still think you failed utterly?"

"No," she ventured, "but I failed often...."

At that the gods laughed. "But you weren't a god," they remarked, "only a queen."

So she looked up at last and smiled at them.

Ryunosuke AKUTAGAWA (1892–1927) has had an immense influence on Japanese literature when one considers that he died at the age of thirty-five. During his short life, he produced over 100 short stories, many dealing with traditional Japanese ideals and cultural values.

Akutagawa's style is that of the objective observer who sketches the scene and leaves the reader to make judgments.

The Akutagawa Prize for Literature has been presented annually since 1935 to promising Japanese authors and is one of the most prestigious awards a Japanese author may win.

Michael ANTHONY, born in Trinidad in 1932, is a popular Caribbean-English novelist and story writer. His stories frequently revolve around the world of the adolescent and initiation to adulthood and responsibility.

Madame Leprince de BEAUMONT of France was not the first person to relate the very special love story, "Beauty and the Beast" (1760). Nor will she be the last to tell the story as the recent success of the animated film testifies.

J. BERNLEF is a pseudonym for the Dutch author Hendrik Jan Marsman, born in 1937. Bernlef has published more than forty books—short stories, novels, plays, essays, and poems. He has won many prizes for his literary works and his work has been translated into most major languages.

"The Black Dog" is a story based on an event from his childhood.

Heinrich BÖLL, born in 1917 in Cologne, Germany, is one of the best known of contemporary German authors. After being drafted into the German army in 1939, he was a soldier for six years until his release from an allied Prisoner of War camp in 1945.

After World War II, Böll turned to writing full time and became a kind of public conscience in the difficult and painful years of Germany's recovery from the war.

His stories, novels, and radio plays have been very popular. His popularity and success were recognized when he was awarded the Nobel Prize for Literature in 1972.

Katharine BRIGGS includes "The Two Pickpockets" in her collection, *British Folktales*. Although an old British tale, the story, like many similar stories from the oral tradition around the world, reflects the modern phenomenon in fiction known as the postcard story. "Brevity is the soul of wit."

I. F. BULATKIN, an anthologizer of folklore from various cultures around the world, retells this Armenian folk tale, which graphically conveys the message that money earned is worth more than money received without working for it.

Laurie CHANNER, presently working in the Toronto film industry, submitted this story to the annual *Toronto Star* Short Story Contest in 1992. From among 3500 stories submitted to the newspaper for the contest, "Las Mantillas" was awarded second prize.

Anton CHEKHOV (1860–1904), recognized as one of the great masters of the short story, was born in a small Russian town on the Sea of Azov.

While studying to be a doctor at the Moscow Medical School, he began writing stories to earn money. By the time he died at the age of 44, he had written over 600 stories and several plays. He never wrote a novel.

In his stories, Chekhov presents the trivialities of daily life in vivid, realistic detail. His "slice of life" style has influenced many contemporary writers of short fiction.

Harold COURLANDER collects myths and stories from the oral tradition of different cultures. "The Departure of the Giants," a myth of the Mensa people of Africa, is from *The Crest and the Hide and Other African Stories*, published in 1982.

This story, passed down through word of mouth among various African tribes, attempts to explain the presence of the many ancient large stone structures in Kenya.

Amparo DÁVILA's enigmatic postcard story "Haute Cuisine" appears in Alberto Manguel's story collection, *Other Fires: Short Fiction By Latin American Women*, published in 1986.

Cyprian EKWENSI, born in northern Nigeria in 1921, studied to be a pharmacist but later began writing novels and short stories. He is one of West Africa's most prominent authors and has been described as the Nigerian Daniel Defoe, chronicling life from colonial days to modern day independence.

His stories, which are often episodic in style, speak of the reality of life in African cities.

Richard ERDOES and **Alfonso ORTIZ**, collectors of Native American myths and folklore, retell in this pourquoi tale the story told by the Tlingit people about how and why mosquitoes came to be.

Alison FELL, born in Scotland in 1944, has worked as a sculptor and a journalist. In addition to stories and novels, she also writes poetry.

"The Shining Mountain" was first published in 1987 in *Close Company: Stories of Mothers and Daughters*.

Robert FOX first published this delightful satiric modern urban fable in the *Midwest University Quarterly* in 1965.

A fable is a short tale intended to teach a lesson. Modern fables like this one are often satiric. The fable begins reasonably, but concludes in a most preposterous way.

Janet FRAME, born in Dunedin, New Zealand, in 1924, has published ten novels and several stories. Two of her most successful novels are *Owls Do Cry* (1957) and *The Edge of the Alphabet* (1962).

In her writing, she leaves what she calls "the safety zones" and ventures to "the edge of the alphabet" where rules and boundaries are less exact.

Gregorio López y FUENTES, not to be confused with the more famous Mexican author, Carlos Fuentes, published this humorous story in 1940.

"A Letter to God" revolves around the foil of the stereotyped peasant farmer who has deep faith and the cynical town dweller. There is a wry, quiet smile on the reader's face after experiencing this gem.

Nadine GORDIMER, born in 1923, lives in Johannesburg, South Africa. Many of her stories, written from a white, middle-class point of view, examine the injustice and pain caused by white supremacist attitudes in South Africa.

"A Company of Laughing Faces," published in 1965, has a more universal appeal as it deals with a sheltered seventeen-year-old girl who learns about life from her experiences at the holiday beach.

HOMER (9th century B.C.) is the author of two famous Greek epic story poems, "The Iliad," about the Trojan War, and "The Odyssey," which recounts the travels and adventures of Odysseus (Ulysses).

Lee MARACLE, born in 1950, is a Native orator, poet, and part-time writer-in-residence at the En'owkin International School of Writing for Native People in British Columbia.

"Dear Daddy," which introduces us to the epistolary genre, first appeared in *Sojourner's Truth and Other Stories* in 1990.

Susan MICHALICKA, born in 1965 in Toronto, now lives in Ottawa. In 1992, "Young Man's Folly" won first prize from among 3500 stories submitted from around the world to *The Toronto Star*'s annual Short Story Contest.

Indro MONTANELLI's story about life, deception, and courage in a Nazi Prisoner of War camp in Italy during the last days of World War II was first published in 1954.

Yuri NAGIBIN was born in Russia in 1920. The original version of "Winter Oak" first appeared in 1953. This translation was done in 1973.

Suniti NAMJOSHI was born in Bombay, India, in 1941. She has published seven books of poetry—five in India and two in Canada where she now lives.

Namjoshi also writes fiction, and in her 1981 book, *Feminist Fables*, she relates some of the traditional fables of India from a woman's perspective.

Aziz NESIN, Turkish short-story writer and dramatist, was born in Istanbul in 1915. Nesin attended traditional Islamic schools and became a prominent journalist and satirist. He published twenty-four volumes of short stories and his writings and political beliefs have led to thirty prosecutions in Turkey. In all, he has served over five years in jail for his acidic political satire.

In his work, Nesin condemns power structures and bureaucracies which control people's lives. He is one of the most popular writers in Turkey and his work has been translated into more than twenty languages.

Alan NEIDLE, has been an American representative at international nuclear disarmament talks. He published his *Fables for the Nuclear Age*, from which "The Fish Who Chose a Magnificent Leader" was taken, to answer some of the questions about the failure of political leaders to solve world problems such as nuclear armament, pollution, hunger, and other international inequities.

Liam O'FLAHERTY was born in 1896 on Inishmore, one of the three Aran Islands off the west coast of Ireland.

O'Flaherty was active in Ireland's political and military struggle to gain independence from Britain. "The Sniper," first published in his collection of stories *Spring Sowing* (1924), comes directly from his involvement in the Irish Revolutionary Movement for Independence.

István ÖRKÉNY, born in Hungary in 1912, trained to be a chemical engineer before turning to writing as a career.

Örkény's favourite topic is the world of the bizarre and the absurd as "There Is Always Hope" aptly illustrates. He writes what he terms "one-minute stories" about odd, grotesque, eccentric characters. His minimal style of "less is more" is part of a modern phenomenon in writing known as "flash fiction" or "postcard fiction."

Pinhas SADEH of Israel bases his story "The Two Friends" on a 17th century Hebrew version of this story. Various versions of this story of friendship exist all over the world.

Samuel SELVON, born in 1924 in Trinidad, is respected as one of the best humorists and satirists in West Indian literature. He has written several novels. "Cane Is Bitter" is from his 1957 collection of stories, *Ways of Sunlight*.

Salma SHALLASH, born in 1941, is a professional film and television scriptwriter in Egypt. Her stories, novels, and scripts frequently examine the lifestyles of contemporary women.

Charlie SLANE's story, "A Catch Tale," appears in the collection, *New Brunswick Folk Tales and Legends*. A catch tale is a story in which the storyteller deliberately misleads the listener. Perhaps more exactly, it is a story in which the teller leads the listener to ask a particular question at the conclusion of the story.

Catch tales contain contradictions and absurdities and conclude with a ridiculous solution. Stories about mixed weather appear in the folk literature of many cultures.

Khalid SOHAIL, born in Pakistan in 1952, studied medicine at the Khyber Medical College in Peshawar, Pakistan. Currently, he is a staff psychiatrist at a hospital in Whitby, Ontario.

In addition to writing stories, he also writes essays, poems, and books on psychology. His stories, translated from the Urdu language, often center around the lonely and isolated members of contemporary society.

Fernando SORRENTINO, born in Buenos Aires, Argentina, has published five volumes of short stories. He says that his stories, although somewhat different and absurd, are the types of stories he himself would like to read. In his first collection of stories, *La Regresion Zoologica*, he wrote stories he thought would please the reading public. In his other four books, he wrote not for an imaginary audience, but for himself.

James THURBER (1894–1961) was born in Columbus, Ohio, and worked for many years as a journalist. Thurber's characters come to terms with the complexities of contemporary life in their own unique ways. His stories have a light-hearted, humorous bent, but they are always perceptive in commenting on the human condition.

Luisa VALENZUELA, born in Buenos Aires, Argentina, in 1938, is a major voice in Latin American fiction today. Much of Valenzuela's writing deals with the horrors of life in a police state. Using a type of fiction termed magic realism, which places fantastic events against realistic settings, she sketches the tyranny, the violence, and the class struggle present in the oppressive regimes of many South American countries.

"The Censors" depicts a society where state repression breeds popular subversion, where distrust feeds on distrust, where restrictions are so excessive that they promote inefficiency, and where surveillance is so severe that it becomes absurd. The main character of the story is at once both victim and agent of the oppressive power of the state.

Adele VERNON bases her story about the poor peasant worker who wins unexpected fortune on the traditional Catalan (Spanish) folk tale, "The King and the Charcoal Maker."

Mai VO-DINH, in retelling this story of the clever child outwitting the powerful man, gives Vietnamese flavour to one of the world's oldest versions of the motif of the trimphant underdog.

Ann WALSH, born in Alabama, U.S.A., now makes her home in British Columbia. She is the author of several plays and novels.

"All Is Calm" was one of 243 stories submitted in 1991 to Thistledown Press in an open story contest. The story appears in the anthology *The Blue Jean Collection* (1992).

Virginia WENG, a Chinese film producer, collaborated with Doctor M.A. Jagendorf, a world-famous folklorist, in collecting some of China's best-known traditional folk tales.

"A True Money Tree," published in their anthology, *The Magic Boat*, illustrates the Chinese work ethic and how success comes from initiative and hard work.

Bing XIN, born in 1905 in Peking, China, attended college in the United States. After graduating with a Master's Degree from Wellesley College, she returned to China and taught at Yenjing University.

Xin lived in Japan for some time but returned to China in 1949 after the People's Revolution. She writes idealistic stories with a stress on family life. "Separation," written in 1931, is a tender mother-child story, but pessimistic in the sense that social class structure is determined by one's birth.

North America

"How Mosquitoes Came To Be" (Canada — First Nations)
"A Fable" (U.S.A.)
"A Catch Tale" (Canada)
"The Princess and the Tin Box" (U.S.A.)
"All Is Calm" (Canada)
"Dear Daddy" (Canada–Métis)
"Young Man's Folly" (Canada)
"Las Mantillas" (Canada)
"The Fish Who Chose a Magnificent Leader" (U.S.A.)

Oceania

"You Are Now Entering the Human Heart" (New Zealand)

INDEX OF ALTERNATE THEMES

Adolescence

"Pita of the Deep Sea" (Trinidad)
"A Company of Laughing Faces" (South Africa)

Birth

"The Two Pickpockets" (England)
"Separation" (China)

Childhood

"Winter Oak" (Russia)
"The Black Dog" (Netherlands)
"The Fly" (Vietnam)

Coming of Age/Changing Values

"Winter Oak" (Russia)
"A Company of Laughing Faces" (South Africa)
"The Tangerines" (Japan)
"All Is Calm" (Canada)
"Dear Daddy" (Canada–Métis)
"Cane Is Bitter" (Trinidad)

Crisis and Survival

"A Letter to God" (Mexico)
"The Sniper" (Ireland)
"You Are Now Entering the Human Heart" (New Zealand)
"His Excellency" (Italy)
"Polyphemus the Cyclops" (Greece)
"All Is Calm" (Canada)

Politics and Power Structures

"There Is a Nut On the Roof" (Turkey)
"Las Mantillas" (Canada)
"The Fish Who Chose a Magnificent Leader" (U.S.A.)
"The Censors" (Argentina)

Outsiders

"Winter Oak" (Russia)
"Heartache" (Russia)
"Island" (Pakistan)
"Las Mantillas" (Canada)

Social Structure

"The Tangerines" (Japan)
"Separation" (China)
"The Riddle" (Spain)
"The Departure of the Giants" (Kenya)

Women's Issues

"A Company of Laughing Faces" (South Africa)
"Dear Daddy" (Canada — Métis)
"The Other Face" (Egypt)
"The Fortunate One" (India)

War and Peace

"How Mosquitoes Came to Be" (Canada — First Nations)
"The Sniper" (Ireland)
"His Excellency" (Italy)
"Las Mantillas" (Canada)

The World of the Worker

"A Letter to God" (Mexico)
"Action Will Be Taken" (Germany)
"The Censors" (Argentina)
"A Rupee Earned" (Armenia)
"A True Money Tree" (China)
"Cane Is Bitter" (Trinidad)

Permission to reprint copyrighted material is gratefully acknowledged. Every reasonable effort to trace the copyright holders of materials appearing in this book has been made. Information that will enable the publisher to rectify any error or omission will be welcomed.

How Mosquitoes Came to Be by Richard Erdoes and Alfonso Ortiz from *American Indian Myths and Legends* by Richard Erdoes and Alfonso Ortiz. Copyright © 1984 by Richard Erdoes and Alfonso Ortiz. Reprinted by permission of Pantheon Books, a division of Random House, Inc.

A Letter to God by Gregorio López y Fuentes. Used by permission of the Estate of Angel Flores.

A Fable by Robert Fox reprinted by permission of *The Midwest Quarterly*, Pittsburg State University © 1965, 1977.

The Two Pickpockets by Katharine Briggs from *British Folktales* reprinted by permission of A.P. Watt Ltd. on behalf of Katharine Law.

A Catch Tale told by Charlie Slane, collected by Carole Spray, from *Will O' The Wisp*, published by Brunswick Press.

The Princess and the Tin Box by James Thurber copyright © 1948 James Thurber. Copyright © 1976 Helen Thurber & Rosemary A. Thurber. From *The Beast in Me and Other Animals*, published by Harcourt Brace Jovanovich, Inc.

Action Will Be Taken by Heinrich Böll copyright © 1966 by Heinrich Böll. Reprinted by permission of McGraw Hill, Inc. and Joan Daves Agency.

The Sniper by Liam O'Flaherty from *Spring Sowing* by Liam O'Flaherty reprinted by permission of Harcourt Brace & Company, the estate of Liam O'Flaherty, and Jonathan Cape Publishers.

Pita of the Deep Sea by Michael Anthony from *Island Voices: Stories from the West Indies*. Copyright Elek Books, London.

You Are Now Entering the Human Heart by Janet Frame from *The Penguin Book of Contemporary New Zealand Stories* reprinted by permission of Janet Frame c/o Curtis Brown (Aust.) Ltd., Sydney.

Winter Oak by Yuri Nagibin reprinted by permission of Ardis Publishers.

The Black Dog by J. Bernlef reprinted by permission of Em. Querido's Uitgeverij B.V.

A Company of Laughing Faces by Nadine Gordimer copyright © 1960 by Nadine Gordimer, from *Not For Publication and Other Stories* by Nadine Gordimer. Used by permission of Viking Penguin, a division of Penguin Books USA Inc.

The Censors by Luisa Valenzuela from *Short Stories: An Anthology of the Shortest Stories*. Ed. Irving Howe & Ilana Weiner – Howe, Kodos, & Godine Publishers, U.K.

A Rupee Earned by I.F. Bulatkin from *Eurasian Folk and Fairy Tales* by I.F. Bulatkin. Copyright © by I.F. Bulatkin.

A True Money Tree by M.A. Jagendorf and Virginia Weng from *The Magic Boat and Other Chinese Folk Stories*. Copyright Vanguard Press, N.Y.

Haute Cuisine by Amparo Dávila from *Other Fires: Short Fiction by Latin American Women*, ed. Alberto Manguel. Copyright © 1986 Lester Publishing.

Cane is Bitter by Samuel Selvon reprinted by permission of the author.

The Departure of the Giants by Harold Courlander from *The Crest and the Hide and Other African Stories* by Harold Courlander. Copyright © 1982 by Harold Courlander. Reprinted by permission of the author.

The Other Face by Salma Shallash from *Egyptian Tales and Other Stories*. Copyright © 1987 American University in Cairo Press.

The Visitation by Fernando Sorrentino from *Celeste Goes Dancing and Other Stories*, ed. Norman Thomas di Giovanni. Copyright © North Point Press, N.Y.

The Fortunate One by Suniti Namjoshi from *A Double Colonization: Colonial and Post-Colonial Women's Writing*, ed. Kirsten Holst Petersen and Anna Rutherford. Copyright © 1986 by Dangaroo Press, U.K.

P H O T O G R A P H S

I L L U S T R A T I O N S